CW00468205

Twilight
at
Croftwood
Library

Victoria Walker

Copyright © 2023 Victoria Walker

All rights reserved.

ISBN: 978-1-7399441-4-8

For everyone who loves libraries

x

1

Croftwood Library was housed in a grand Victorian building with an overgrown, slightly neglected garden at the front. The windows were so high up that there was no way to sneak a look inside, so Lois Morgan propped her bike against the wall, locked it up, and took a deep breath as she stood in front of the heavy oak doors.

When she'd gone to work that morning at the Hive, a city library in Worcester that encompassed the Worcester University library and was and one of the biggest in the Midlands, it had been a normal day. Now here she was in a little town that was only six miles from Worcester but which in terms of the library might as well be on the other side of the world, it was so different from the huge library she was used to.

As she took a step closer to the doors, they opened automatically and the scent of an old library which was ingrained in Lois's memory enveloped her and briefly transported her back to the Saturday mornings of her childhood. It was a combination of things that were indescribable and had been lost from the library where she

1

worked now because it was too new. It was stillness, silence, time and so much more, as well as the books themselves, all wrapped up in that smell that hits you when you walk into a library of a certain age.

She inhaled deeply and took a second to enjoy the nostalgia that washed over her. A million tiny memories flashed through her mind too quickly to dwell on but leaving her with a sense of contentment at being somewhere that felt so familiar.

The information desk was centred in the entrance so that customers were channelled down one side to enter and deposit their returned books, and down the other side to exit. It was like entering a time warp. It had been years since she'd been in a library like this one. She could see why it was listed for closure because it was so behind the times. It had been forgotten and overlooked in the wave of modernising and computerising of libraries and Lois knew it would be impossible to get any funding to help it now. It would always be cheaper to close it.

'Are you a member?' a woman barked from behind the desk.

'Yes,' said Lois, extracting her Worcestershire Libraries card from her purse.

The older woman peered at the card through her half-moon reading glasses. 'No,' she said.

'Sorry, no?' The card allowed membership to all the county's libraries.

'We don't accept those new-fangled cards here. You will need to join this library.'

Lois wasn't about to start an argument which she wasn't sure she would win, even though she knew she was right. 'Okay, thank you. I just wanted to browse today.'

The woman tutted and went back to what she was doing. Lois took that as a sign that she was permitted to enter and hurried past the desk.

She spotted another lady re-shelving some books in the fiction section.

'Hi, can you recommend a good crime novel?' Lois asked, smiling.

The woman looked like a rabbit in the headlights. 'Can I recommend a crime book?'

Lois suddenly felt like she was in an alternate universe where libraries weren't what she thought they were at all. If not that, it was certainly like stepping back forty or fifty years in time.

'Or whatever you've read recently that you enjoyed?' Maybe it was the crime request that had thrown her.

'Gosh, I can't remember the last time anyone asked me to recommend a book to them. How lovely,' she said in hushed tones. 'I don't read much crime, but I very much enjoyed *The Flatshare* by Beth O'Leary.'

'Oh, I've read that, it's brilliant,' said Lois. 'Clever concept.' Lois would never have expected that to be on this woman's reading list which just went to show that you should never judge a book by its cover.

'I have to admit,' the woman said, glancing over her shoulder before she continued, 'I love contemporary women's' fiction.'

'Do you have a section for that here?'

'Goodness no. Barbara Taylor Bradford is about as contemporary as we get in these parts.' She smiled, then realising she had relaxed for a nano-second too long, immediately became flustered and said, 'Anyway, I must get on.'

'It was nice talking to you,' said Lois, slightly stunned to hear that less than six miles from Worcester, contemporary fiction was considered racy.

The only nod to modern times was a large table with a

cluster of four elderly computer terminals and a printer on it, all of which were switched off. Not that there was anyone in the library to use them. Despite the nostalgia that Lois had felt when she walked in, now she felt like it was quite a sad and lifeless place. Could she bear to spend the next six months here?

'I've had a request from County Libraries,' her boss, Robert had said when he'd called her up to his office earlier that morning. 'It seems they are suddenly lacking a librarian in Croftwood. I have been tasked with lending them a capable member of staff until such time that it's resolved.' He'd looked expectantly at Lois.

'Oh right. So, you want me to fill in for a couple of weeks?'

'Actually, it's a little longer than that. To be completely frank, Lois, Croftwood Library is on the list for closure. Their librarian is retiring, and they need someone to step in for a few months. Just until the decision is made one way or the other.'

It was always sad when a library faced closure and Lois's heart had gone out to the little town that could lose its hub, but now that she had seen it for herself, she could understand why the decision had been made. It could be a particularly depressing secondment with nothing to do apart from wait until the end came.

'Can you do without me here?' Lois had asked, uncomfortably. She hated to over-estimate the value of herself to the Hive, but could they really lose a deputy manager without noticing?

Robert had exhaled loudly and kneaded his forehead with his finger and thumb.

'The thing is, I'm between a rock and a hard place. There is always the pressure to cut costs here and you're right, we can't do without you but moving the cost of a deputy manager off my payroll for a few months would make all the difference. Obviously, it will be very difficult to work around your absence but the library in Croftwood needs a solid librarian, old school as it were. I could send Andrew, but you know how awful he is at cataloguing and he hates re-shelving. I wouldn't want to inflict that on any other library. I appreciate it's a big ask, Lois but you're the only person who fits the bill.'

Lois hadn't been sure whether she was flattered or offended but when she snuck out of the exit of Croftwood Library, breathing a sigh of relief at managing to avoid the scary librarian, she couldn't help but think that Robert had picked her as the person who would make the least fuss.

'Take tonight to think it over, and why not take the afternoon off and pop over there,' he'd suggested.

The bike ride to Croftwood in the autumn sunshine had turned out to be the best thing about the visit and she wasn't sure what she was going to say to Robert.

Oliver Jones began every week at his eponymous coffee house expecting Monday to be quiet whereas, in fact, Monday could sometimes be busier than Saturday, not in takings but in footfall. People were lingering, meeting friends, easing themselves into the week which meant the exact opposite for him.

'One-shot espresso, please,' his next customer said. An unusual request after midday but one that Oliver sympathised with.

'Drink in?' It definitely would be. Hardly anyone had take-outs on a Monday.

'Yes please.'

Oliver put two espresso cups under the porta-filter and once he'd handed one to his customer he took the other himself, leant against the counter and gazed out of the window, taking advantage of the nearest thing he was going to get to a break for another few hours.

There was a steady stream of people walking up and down the high street. Croftwood wasn't a big town, but it was a loyal town and the high street was thriving compared to other places. It heartened Oliver to know that having sunk every last penny of his savings into the coffee house and more recently the cinema, the town was behind him.

He was drawn out of his trance by the sight of a woman riding an old-fashioned bicycle past the window. She was wearing a floral dress and Doc Marten boots both of which were at odds with the safety helmet she also wore. The basket on the front of the bike was only just containing a sweater; the sleeve was hanging down, threatening to become caught in the spokes. Something about her lifted his mood and he smiled to himself.

A couple of customers later, he checked his phone. He tried not to look at it too much during the day because he liked to emit a laid-back vibe for his customers. If he stood there checking his phone it was hardly attentive and he prided himself on his customer service. It was the only thing that set him apart from the chains.

Amongst the numerous emails from companies he had been interested in for a fleeting second and whose emails he kept meaning to unsubscribe from, there was an email from Amy. It was the first time he'd heard from her in a couple of months. The subject was 'Catch Up?'.

'Skinny latte please and a chocolate muffin.'

'Sorry.' Oliver dragged his face into a smile and pushed his phone into his apron pocket. 'Drink in?'

'Yes please.'

'Take a seat, I'll bring it over.'

He turned to the coffee machine and went through the familiar motions while his phone burned against his hip, willing him to look at the email. But it would have to wait.

2

On balance, Lois had decided it would be better to go along with Robert's request that she transfer to Croftwood Library for six months. It wasn't for that long and she couldn't quite bring herself to say no.

'Rather you than me,' said Andrew, as they stood at the information desk together. Lois waited in vain for him to offer to re-shelve the returns from last night before she gave in and did it herself, the same as always.

'I think it'll be fine. With Alex gone, it's a good time to take on a new challenge.'

'It's hardly going to be a challenge, Lois. You literally just have to make sure the doors are open Monday to Saturday for the next six months.'

'Well, why didn't you want to do it then?'

Andrew was the laziest person she'd ever worked with. It could have been his dream job.

He screwed up his face as if he had just smelled the inside of used dog poo bag. 'Can you see me somewhere like that? Please.'

Lois took a moment to imagine the reaction of the old

librarian if Andrew had turned up at Croftwood Library yesterday instead of her. He definitely would have given her a run for her money.

'Anyway, Robert didn't ask anyone else, he wanted you.'

A wave of paranoia swept over Lois. The more she thought about it, the more she was talking herself into thinking that there was some ulterior motive in having been chosen. Was she the person they would miss the least? The most easily replaceable? Then she forced herself to remember the reason Robert had given her; that she would be helping him to lower his wage bill which might save someone else's job in the long run.

Talking it through with Andrew wasn't helping her to be at peace with the decision and it actually made her realise that it was the first time she had missed having Alex at home. Her now-ex-boyfriend had moved to London a couple of months ago and their relationship had very quickly fizzled out. Lois had been surprised by how easily she had bounced back from the break-up, but her friend Steph had insisted that was because Alex wasn't The One. Regardless of whether he was The One or not, he had effectively been her closest friend for the two years that they'd lived together and that was what she missed the most.

She wheeled the returns trolley over to the lifts, hit the button for the first floor and then pulled her phone out to look at while she waited. There was a text from Steph who as well as being her best friend was in charge of the mobile library van.

Want to come on a jolly tomorrow? Doing the school round and could use a hand. X

The mobile library visited a lot of the smaller rural primary schools. It gave schools the opportunity to refresh their books more frequently than their budgets would otherwise allow. The children were allowed out of class to come and choose books, and sometimes Steph needed a hand to help with the children as well as do the necessary admin side of the visit. Lois always jumped at the opportunity to go out and about and Robert was really good about letting her go out on the mobile library whenever she wanted to. It might be her last chance before she started working at Croftwood.

Count me in! x

Do you think I'm mad?' Lois asked Steph as they meandered along the country lanes in the mobile library van.

'Oooh, that's a hard one. Mad to be taking the Croftwood job when you don't want to, or mad to say yes to Robert when you could wrap him around your little finger if you tried? Tough…'

'Come on Steph. You know what I mean.'

'I do know, Lois. I know that you need to do whatever feels like the right thing for you.' She was very pleased with her diplomatic answer.

'Well, I think I quite fancy it. It's a proper library at least. It'll be a challenge and I think that's what I want. I love the Hive, but this is a chance to do something different for a little while. It'll be like having a new job for a few months without actually having to get a new job.'

'You're right. A change is invigorating, makes you feel like you're really living life.' Steph didn't think for a minute that Lois was going to find working in Croftwood Library invigorating or challenging but it was her job to support her friend. She was probably still feeling a bit adrift since Alex left, although in her opinion it had been good riddance, so doing something different was a good idea.

Steph had worked on the mobile library van for fifteen years and contrary to the advice she was happy to dish out to Lois, had never wanted to do anything different at all. It sounded boring to have been doing the same thing for so long, but she was way past the point of caring about that. She knew she was lucky to have a job that she loved. It was her customers that made the job so fulfilling. The regulars saw her as a lifeline which meant more to her than just being a librarian.

'It does bother me that Robert is so...' Lois was wavering for the right word.

'Wet.'

'I was thinking, presumptive,' she said, looking pointedly at Steph who concentrated on the road and pretended she hadn't seen. 'He knew he was onto a sure thing asking me to do it.'

'Well, I hate to point out the obvious, but you are doing it and didn't put up much of a fight, am I right?'

Lois hated confrontation and was particularly bad at putting her foot down about anything. In fact, Steph knew that Alex had left most of his stuff behind and Lois was keeping it in the spare room for him.

'Yes, but I don't want people to think I'm a pushover.' Lois sighed.

'Well, don't let yourself be pushed over so often.' Seeing Lois's face fall she said, 'Come on, it'll be fun. You'll get to ride your bike to work every day. Think what that'll do to your bum, it'll look amazing by Christmas,' said Steph.

Lois laughed as they pulled up at St Hilda's Primary School, parking the van in the playground. Steph went in to let them know they'd arrived while Lois got the steps down. A few minutes later Steph appeared with four small children who were walking behind her in a line, holding each other's hands.

'Right, you're allowed to choose one book each,' she said, as they came into the van, their eyes wide with reverential excitement. 'If you want to sit down and look through some

11

different books before you decide you can sit here.' Steph gestured to the carpeted area at the back of the van.

The children began to cautiously look at the bookshelves, one little girl turning to look at Steph as she tentatively put out a finger to take a book. Steph nodded encouragingly, seeing the girl's relief as she realised it was okay to touch. She went over and crouched next to her, picking out a Mr Gum book.

'Have you read any Mr Gum books before?'

'No.'

'They're really funny.' Steph handed the book to the girl who flipped through it.

'It hasn't got many pictures,' she said doubtfully.

'It hasn't,' Steph agreed, 'but you know when someone reads to you and you make pictures of the story in your head? Well, this book is really good at that.'

The girl nodded. 'I'll choose this one,' she said, very seriously, holding the book to her chest.

'That's a great choice. If you take it to my friend, Lois, she'll stamp the date in it for you.'

'Chosen already, Clara?' Mr Reeves, the Literacy Leader and the class teacher came into the van followed by another four children. 'Time to make your choices, Harry, Maia and George!'

'Morning, Mr Reeves.' Calling him that made Steph smile. She knew his name was Tom, but she had to refer to him by his teacher name when he was at school.

'Hi, Steph. How's it going?' He was a nice bloke, too nice for her but perfect for Lois. Steph's tastes ran to grungier, edgier men and Tom definitely wasn't either of those things, well-groomed in his smart suit.

'Great, thanks. I've got my friend Lois with me today.'

'Ah, nice to meet you, Lois.'

Lois blushed and said hello before turning back to the

children who were waiting with their chosen books. Clearly, she thought Tom was pretty nice too.

'Right, I'll take these four back and send Miss Briggs in to fetch the others in a few minutes. Thanks so much, Steph. Nice to see you both. 'Betsy, William, Rosie and Charlie, quick choosing please!' he added in an authoritative teacher voice.

'Wow, he doesn't look like a teacher,' said Lois, lowering her voice so that the children wouldn't hear her.

'I know, he's quite fit, isn't he?'

'Steph! You can't say that about him.'

'Don't be so prissy, Lois. He is. And he's a nice person.'

'He does seem nice,' said Lois, gazing at the door.

Steph smiled. At least Lois wasn't completely blind to the wider world.

After another hour or so of entertaining groups of children, Miss Briggs collected the final four and Steph and Lois packed up and set off for their next destination.

'Do you think he's single?' asked Lois. Steph looked vague on purpose, forcing her to add, 'Mr Reeves?'

'Hmm, I think he is. Interested?'

'No, of course not. I was thinking of you.'

'Do you know me at all? He's too clean-cut, we'd look ridiculous together.'

'Aren't you fed up of falling for bad boys, Steph? Maybe it's time to go for it with someone who you know is a nice person. It's got to be worth a try.'

'I think it'd be boring.' Steph had been out with enough guys to know what she didn't like even if she hadn't quite worked out what would make the perfect man. And respectable, professional, well-turned-out men usually had very little to offer her in the way of excitement. She needed a risk-taker, a bit of rough and someone who was going to constantly surprise her. All of that and something else as well but she wasn't sure what the secret ingredient was, that was the problem.

'I think it'd be less stressful.'

That was probably true, but Steph was nothing like Lois. Maybe that's why they were such good friends.

3

Just two weeks later Lois was on her way to Croftwood, on her bike, for her first day. The old librarian, Rosemary, who Lois had discovered was the battle-axe behind the desk when she'd visited, had retired on Friday.

She was glad it was a fine day as she really didn't want to arrive wet and dishevelled. It had been hard enough deciding what to wear and, in the end, she had gone for a floral blouse, jeans and a cardigan with her well-worn but highly polished pair of black Doc Marten boots because they were practical for bike riding and went with everything.

Once she arrived in Croftwood she dismounted and pulled out her phone to ring Steph who she knew would be busy stocking the mobile library with help from Andrew.

'Are you missing me?'

'You have no idea. He seems incapable of placing any book on a shelf.'

Lois laughed. 'He's famous for it.'

'Lucky me. Are you there yet?'

'No, I'm delaying the inevitable by strolling through town first. And I need to know how your date went on Saturday night.'

'The loser I was waiting for never showed up. His name was Sylvester.'

'Sylvester?' said Lois as she waited to cross the road to the library. 'No-one's called Sylvester.'

'Exactly,' said Steph. 'It's a sign which I should have seen as soon as he came up as a match. I'm sending you the picture of him.'

'Oh God, Steph.' Sylvester was a thick-necked, shaven-headed man with quite frightening eyes.

'I know. Lucky escape.'

'Definitely.' said Lois smiling to herself as she headed towards the library. She loved hearing about Steph's dating so much that part of her would be sorry if she ever found Mr Right. 'I need to go. Tell Andrew I said he should pull his socks up.'

'Will do. Good luck, Lois.'

'Thanks.' She wheeled her bike into the library figuring that there must be somewhere she could leave it rather than outside.

'You can't bring that in here!'

It was the retired librarian. What was she doing here? Behind the desk? Quickly, Lois decided that this moment could make or break how today and maybe the rest of the job went for her.

Seeing a door marked 'Office' to her left, she said, 'I'm going to leave it in the office in case it rains.' She purposefully manhandled the bike through the office door, closed it behind her and sighed heavily. This wasn't how she thought the day was going to go.

She pulled out her phone and called Robert.

'Morning Lois,' he said jovially. 'What can I do for you?'

'Robert, I thought Rosemary at Croftwood Library had retired on Friday?' Lois said in a low voice so as not to be overheard by anyone who might be listening on the other side of the door.

'Well, yes. Why do you ask?'

'She's here, Robert. Behind the desk as if nothing's changed.'

'Oh, I see. Yes, we did wonder whether something like this might happen.'

Brilliant. And absolutely typical that despite thinking this might happen no-one did anything to stop it or at least warn her.

'What am I supposed to do? I can hardly throw her out, can I?'

'On the contrary, Lois. I'm not condoning forcibly removing her, but you are the interim manager and must run things as you see fit.'

Somehow, she hadn't expected that. 'Oh, right. Thanks, Robert.'

She ended the call, took off her cycle helmet and pulled her hair into a bun. She could do this. What had she said to Steph about not wanting to be a pushover anymore? With a smile plastered on her face, she opened the door and headed for the desk.

'Good morning, Rosemary. We haven't met officially, I'm Lois Morgan. Interim manager.' She held her hand out and looked Rosemary firmly in the eye. 'What can I do for you this morning?'

Rosemary did at least have the good grace to look taken aback and Lois smiled inside, feeling that she had managed a tiny victory.

'Well...I imagine that you will need help to find your feet. Linda will be of some help of course but –'

'Thank you so much for thinking of me but Linda and I will be fine.' Lois made sure to sound firm, then added conspiratorially, 'This isn't my first time working in a library.'

'Oh, I see.' Rosemary looked downcast and for a split-second, Lois felt a pang of guilt. 'Well, I must be going then.'

Lois felt it was best not to say anything more in case she caved in and offered Rosemary an extra couple of weeks work as a handover. After all, if she wanted to be here so badly, why hadn't she stuck it out until the library closed down instead of retiring?

Once Rosemary had gone and Lois could get behind the desk, she was shocked by the amount of paperwork everywhere. She removed a sheaf of paper from the computer keyboard, switched it on and logged in. Out of interest, she went to look at the borrowings from the Saturday that had just gone. Nothing.

When Linda appeared from some re-shelving she'd been doing, Lois asked her about it.

'Oh, we were very busy on Saturday, but I haven't had a chance to put it on the computer yet.'

'What do you mean?' asked Lois with a frown. 'Don't you just scan the books out as and when?'

'Well, no. They did want us to start doing that but Rosemary thought we would lose track of things, so we carried on doing it the normal way. Then every so often, when I have time, I update the computer.'

Lois was astounded. Aside from the insane duplication of effort that caused, it meant that the whole county library system was being compromised by this one branch. Someone could go onto the online catalogue and think there was a copy of something available when it could well have been lent out from Croftwood.

'And the returns?' she asked reluctantly.

'Yes, the same,' Linda nodded as if it were perfectly alright.

'Right. Well, we're going to use the computer, Linda. Starting from now.'

Lois asked Linda to get the computer records up to date as

a priority and began doing some re-shelving herself. It was therapeutic and gave her chance to get acquainted with the whereabouts of various sections as well as calm down her inner rage at Rosemary's blatant indifference to the workings of the county library system.

When Linda came to find her and announced that she was up to date and would it be alright to have her lunch break, Lois couldn't believe that the morning was already over. She also couldn't believe that they had only had two people across the threshold that morning. It was Monday in a smallish town but still, she had hoped for more.

She settled herself back behind the desk and started sifting through some of the paperwork in a vain effort to see what else had been left to more traditional methods. Judging by the number of emails in the inbox and the sent items, almost everything relied on good old-fashioned snail mail. There was even a pile of cards ready to post notifying customers that their reservation was ready to collect. Lois couldn't remember the last time she had even seen one of those cards.

Once Linda was back from her lunch break, Lois grabbed her book and purse out of her bike basket and headed out for a break herself. She headed up the high street, looking more carefully at the shops she'd not had chance to notice when she'd been past on her bike. There was an amazing fabric and wool shop, The Croftwood Haberdashery, which was begging her to go inside but she had a few sewing projects on the go, so she decided to save that treat for another day. After Alex left, she'd thrown herself into dressmaking to fill the quiet evenings.

Her stomach rumbled, making her wish she had thought to bring a packed lunch but as she strolled further up the high street, she came across a trendy coffee shop that looked inviting. Oliver's was all metal table frames with scrubbed wooden tops, mismatched metal and wooden chairs, filament lights, plants trailing from the shelves and a very cool bar across the length of the front window with stools, begging the customers to while away some time by people-watching. A huge blackboard behind the counter announced the menu and Lois noticed there were lots of smaller blackboards around the place with funny quotes chalked on them; 'A yawn is a silent scream for coffee', was one that caught her eye.

The woman behind the counter had a mane of thick chestnut hair which she had wound into a huge bun on the top of her head. She was wearing a canvas apron with 'Oliver's' emblazoned across the chest and she had a warm smile.

'Hi there, what can I get you?'

'A skinny latte and an avocado and tomato toasted sandwich, please.'

'Are you eating in?'

'Yes, please.'

'That'll be six twenty-five.'

Lois put her book down on the counter while she ferreted in her purse for her card and tapped it on the machine.

'Great, thanks. Take a seat and I'll bring it over.'

Lois thanked the woman and headed over to a table in the back corner of the shop, underneath a shelf which was full of ferny leaved plants, lit dimly by an old industrial bulkhead wall light. Just as she realised that she'd left her book on the counter, her phone rang. It was Robert calling for an update on the Rosemary situation. As she explained what had happened to a relieved sounding Robert, the barista delivered her latte and toasted sandwich. Lois finished the call, ate her lunch and with no need of her book to fill the time, forgot all about it.

It was when she came to pack her bicycle basket as she was leaving the library that she realised she must have left her book at the coffee shop. Never mind, it was on her way home, so she'd pop in and collect it. The woman was so lovely, Lois felt sure she'd have put it somewhere safe.

Lois parked her bike opposite Oliver's and locked it to the railings which enclosed the church grounds. It was much quieter in the coffee shop there than it had been at lunchtime and this time there was a man behind the counter, who could possibly be Oliver, thought Lois. He had a relaxed, happy kind of aura around him. He wore faded jeans, a floral shirt and brown boots and an 'Oliver's' apron. His brown wavy hair was expertly swept up off his forehead in a manner that looked effortless but somehow made Lois imagine him peering at it in the bathroom mirror of a morning. Basically, he was as trendy as the place itself. He looked up from the book he was reading.

'Coffee?' he asked, giving her a lopsided smile and not seeming to be in any hurry.

'Sorry, no. I came in at lunchtime and left my book behind.'

He blushed slightly and said, 'Oh, I think this is probably yours then.' He closed the book and handed it to Lois. 'Shame, I was just starting to enjoy it.' It was called *The Perfect Couple* but it was a crime novel so possibly the couple would turn out to not be perfect at all.

'Oh, well, you're welcome to borrow it if you like,' she found herself saying. 'I've barely started it.'

'That's really nice of you but despite you catching me just now, I don't get much time to read. Maybe I could borrow it after you've read it though?'

This time Lois blushed, feeling foolish for doing so when there was absolutely no reason but at the same time realising that this man was having a strange effect on her. 'Sure. I'll drop it in.' The thought of him borrowing her book made her feel like a teenager with a crush.

'And I can tell you, by the time you get to chapter three

there's no way you'd be leaving that book anywhere.'

'Well thanks for holding onto it for me.'

'No problem. Sure I can't get you a coffee?'

Lois couldn't think of anything she'd rather do than stay and have a coffee with him, but she felt thrown and flustered.

'No, I need to get home, but thanks anyway.'

'Nice to meet you…'

'Lois.'

'Lois. I'm Oliver.'

Her heart was thudding as she crossed the road back to her bike, forcing herself not to look back to see if he was watching her. She tucked her book in the basket, unlocked the bike and didn't look at the coffee shop again. As soon as she'd left the high street and started on the road back to Worcester, she smiled to herself. It had been a long time since a man had made her feel like that. He was lovely and he'd been reading her book. Maybe working in Croftwood was going to be better than she'd thought.

4

Steph was on the way to her stop at the Red Lion Inn car park on Old Station Road. She passed one of her customers and gave a gentle peep of acknowledgement on the horn. He raised a hand in reply. She could have stopped to give him a lift, but she knew that walking to see her was one of Bill's rituals. Lots of her customers had them. Her visit was often the highlight of their week or even month and she wasn't about to ruin that.

Bill didn't consider himself to be a reader. He'd admitted to Steph that he hadn't read more than five fiction books in his whole life. But he loved non-fiction and biographies, particularly books about how things worked so she made sure there was something new of that nature on the van every time she called at Old Station Road. She insisted that he was indeed a reader. What you choose to read doesn't matter, it's still reading, she told him.

He'd found the mobile library by chance one Thursday. Since his wife had died, he'd taken to walking to the village shop once a week to buy his lottery ticket. That particular Thursday he'd had taken a different route to usual, simply because it was raining. He came across the mobile library parked up at the pub and on a whim, went inside. It became clear quite quickly that this was going to be a brand-new reason for an outing each month.

'Good morning, Steph,' Bill called as he climbed the steps into the van.

'Morning Bill, cup of tea?' Steph always carried a couple of flasks of hot water, milk and teabags so that she could make her regulars a nice cup of tea. After all, sometimes they braved the most awful weather to visit her so it felt like the least she could do.

'Lovely, I'm parched. I've come the long way round as it's such beautiful weather.'

'Got your lottery?' Steph knew that sometimes she was the only person her customers spoke to on a regular basis, so she made an effort to remember what they told her.

He smiled. 'Yes, got to be in it to win it, eh?' he laughed.

'Well, talking of luck, I managed to get you a copy of that Lady in Waiting book you wanted. It's like gold dust, Bill. I had to pick it up from Evesham yesterday. They had the only copy not on loan.'

'I appreciate that Steph, thank you.' He sat and sipped his tea while Steph chatted about the other people she'd seen that week.

'Gloria from Beech End borrowed that Hillary Clinton book. You read that a couple of months ago, didn't you? I didn't think that'd be her sort of thing.'

'It's always tempting to have an insight into other people's lives, particularly someone as high profile as Mrs Clinton. I expect Gloria was after her take on the incident in the Oval Office,' he said tactfully.

'Oh, the Monica Lewinski thing? I bet that's it. Gloria is such a devout romance reader, I was shocked that she'd chosen something so out of character but that explains it.'

Bill finished his tea and handed Steph his returns then began browsing for another couple of books to see him through the next few weeks.

'Quiet today, isn't it?' he said as he ran his finger along the shelf as he browsed.

Bill was her only regular at this stop and it was a mystery to her. She lived in fear of any of her stops being deemed unnecessary by someone who wouldn't care that they were removing someone's lifeline and maybe their only social encounter of the month. There was more to it than books. At least here Bill borrowed enough books on a regular basis for it to look consistent.

'It's been quiet everywhere this week. People are probably busy getting ready for Christmas.'

'Ah yes. That's probably it.'

Steph wondered what Bill would do at Christmas. She worried about some of her more isolated customers who didn't live with anyone. Not only the older ones; there was a woman who often came to the Old Hollow stop who wasn't that much older than Steph. She lived alone and had no family close by, although to be fair she did have a very healthy social life.

Another couple of people turned up while she was there, they'd never been before, and Steph suspected she'd never see them again as neither of them borrowed anything. It was a far cry from some of her other stops, like Hawthorn Lane where her regulars had become friends with each other. She wished that could happen here, for Bill.

He handed Steph his other choice, a biography of the England cricket team.

'That'll keep me going until next time.'

'Good choices, Bill. I fancy reading the Lady Glenconner one myself.'

'Wonderful woman,' said Bill.

He sounded like he knew her. Steph laughed. 'I'm sure she is.'

'Thank for the tea and books, Steph. Until next time.'

He pretended to doff his cap and left. Steph was sorry to see him go. Did he really know Lady Glenconner? She rolled her eyes and laughed. Of course he didn't.

5

The rest of the week went by in a flurry of re-organisation and Lois was relieved that Rosemary seemed to have got the message and wasn't manning the desk every morning when she arrived.

When Linda came back from lunch on Thursday, she looked like there was something she wanted to say. Lois could tell by the sideways looks she kept making while biting her lip and the little sighs that kept escaping from her.

'Is everything alright, Linda?' she asked eventually.

'I wasn't going to say anything,' began Linda, 'but I saw Rosemary at lunchtime and she's just not herself. I know she comes across as tough, but I think she's actually quite lonely. Now that she's not working anymore, well, I thought she looked lost.'

'It's bound to be difficult for her,' said Lois, trying to be sensitive. After so many years of working together, Rosemary and Linda might even be friends, as unlikely as that seemed. It was hard to imagine anyone being able to live up to high enough standards to become Rosemary's friend.

'Do you think there's anything we could do?' said Linda,

making Lois's heart sink a little as she imagined being guilt-tripped into letting Rosemary come back.

'I don't know,' she said, carefully. 'The thing is, even as a volunteer, I'm not sure she'd be willing to go along with the changes we're making. I know they are planning to close this library, but it has to be run properly until then. I'm not sure Rosemary would be behind that.'

'Oh, I think if it meant she could come back, she would be all for it. She'd planned her retirement before the closure was announced and I don't think she realised how much she would miss the place.'

Lois had her doubts about whether Rosemary would get behind any of the changes she'd made, even though that's how it should have been done all along anyway, but faced with Linda's pleading tone, she felt she didn't have much option.

'Why don't you ask her to come in on Monday, after lunch when it's quiet.' It was always quiet, but she couldn't face Rosemary first thing in the morning. If she was going to do this, Lois knew it was important to make sure it was on her terms. 'The three of us can have a chat about the ideas I've got and if Rosemary's onboard we can go from there.'

'Thanks, Lois,' said Linda, looking relieved. 'Thanks for giving her a chance.'

Lois went to Oliver's for a coffee. She had bought her lunch with her every day since Monday, mainly because she always used to take her lunch to work to save a bit of money and there was no reason to stop now. But she wished she was going in there every day. Since her visit, she hadn't been able to stop thinking about him. Every time she picked up her book, the image of him engrossed in reading it popped into her head. That slightly bashful smile he'd given her when he'd realised it was hers. She'd been hugging that image close ever since. She only wished she'd had more to say but he'd caught her off guard and anyway, she wasn't great at thinking of the wittiest thing to say. It had been a long time since a man had caught her attention like that.

It was busier in there than it had been on Monday, but he was working alone, unflustered and relaxed yet supremely efficient. His demeanour seemed to radiate out into the rest of the shop. No-one was in a hurry, people chatted in the queue and were happy to wait.

'Please tell me you're staying for a drink today?' he asked with a lopsided grin once he'd thanked the customer in front of her.

'Definitely. Skinny latte please,' she said in response to his expression, asking her what she wanted by way of raised eyebrows and the slightest parting of his lips.

He smiled and turned away to make the coffee. 'You having a good week?' he asked over his shoulder, raising his voice over the noise of the coffee machine.

'Yes, thanks,' she said, trying not to think so hard about his lips. 'I've just started working at the library.'

'Really? That explains the book then.'

'It's not just librarians that read.' It wasn't the best comeback, but she felt brave for attempting something more than a smile which is what he'd have got otherwise.

'True, yours isn't the only book that's been abandoned here.' He nodded towards a modest shelf of books with a sign underneath which said, 'Take one or leave one'.

'See?' she said, 'There aren't enough librarians to account for all of those.'

'That's true enough around here. Rosemary's a regular.' He gave her a knowing look.

'Oh right. Well, I'm probably not her favourite person at the moment.'

'That's an understatement,' he said with a grin.

Lois had forgotten how it could be in a small town. She

had grown up in a place like Croftwood and remembered the downside of living in a small community where everyone knew everything about everybody.

'I'm working on winning her over,' she said, feeling the need to explain herself.

'Good for you. Let's see how that goes.' He smiled and handed her the coffee. 'This one's on the house. Welcome to Croftwood.'

'Thanks, that's really nice of you.'

'Us outsiders have to stick together.' He winked at her and feeling herself blush, she gave a tight smile and turned away, heading over to the same place she had sat on Monday.

She saw Oliver glance at her as he listened to the next customer's order and felt a shiver of excitement. What was going on?

She headed back to the library with a spring in her step. Things were going really well, she concluded. It had been a good first week.

Oliver was struggling to concentrate on the customer he was serving. He glanced across at Lois. Since she'd come in to get her book with all her bike gear on, he'd known she was almost definitely the girl he'd seen ride past a couple of weeks ago. Funny how that had stuck in his mind. And funny that she was working at the library. He'd heard quite a lot about the new manager of the library from Rosemary who unsurprisingly didn't have a good word to say about her. But looking at her now, he was finding it hard to imagine that this Lois, who seemed particularly shy and unsure of herself, had managed to stand up to Rosemary so effectively.

He'd hoped to have more of a conversation with her when he'd dealt with the queue and could have gone over with the excuse of clearing the table, but it was busy and he was still serving when she'd left. But there was no rush. She'd probably be in all the time now that she was working in the town.

That evening, once he'd locked up and retreated to his flat upstairs, he ate a bowl of pasta then sat down to consider his reply to Amy's latest email. The first email from her, on the day he'd seen Lois, had taken him by surprise. They'd ended their relationship that summer while he was renovating the cinema. His purchase of the cinema, without telling her, had been the beginning of the end. Looking back, Oliver could see that they'd grown apart way before that and it had made sense to move on. He hadn't actually started seeing other people properly, but he'd dipped his toe in the water and he wasn't blind to the fact that the amount of time he'd spent thinking about Lois today was another sign that he was ready.

Amy's email had been an apology, but he wasn't sure what else. She didn't explicitly say she wanted to see him or anything but if she wasn't thinking along those lines what was the point of contacting him in the first place? He'd replied saying simply that it was nice to hear from her and he was glad she seemed to be doing well. It was friendly but brief. In return, she'd sent a very chatty, newsy email that seemed to require the same kind of thing in return. The problem was, it felt like he was opening the door to somewhere he didn't really want to go.

In the end, he decided on another brief reply. He wasn't one for wordy emails to anyone, she should know that and besides, he didn't know what to say. What was the point of telling her anything about his day-to-day life? He understood that maybe she was testing the waters with him. Being together for so long meant that it wasn't the cleanest break and with no third parties involved, some time apart inevitably led to wondering if they'd done the right thing.

He'd be lying if that hadn't crossed his mind more than once.

He pressed send on his email to Amy, put his phone down and lay out on the sofa ready to watch *The Walking Dead*. His phone pinged.

Can we meet? A x

Meeting was something he wasn't sure about without knowing what the agenda was first.

Really busy with the coffee house. What do you want to meet for?

Okay, it was blunt, verging on rude but he needed to know.

Just to catch up. Talk? A x

If he said no, that wouldn't be the end of it. It was probably simpler to just arrange to meet for a drink somewhere.

OK. Bolero 7.30 Friday?

Perfect. Thanks A x

He sighed. The kisses weren't a good sign.

6

By 7pm on Friday, Lois and Steph were sat in a super trendy bar in Worcester sipping extortionately priced cocktails. Steph had insisted that they go out rather than stay in.

'When was the last time we went out together? Not counting Monday morning coffee after we've loaded the mobile library,' she added, guessing what Lois was going to say. 'Because that's not going out, it's work.'

Lois couldn't actually remember so it was decided, it had definitely been too long. It felt quite nice to be going out knowing that there was no chance of seeing Alex. Back when they were together and he still lived in Worcester, if Lois was out in town it was inevitable that Alex and his friends would be too and would end up tagging onto her so it ended up feeling like a night out in a big gang rather than a night out with whoever she had started out with. It was usually Steph and she had complained loudly whenever it had happened.

'So, how's the first week been out in the sticks?' Steph asked.

'It's hardly the sticks.' Lois had already developed a bit of a soft spot for Croftwood.

'In the comparative sticks,' she said, rolling her eyes. 'Pedantic,' she added under her breath.

'It's been okay. There was a tiny blip on the first morning when I turned up and the retired librarian was sat behind the desk, but I think I've got that sorted out now.'

'Oh, god. I've come across her before. I think it was on a training course. Quite a tough old bird. Rosie is it?'

'Rosemary. She is quite formidable. I thought Linda was scared to death of her, but she has talked me into letting Rosemary come back to help out.'

'You're not going to do that are you? It'll be a nightmare with her telling you what to do and thinking experience beats anything else.'

'I know, I thought the same, but Linda reckons she's lonely and would come back on my terms. Anyway, she's coming in on Monday, so I'll see how receptive she is to a few new ideas before I offer anything.'

'Be careful. I'll be annoyed if you start moaning about how you couldn't say no to her.'

Lois laughed. 'I did throw her out that first morning, Steph. You would have been impressed.'

'Good, that's what we want. Take charge, Lois,' Steph said confidently, slurping the last of her cocktail. 'Ready for another?'

Lois nodded and finished the last of hers before fishing the slice of orange out of the bottom of the glass and furtively sucking the juice out of it.

'Hi, Lois.' She looked up to see Oliver standing next to her, amusement washing over his face as she hastily pulled the rind out of her mouth and deposited it back in the glass.

'Hi. Sorry, just getting my money's worth,' she said blushing.

He laughed. 'Quite right.' Without his apron, he looked different. Smarter, Lois thought and although he had been well-groomed when he was at work, he looked extra polished tonight wearing smart jeans and a jacket. 'I didn't expect to come across any librarians in here.'

'We're allowed in most places, actually.

'You're not by yourself, are you?' he asked, glancing around.

'No, I'm not a sad librarian. My friend's gone to get the drinks.'

Just as she was about to ask if he was alone, Steph arrived back with the drinks. She sat down, looking expectantly at Lois, waiting for an introduction.

'Are you a librarian as well?' Oliver asked her.

'I am indeed. A roving librarian.' She raised her eyebrows at Lois.

'Oliver owns a coffee shop in Croftwood.'

'It's a coffee house, actually. You know, like in *Friends*.'

'Ah, I see. Good job you said. Who knows the chaos that could have come from me getting that wrong,' said Steph.

'Well, you know, a coffee house is just cooler,' said Oliver. 'That's important.'

'Do you want to join us?' Steph asked him, ignoring the daggers that Lois was making at her.

'No, that's okay. I'm with someone. I'd better go. Enjoy the rest of your evening.'

'Oh my god,' Steph began after Oliver had walked away. 'No wonder you're enjoying working there, you've already met the fittest man in town.'

Lois smiled. She couldn't disagree. Oliver was good-looking and charismatic with it. 'I'll give you that. He's really nice.'

'He should have been at the top of your report about the first week, Lois. What is wrong with you?' Steph said affectionately.

'Just because I think he's attractive, it doesn't mean I want to go out with him. I've only met him twice.' Three times now. Not that she was counting but that wasn't enough times to know someone and despite her cringing when Steph asked him to join them, she was sorry that he hadn't.

They finished their second cocktail and decided to find somewhere to have dinner. Lois scanned the bar as they left, hoping to catch a glimpse of Oliver, planning to wave goodbye. She spotted him standing at the bar with his back to her. Steph nudged her and nodded towards him. Lois nudged her back, shooting her an exasperated look which just made Steph laugh. Then as they walked past him, they could see that he was talking to a woman who was looking up at him in a way that told Lois she was in love with him. And the jolt that Lois felt as she realised that, made her wonder why it mattered to her so much.

'Bloody hell, he's got a girlfriend,' said Steph and they linked arms and walked along Foregate Street towards their favourite Mexican restaurant. 'Of course he has,' she carried on. 'There are no single blokes like him.'

And as much as Lois tried to shrug off how much it bothered her to see him with someone, she couldn't. And that bothered her just as much.

As soon as Amy arrived at the bar, Oliver gave her a quick peck on the cheek then excused himself and went to the bathroom. He stood, leaning on the edge of the sink looking at himself in the mirror, taking deep breaths. It had been overwhelming to see her again. Everything had flooded back suddenly, and he just needed a minute.

Because they'd split when he was so engrossed in the cinema project, he hadn't had much time to think. With Amy driving the decision, he'd just gone along with it. Practical things like having to buy her out of the coffee house, he'd dealt with, with the help of Patsy, his business partner and he hadn't allowed himself to think too hard about how he felt. The cinema was finished but there were still plenty of teething problems, as there were with any new business so there hadn't seemed like a good time to try and resolve things with Amy. Tonight was the first time he'd seen her since the last bitter row they'd had months ago and all the reasons why he'd fallen for her in the first place had just floored him.

He exhaled, shook his hands to try and alleviate his stress, and then washed them because it felt wrong to leave the toilets without doing that. He looked himself hard in the eyes, willing himself to remember that Amy had turned into someone who didn't trust him. She hadn't wanted to be part of the cinema project, even though it had meant so much to him. It was going to be important to remember that tonight when she was right in front of him looking like the woman he fell in love with, none of the bitterness in her face. At least not yet.

He walked back into the bar and saw Lois sat alone at a table, looking as if she was sucking an orange slice, the rind giving her an orangey smile. Having a quick chat with her and then her friend relaxed him. He could do this. It was just Amy. After all, he had pulled off a one-minute conversation with Lois and he thought – hoped - he'd come across as charming and witty. That was easily more nerve-wracking than talking to his ex.

'I got us a couple of cocktails to start with, I hope that's okay,' said Amy when he went back to her.

'Fine, thank you.'

'Cheers.'

'Cheers.' She looked the same. Maybe more sparkly somehow but pretty much the same.

'Who was that you were talking to?' She nodded to where Lois and her friend were sitting.

'She's the new librarian at Croftwood Library. She's been into the coffee house a couple of times.'

'Oh right. The one that's taken over from Rosemary?'

'Yes, you heard about that did you?' He smiled. They were on safe ground.

'God yes. I don't know who I feel sorrier for, her or Rosemary. I know she's a nightmare but it's such a shame she couldn't delay her retirement to coincide with the library closing.'

'Well, maybe it won't close.'

Amy looked at him as if she thought that was unlikely, then in an out of character move when there was conflict on the horizon, she changed the subject. 'So how are you? It's great to hear that the coffee house is busy.'

'Yes, thanks, really busy. And how are things with you?' Even though he felt more at ease, he wasn't sure whether he was ready to hear about how things really were with her, but it was only right to ask. And it hadn't gone unnoticed that she'd avoided asking about the cinema.

'It's been a tough year.' She looked at him with an expression on her face that transported him back to the last time he'd seen her when they'd decided it would be for the best to end things.

'Yes,' he said quietly.

'But I'm ready to think about working again…'

They'd started the coffee house together but gradually she had lost interest and stopped being involved, relying on Oliver to run the place even though she wasn't working elsewhere instead. It had been another bone of contention.

'That's great, Amy.' He meant it. She needed to feel able to move on just as he had.

'And I suppose, now that things are… more normal, well I just wanted to see you. It was bad for both of us, and I just wanted to make sure we could be friends.'

'Of course.'

She smiled and rested her hand on his. 'Thanks, Oliver. It means a lot to me.'

It meant a lot to him too, he realised then. You couldn't end something so suddenly without feeling like there was some closure to be had. Meeting up had been a good idea from that point of view.

The rest of the hour or so they spent in the bar was a careful reminiscence of the good old days. When Amy said she had a taxi booked at nine o'clock, Oliver was part relieved that he had made it through the evening and part sorry it was over.

He glanced behind as he ushered Amy out of the bar, but he couldn't see Lois. She must have already left.

They walked along the pavement to where Amy's taxi was waiting. He pecked her on the cheek then wrapped her in a brief hug.

'It's been great to catch up, Ames,' he said, falling into using his pet name for her before he could stop himself.

'Night, Oliver.'

He turned up the collar on his jacket against the cold of the late Autumn evening and pushed his hands into his jeans' pockets. The queue at the taxi rank thankfully wasn't that long and he was relieved he was going to be able to have an early night as he was opening up the coffee house in the morning.

Where did Lois live, he wondered as the taxi headed out of the city. Not in Croftwood if she rode a bike to work. Maybe in Worcester. He seemed to remember that Rosemary had said she usually worked at the Hive. He wanted to find out, to know everything about her. Most of all he wanted to find out if she was feeling the same way as him.

7

Lois, Linda and Rosemary sat around the big table in the reference book area of the library ready for their meeting. Rosemary looked a little out of her comfort zone which Lois couldn't help but feel pleased about; at least it meant she might be more receptive than she'd expected.

'Shall I start by outlining a few of my ideas?' began Lois, keen to end the awkwardness.

'By all means,' said Rosemary.

'Linda and I have already switched over to using the live system for checking books in and out.' She paused to gauge Rosemary's reaction to this. Lois had thought she'd take it as a snub on the way she'd done things before, but her expression didn't change. 'And we've been issuing county library cards.' So far, so good.

'It's gone very smoothly,' added Linda, bravely.

'So, I think the next thing I'd like to do is to add a bit of colour to the library with some genre-specific displays. In the Hive, we have small table-sized units with shelves underneath dotted around with a selection of similar titles grouped together. You might have one with thrillers, crime, romcoms, you know. It helps people find something new from a genre they already know or perhaps tempts them into trying a new genre altogether.'

'I love that idea!' said Linda. 'When it's Christmas we can have all the Christmas books in one place.'

'Exactly. How do you feel about taking that on, Rosemary?'

'I suppose I could...it's quite unorthodox and it seems like a waste of effort given the future of the library.'

Lois took a breath. 'I know you haven't done it here before, but I think it could help to increase borrowing rates because it saves people from trawling through the shelves. It's much easier for a cover to catch their eye. Once we get known for it, I think it will be a real draw. And I take your point about whether it's worth us bothering but we're here for six more months. Let's send it out on a high.'

Linda looked thrilled. 'Quite right, Lois.'

'And how much time do you think it will take?' asked Rosemary.

'I know you must be very busy. Why don't we go with Tuesday and Thursday mornings, if that suits you?'

'That will do nicely. Thank you.'

'Great, thank you, Rosemary. It'll be a great help because Linda and I will struggle to find time for that. Probably why it hasn't been adopted before,' she said kindly.

'Indeed. I shall see you tomorrow morning.' Rosemary buttoned her coat and picked up her bag. She waited for Linda to return to the desk before she said, 'Thank you, Lois.' A little nod along with complete eye contact showed Lois how much she meant it.

'No problem. See you tomorrow.' She had made the right decision and had a feeling that it was going to work out just fine.

The next day, Rosemary was in the library when Lois arrived, though thankfully not behind the desk. She was browsing the shelves and had begun making a pile of books. Lois had already decided not to interfere but was pleased to see a CL Taylor title in amongst a pile of other thriller and suspense novels.

'Morning, Rosemary.'

'Good morning, Lois.' Rosemary left what she was doing and came over to Lois. 'I had a thought. I happened to be in Waterstones last week and they have recommendations written by the staff for various books. I wondered whether we might do something similar to put on the displays?'

'Brilliant idea, Rosemary. Yes, if any of us have read anything you choose, we'll write a brief review.' Lois felt like she'd won something, she was so pleased that Rosemary was on board. 'In fact, I could start you off with a review for that CL Taylor book.'

'Wonderful,' she said and went back to browsing the shelves.

'I think you could call that a breakthrough,' said Linda when Lois sat down behind the desk.

'Let's not get ahead of ourselves.'

Linda grinned. 'Honestly, I've never seen Rosemary so willing to go along with anything before. It's amazing.'

'Well, thanks for suggesting it.'

Linda looked as pleased as anything as she got on with arranging the small number of reservations that had come through on the system while Lois went back to sifting through the mountains of paperwork to make sure everything had been dealt with properly before they got rid of it and went completely digital. Her thoughts drifted to Oliver. She was still feeling thrown by having seen him with the woman at the weekend. Rationally she knew that Steph was right, of course someone like him would have a girlfriend but until then, she had honestly felt like something was beginning between them. She should force herself to go into the coffee house sooner rather than later if only to prove to herself that seeing him was no big deal. There was no reason for her to avoid going in there whatsoever.

At lunchtime she strolled along the high street, telling herself that if there was a queue it wasn't worth waiting. If there was no-one queuing at all then she would go in and have a coffee. Secretly, she was hoping that the queue would be out of the door because she didn't know what was the matter with her.

There was no queue. It was Tuesday after all. She took a deep breath and went in. It was so quiet that Oliver was sat at one of the tables nearest the counter with his laptop open.

'Lois,' he said, looking pleased to see her. 'Have a coffee with me to save me from having to get on with my accounts.'

She hadn't expected that. 'Okay, thanks.'

'How's your week going?' he asked as he made coffees for them.

'Rosemary's back in the fold,' she said with a smile.

'Really? Is she driving you mad yet?'

'Surprisingly not. She seems keen to go along with the changes I'm making and has even had her own ideas to help it along.'

'Wow. Well, that's good, isn't it? She's nice enough, maybe just a bit stuck in her ways. I guess it's easier for her to work to your changes than to have to change the way she'd always done things herself.'

'Hmm, maybe.' Lois had never thought of it like that.

'Good night out on Friday?' They sat down at his table and he closed the lid on his laptop.

'Yes, brilliant. You?'

He looked up at the ceiling as if he was trying to find the right words. 'Yep, good,' he said finally, sounding as if even saying it was good was an effort.

'Really. That good?'

'No, not really,' he smiled. 'She's an old friend, it's complicated.'

An old friend who was completely besotted with him. Clearly, there was more to it, but she was quite pleased by his lack of enthusiasm.

'Right.' This subject was stalling the conversation, it was so awkward.

'Anyway,' he shook his head and smiled. 'Did you go somewhere after the bar?'

'Steph and I went to that Mexican place on New Street. I had one too many tequila shots, but we had a good time. How about you?'

'I had an early night. Boring, I know, but I had to open up on Saturday morning.' He looked down at his coffee and a lock of hair fell over his eyes.

Her fingers twitched as she imagined weaving it back where it had come from, into the rest of the dark waves. 'What time do you open?'

'Seven-thirty. It kills the Friday night vibes but,' he shrugged, 'not a problem for a singleton like me.'

He was single. She was ridiculously pleased to hear him say that. 'I think it'll be a shock to the system when I have to start working Saturdays again. I can't expect Linda to do them forever.'

'It's people like us who keep the wheels of the weekend turning for everyone else, Lois. We're special, invaluable even.' He grinned, then stood up and took his empty cup over to the counter.

'I'll remember that in the middle of winter when I have to drag myself out of bed in the dark on a weekend.'

'That's exactly why I live upstairs,' he said, flicking his eyes to the ceiling. 'I just roll out of bed and down the stairs and I'm good to go.'

He never looked like he'd just rolled out of bed. He pushed his hand into his hair, the stray lock now back where it belonged, the gesture making Lois a little weak at the knees.

'Well, I'd better get back.' She pulled her purse out of her pocket.

'It's on the house. It was good to see you, Lois.' He leaned his hands on the back of his chair and looked at her with an intensity that said it actually was good to see her and not just something he was saying as a goodbye.

'Thanks. That's really nice of you.'

'Anytime.' He tilted his head and gave her a lop-sided smile then sat down and opened his laptop back up.

She left the coffee house with a spring in her step, completely forgetting that she'd gone in for lunch and hadn't eaten anything.

8

Steph couldn't believe she was facing another Friday night with nothing to do. She was on her way to the last stop of the week, a small village called Old Hollow. It was one of her favourites, although she thought of most of her stops fondly. There was one customer, Zoe, who worked from home on Fridays, so she always called in and Steph was hoping to see her today. They usually put the world to rights over a cup of tea and a few biscuits.

The stop was in a visitor's car park for people visiting the Malvern Hills. In the summer Steph sometimes had trouble finding enough room to park the van. It was the same with the Red Lion Inn car park which could be heaving on a hot summer's day but today, there was a light mist which had settled over the hills and there were just a handful of cars.

Steph got the tea and biscuits out and busied herself with some admin which was left from the previous stop that day.

'Steph! Got the kettle on?' Zoe was wearing her usual high-end excuse for a tracksuit which was cream and probably cashmere, with her perfectly highlighted blonde hair piled in a neat bun on the top of her head. She was probably in her late thirties and her job was something to do with PR for a cosmetics company.

'Course! How are you?'

Zoe rolled her eyes dramatically, sat down on one of the stools and started nibbling at a custard cream. 'Oh, god. Date from absolute hell last weekend, Steph,' she said, picking up a stray crumb from her lap and licking off her finger.

'Tinder disaster?' asked Steph. This was just what she needed. A good gossip about terrible dates would confirm that it was safer to stay in tonight.

'If only. I could have buggered off after ten minutes if it was. No, it was a friend of a friend, so then you have to see it through, right?'

Steph nodded sympathetically.

'Honestly, if Sasha really thought we'd get on I'm not sure she actually is a friend. He was shorter than me. Shorter! I mean, that is not okay.'

'But aside from that?'

Zoe took her phone out and showed Steph a picture. The guy was attractive. Not rugged enough for Steph's taste but she could appreciate that other people, lots of other people would think he was a catch. 'See?'

'Um, he looks okay...'

'Exactly! He does in that picture. I mean I might as well rely on Tinder if my friend,' she did air quotes, 'thinks this is representative.'

Steph handed her a cup of tea. 'So he didn't look like that?'

'He did not. He has shaved his hair. Short. This,' she pointed to his blonde quiff in the picture, 'is gone. Honestly Steph, I could have cried. Is it too much to ask for men of a certain age to just try using caffeine shampoo before they resort to shaving their heads?'

She was so affronted that Steph had to muffle her giggle with a bourbon biscuit.

'I've had a very similar experience recently.' Steph took her phone out and presented the picture of Sylvester.

'God!' Zoe recoiled from the phone then laughed. 'You win! That's the definition of a Tinder disaster. It just makes you want to jack it all in and stay single, doesn't it?'

While Steph could see where Zoe was coming from because all the evidence pointed to the fact that it seemed to be near on impossible to meet anyone normal in the world of digital dating, Steph was a believer. She really believed that somewhere there was a man who was The One and she knew, she believed she'd find him. One day.

'Mmm,' said Steph as she munched on yet another biscuit. 'But when you find the right man, it'll have all been worth it.'

Zoe shot her a dubious look. 'Well, he'd better show himself soon, that's all I can say.'

A couple of other regulars called in and Steph chatted to them while Zoe chose a selection of books.

Chatting to Zoe had given her the lift she needed. After she dropped off the van at the Hive, she walked home via Tesco Express and picked out a nice bottle of red then as soon as she got in, ordered a pizza. All she needed was this - good wine, good food and BBC iPlayer. She flicked down the listings until she found Gavin and Stacey and settled in for the evening. It didn't matter how many times she watched it, she still loved it as much as she had the first time. And it gave her hope that there really was one person out there. The right person. And you might see them lots of times without realising they were they one straightaway, like Smithy and Nessa, but the universe would sort it out for you in the end. That was all she had to do. Keep looking and eventually, she'd find him.

9

It was a crisp late Autumn day which made Lois's bike ride to Croftwood a lot more pleasurable than the past couple of days which had been drizzle all the way, and the fact that it was a Saturday meant that the roads were a lot quieter than in the week.

It was the first morning that she had opened the library up by herself. Linda was usually there first and as she lived so close by, had even been opening up on her days off until Lois got the hang of the alarm and knew what needed switching on and off.

Lois found there was something magical about being the first person there in the morning. The stillness as she walked in was incredible and she found herself tiptoeing around the place as she turned everything on. It was like waking the library up from a peaceful slumber.

She got straight on with her morning chores, thinking that a Saturday could easily be much busier than she was used to in the week. It was a couple of years since she'd routinely worked on Saturdays. Once she'd been promoted to deputy manager at the Hive, she had Monday to Friday shifts and having Saturdays off had been a relief because Alex constantly complained that she wasn't around at the weekends. Even though she'd had every fourth Saturday off, he'd inevitably spent it watching football at the pub with his mates. Now that he had left, it was nice to have something to fill the weekend again and nice not to have to battle with anyone about it.

By half-past nine, a trickle of parents and children began, turning into a steady stream by late morning. In the Saturday morning tradition of many households with young children, lots of them had clearly been swimming at the local pool on the way. It was the most buzzing that Lois had seen the library since she'd started there.

She was surprised that no-one was asking anything of her. In the Hive, they were inundated by children asking to reserve copies of the latest David Walliams book or the endlessly popular Harry Potter books but here, everyone was very quiet and reverential. It was weird. When Lois then heard a parent shush a child who was exclaiming about a book they had found, she decided to step in.

'Morning everyone!' she said in a loud voice. Everyone turned to look at her, clearly stunned that anyone should use such a loud voice in the library. 'Just to let you know, we are making a few changes to the library, so please don't feel it's necessary to keep your children quiet. The library is for everyone.' A few parents mumbled a thank you and then they all went back to what they had been doing, just as quietly as before. Oh well, it wasn't going to change overnight.

Because she was alone in the library, Lois couldn't have a lunch break. She had planned for it and bought food that was easy to snack on behind the desk when she had chance in between customers. She had just opened a packet of crisps when the door opened, Oliver walked in and placed a brown paper bag on the desk in front of her.

'Lunch is served,' he smiled.

'But I didn't order lunch,' said Lois.

'It's a standing order on a Saturday. I used to do it for Rosemary and I do it for Linda on days when there's just one of you working. Rosemary mentioned this would be your first Saturday by yourself so I just thought, you know,' he said, looking slightly awkward.

Lois was touched not only by his thoughtfulness but by Rosemary's in tipping him off. 'That's great, thank you. How much do I owe you?'

'Nothing this time. I did spring it on you, after all. Let me know if you don't want to carry it on but if you do, I'll put it on your tab next time,' he said as he backed out of the door.

'Do you want to stay for a cuppa?' she asked, before realising how ridiculous it was to be offering him a drink when he'd just bought one for her.

'Another time, I need to get back. But thanks.'

Lois opened the bag to find a deliciously warm avocado and tomato toasted sandwich. It gave her a glow inside when she realised he had chosen for her exactly what she would have chosen for herself and thank goodness, there was nothing she had to do, no-one to serve so she sat back and enjoyed it. Oliver must have a helper at weekends then, she thought. It must be the busiest day of the week for him, and he wouldn't have closed the place while he popped her lunch in. He was so thoughtful.

When Lois left that evening it was dark and cold. She cycled up the high street and saw that Oliver's was still open. It looked warm and inviting. Perhaps she would just pop in to thank him properly for her lunch. She pulled up on the opposite side of the road but while she was waiting to cross, she saw the woman from the bar inside, his old friend and she was wearing an Oliver's apron. They were clearing tables together. He was smiling and she was laughing at something he'd said.

Lois got back on her bike and cycled. The high she'd been on since lunchtime rapidly dissipated as she taunted herself by remembering how that woman had been looking at Oliver in the bar. She was some kind of old friend who'd been a lot more than that at some point, Lois was certain. Every moment that she'd felt something between her and Oliver was cast into doubt as she rode along the road that had become so familiar. There was nothing to distract her from doing anything other than convincing herself that she'd imagined everything.

The house was in darkness and once she'd pulled off her coat and helmet, she made herself some beans on toast with plenty of cheese and lashings of Worcestershire Sauce, poured herself a glass of wine and settled herself on the sofa ready for *Strictly*, trying not to think about how envious she was of the evening that the woman in Oliver's was enjoying right now.

10

Rosemary had done a great job of making three genre-specific displays. They'd gone for crime/thriller, contemporary women's fiction/romcoms and biographies/autobiographies. Between the three of them, they'd managed to write a few reviews to stick on the shelves and they had begun suggesting to customers that they may want to submit their own reviews.

On Tuesday, when Linda had gone to lunch, Rosemary came over to the desk.

'Lois, I owe you an apology.'

Lois opened her mouth to object, but Rosemary raised her hand and made a face that meant she didn't want to hear anything from Lois.

'I can see now how things should have been run here,' she began. 'What you have done has only enhanced the library and I wish I had been more open to such ideas while I was Librarian, then we may not be in the situation that we find ourselves in now.'

Lois was stunned that Rosemary should be so frank about what she thought. 'I really appreciate that Rosemary, and we couldn't have done it without you. The displays have been a big hit. We'll see what else we can come up with. Perhaps the three of us could have a brainstorming meeting on Thursday when you're here.' She stopped, then said more gently, 'I'm not sure you could have stopped the library being on the closure list, Rosemary but let's give it the best send-off we can. At least make County Libraries wonder what they're giving up.'

'Wonderful, thank you, Lois.' Rosemary managed a smile then went to collect her things from the office.

What if they did make enough changes at Croftwood Library to turn things around? Was it possible to reverse the decision with less than six months until the closure? It was already a far cry from what Lois had expected the job to be like when she'd first looked round. Even implementing the few changes they had so far seemed like a huge step forward. Maybe they could make enough of a difference. She resolved to talk to Robert and get his take on things.

While Linda was still gone, Lois began to pick at her lunch. A gorgeous, toasted sandwich from Oliver's would have been much nicer than the limp cheese sandwich she'd half-heartedly made that morning but she picked tiny bits of bread and cheese from it as she sat there, with no drive left to do anything.

'Hey.' A voice broke into her thoughts. It was Oliver, strolling through the door as he unbuttoned his coat. It was a surprise to see him walk straight from her daydream into the library. It just went to show how much she was still thinking about him at the moment despite her vow to forget about any possibility of romance with him once she'd forced herself to stop moping at the weekend.

'Hi. Are you not open today?'

'I am open but I'm not working. Day off. Patsy's in today.'

Patsy must be the friendly barista she'd met on her first

day.

'What can I do for you?' She tried not to be disappointed that he hadn't bought her any lunch.

'Rosemary suggested I call in to choose a book. She said you have some new displays and she was keen for me to be a guinea pig.'

'Oh, right. What kind of books do you enjoy?'

'Like I said before, I don't have that much time to read.'

It always annoyed Lois when people said that. How could anyone not find ten minutes to pick up a book? It wasn't as if you had to devote days at a time to it unless you wanted to. She came out from behind the desk and headed towards the display of crime and thriller books.

'Maybe something along the lines of the book of yours I started?'

She shrugged off a pang of guilt as she remembered she'd promised to lend it to him after she'd finished it. She hadn't forgotten but she'd got distracted by another book and not picked it up again yet.

'You could try this one.' She handed him a copy of *Sleep* by CL Taylor. He turned it around in his hands and nodded.

'Have you read it?'

'Yes, I enjoyed it. It's quite pacey, keeps you interested.'

'Okay, I'll take it. Maybe we can have a coffee and talk about it after I've read it,' he grinned.

'That'd be good.' She was momentarily distracted as she pondered what a good idea that was, not just because she couldn't think of anything she'd rather do but it sparked something that she thought could work for the library too.

Oliver looked surprised. 'I mean, we don't have to do that.'

'Sorry. It'd be great to do that. I was just having an epiphany.'

'That sounds like it ought to be good?' His brow furrowed.

'It is good. You've just given me an idea.' She laughed,

feeling on a high like she did on the rare times she knew she'd hit on something special.

'Right,' said Oliver, looking amused with a hint of frightened. 'Anyway, shall I check out my book?' He flipped his wallet open and handed her one of Rosemary's old-fashioned paper library cards. 'It's been so long since I came in, does that still work here?'

Suddenly, even though the same thing had been happening on a daily basis since she'd started working at Croftwood Library, it seemed hilarious that Oliver was quite seriously offering her this scrappy piece of paper and she burst out laughing.

'Sorry, I'm not laughing at you,' she said, trying to pull herself together. 'It's just so funny that you...' she bent over, holding her stomach as the laughter gripped her and she could hear Oliver begin laughing along with her which made it even worse. '1970s...' she managed to blurt out. Then a wave of embarrassment flooded over her as she remembered that she was at work, she was the manager for god's sake. She managed to sober her mood by imagining Rosemary's expression if she was stood there instead of Oliver and she stood up, wiping the tears from her cheeks trying to ignore the fact that now she thought she may burst into tears right in front of Oliver and for no reason at all.

'Gosh, I'm so sorry. No, we're not taking those anymore as they're a relic from the 1970s.' She risked a smile, hoping that it wouldn't lead to full-blown hysterics again. 'But I can sort that out for you.'

She sat down at the desk and asked him the few questions necessary to set him up with a digital account. His whole name was Oliver Jones. Somehow finding that out made her feel closer to him. She handed him his new card along with his book. 'Enjoy it.'

'Thanks, Lois.' He turned to leave, then paused and turned

around to look at her, his expression telling her that he was weighing up whether or not to say something. 'Anytime you want a coffee...you know.' He looked like he was going to say something else then shook his head slightly and smiled. 'Take care.'

'Bye, Oliver,' she called to his back as he walked out.

How mortifying. She didn't know what had come over her. And how long had it taken for her resolve over Oliver to crumble? A matter of minutes in his presence and she was willing to open herself up to goodness knows what and she didn't seem able to stop herself from feeling like... like she was falling for him. Was that what it was? And had he come here today to see her or to do Rosemary a favour? Either way, the germ of an idea he'd given her was well worth another go on the emotional rollercoaster she seemed to be on at the moment. She was going to start a book club. Not any book club, this one was going to be different, and she already had a feeling that it was going to change everything.

11

'I think the displays are working out really well,' said Lois at the Thursday meeting with Linda and Rosemary. 'It's been great to be able to point people in their direction for them to browse through.'

'It's a huge time-saver if someone doesn't know what they want and are after us to help them choose. It used to take ages when everything was shelved away.' Linda blushed as she realised Rosemary might take that as a criticism but actually Rosemary looked much happier than she had even the week before. She seemed to be enjoying her new role at the library and was managing to be very positive about most of the things that were improvements on the way she'd run things before.

'The next thing I'd like to concentrate on is building our social media presence. We need to have a Twitter account so that we can network with other libraries and it's an easy way for customers to get in touch with us. And an easy way for us to publicise the library. I know we're faced with closure, but I really would like us to go down in a blaze of glory.'

'I'm not very good at social media,' said Linda, 'but I'd

love to have a go at that.'

'Great, I'll put you in touch with Claudia at the Hive. One session with her and you'll be away. I'd also wondered about starting a book club.'

'There are so many book clubs, Lois. Do you think it's necessary?' asked Rosemary, her tone of disapproval back, it seemed.

'That's true,' said Lois patiently. 'Our book club needs to be different. I haven't quite got it sorted in my mind yet, but I was thinking of some sort of date-with-a-book kind of thing? We pair readers up with someone who has read the same book as them and they discuss it over a coffee or something. It might be less intimidating for people who aren't keen on groups; you always get the odd one or two who dominate things. I don't know, it's just something that came to me, something that Oliver said gave me the idea. I haven't quite thought out how it would work yet but it's a start.'

'I think it's a delightful idea,' said Rosemary, surprising both Linda and Lois with her renewed enthusiasm. Perhaps the mention of Oliver had changed her mind. 'Some book clubs can be dreadful and often never even discuss the book, it's just an excuse for a gossip and can be very cliquey. The idea of going for a coffee or what-have-you with a fellow book lover, well that's wonderful.' She was smiling and shaking her head. Lois hadn't expected the idea to be so well received.

'Would you mind having a think about how we can do it, Rosemary? I also thought we could get my colleague Steph involved somehow with the mobile library so that people who don't find it easy to get into town could still join in.' The more Lois thought about it, the better the idea was forming in her mind.

'Thank you, Lois,' said Rosemary, as if Lois had bestowed some marvellous honour on her. 'I will enjoy that very much.'

'Great. Now that we've all got something to get our teeth into let's make this meeting weekly so we can keep track of our progress. Linda, do you mind if I have lunch first today?'

'Not at all. I'm happy whatever you want to do.'

Lois headed straight for Oliver's, no longer able to remember why she'd been avoiding it for the whole week.

'Hey Lois, good to see you. Skinny latte?'

'Great, thanks.' There was no queue behind her. 'Have you got time to join me?'

His face lit up. 'Give me two minutes to get this sandwich made and I'll be with you.'

Lois went and sat down in what had become her usual seat. Oliver worked quickly, scooping the sandwich onto a plate and cutting it in half before delivering it to a guy who was working on his laptop at one of the tables near the window. Then he picked up the two coffees he'd already made and came over to join her.

'How are you getting on with the book?' she asked.

'Oh, god. You haven't come to talk about it already, have you? I've only had it a couple of days.' He'd gone pale and looked so genuinely frightened that Lois couldn't help laughing.

'I was just wondering, making conversation. I just fancied a change of scenery.'

He stared into his coffee for a few seconds then lifted his eyes to look straight into hers. 'So, the other day at the library…are you okay? It seemed like it might have been one of those times when you start off laughing but end up crying.'

Lois was touched that he cared enough to ask although it was quite worrying that he'd thought she was that emotionally unstable that she'd end up hysterically crying in the library, even if that's exactly what she'd thought was going to happen too.

'Sorry, I didn't mean to make you uncomfortable. Quite a lot has changed for me recently. The job, obviously, and I split up with my boyfriend a couple of months ago.'

'Sorry to hear that.'

'It's okay. It was probably a long time coming. Anyway, I think sometimes, things just build up and I don't know why I thought it was so funny, you getting that old library card out of your wallet...' she couldn't help giggling for a second, 'but it was funny and I just let myself go...or something.'

'You certainly did that.' His eyes were sparkling, and she was relieved to see he thought it was endearing rather than bonkers.

'Well, so often you can be thwarted in letting your emotions take their natural course.' He was so easy to talk to, she felt like she could tell him just about anything.

'Thwarted is a great word,' said Oliver smiling. 'And allow me to welcome you to the singles club.'

So, he was still single despite the Old Friend.

'Thanks. That sounds appropriately tragic.'

He laughed. 'It is a bit tragic once you get to our age, I suppose it's harder to find the right person. I'm probably too hard to please. Once you hit thirty and you're still single, you're kind of set in your ways.'

'Speak for yourself. Anyway, you haven't been single that whole time surely?'

'Surely because I'm a great catch?' He grinned then looked embarrassed and said, 'Sorry, don't answer that.'

Lois smiled. 'Surely because it's highly unusual for someone in their thirties to have been single forever. Everyone's had at least a dalliance by then.'

'Gosh, you're full of words no-one else uses any more today,' he teased. 'Now you're single are you going down the Tinder road?'

He hadn't answered her.

'No, I don't think I can face it. My friend, Steph, you know, from the bar, has had some shocking Tinder dates but she sticks with it, reckons it's the only way things are done now.'

'I'm sure it is,' he said. 'It wouldn't be for me though. Have you done it before?'

'No,' Lois admitted. 'I met my ex-boyfriend in the pub which isn't that surprising once you know him.'

'You see? That's how it used to be done. Meet in a pub or club. Always used to work for me.'

'Well, the thought of that terrifies me just as much. But you know the other day when you were saying we should have a coffee sometime when we talk about that CL Taylor book? I'm thinking that might work as an idea for the library. We're going to try a book club where just two people meet to talk about the book. A date with a book.'

'Do I get commission?'

Lois rolled her eyes.

'Seriously, I'm glad you're thinking of things to revitalise the library. As much as I love Rosemary, she did have it firmly planted in… the 1970s, was it?'

Lois grinned and managed to hold in the laughter that threatened to bubble up again. 'Thanks for the idea. I'd better get back to the time warp.'

As she was leaving, the guy with the laptop intercepted her.

'I couldn't help but overhear you talking to Oliver about a book club.'

'That's right, we're starting one at the library. Just pop in if you want to sign up.'

'Great, will do. I'm Toby.'

Toby held his hand out for Lois to shake.

'Lois.'

'You'll see him again, Lois. He practically lives here during the week,' Oliver called from behind the counter.

'Sadly, that is true.' Toby smiled. 'Anyway, thank you. I'm quite keen on the idea of the book club.'

'Because you heard the word 'date'?' Oliver teased him.

Toby blushed but grinned good-naturedly. 'I need all the help I can get in that department,' he said.

'It's not meant to be a romance thing but you never know,' said Lois.

Lois glanced at Oliver who was also grinning as he rolled his eyes. 'He's avoiding Tinder, like the rest of us.'

'Anything involving books has got to be worth a try.'

Lois left Oliver's hoping that Toby's enthusiasm for the book club was a good sign that people would be as interested in it as he seemed to be.

12

Linda took to using Twitter like a duck to water and it had definitely helped to spread the word about the new displays. By the time they had their next Thursday meeting they had over a hundred followers and Linda was keen to try out Instagram, to 'get with the kids', she said. They'd also been pushing the fact that they had computer terminals that could be used – they were even switched on these days - and that had drawn a few people in. Lois had helped a few of the more elderly customers to set up email accounts.

Oliver had dropped in some loyalty cards and said he'd do a discount for anyone who wanted a coffee to take to the library given that they didn't have their own café like some of the bigger libraries. Lois couldn't believe the effort people were willing to make to help out and she began to wonder whether they could do more than just go out with a bang.

Rosemary had come up trumps with a plan for the date-with-a-book club. She thought they should choose one book from each of their three displays each month which would give people a choice of genre. They could then make sure they got extra copies of those books into the library. Readers who wanted to join in would fill in a card when they had finished the book and then everyone who had read a particular book would be matched with someone else and would meet their coffee buddy at a designated book club meeting.

Lois was so pleased that Rosemary had got the whole thing planned out so thoroughly. She had taken Lois's, well Oliver's idea and turned it into something that would work. The three of them chose the books they would start with after checking on the system for availability of extra copies, then Linda launched it on Twitter.

Rosemary had also asked Oliver if he would be willing to host the club in the coffee house one evening a month so that people who worked during the day could join in. It was a more relaxed atmosphere and more comfortable than the library with the added benefit of refreshments on hand. The logistics of organising it for the mobile library were a little trickier so they were going to have a meeting with Steph at some point to see if she had any bright ideas.

Feeling as if she was making progress at work made Lois want to extend that into the rest of her life so she spent the weekend sorting out all of Alex's things which she moved from around the house and put in the spare bedroom along with the tidy piles of his clothes she'd already put on the bed. She wondered how he had been managing with just the clothes he had taken with him for the one week when now it was two months since they'd split up and he hadn't done anything about collecting everything.

It felt surprisingly cathartic to clear the house of traces of him. The fact that she wasn't overwhelmed with nostalgia or sadness was yet another sign that they'd made the right decision.

Got your stuff ready for you whenever you want to collect it. L x

He didn't reply, not that she'd expected him to, but it was starting to niggle her that he seemed to think it was okay to leave all his things with her as if she was just sat at home looking after it for him.

The weekend dragged with not much going on. She was restless and what had started out as a cleansing experience was annoying her now. She wanted it all out of her house and the fact he'd ignored her text for the whole day had ignited an unusual rage in her.

On Sunday morning she went to the corner shop for the papers, which she never normally did, and had a lovely relaxing morning idly reading and watching the television. But by lunchtime, the novelty had worn off and she was bored and twitchy again. She looked around the lounge. Her lounge. Now that Alex was gone, this was her house again, she realised.

Gulping down her seventh cup of tea of the day, she ran upstairs and changed out of her leggings and sweatshirt into jeans and a Fair Isle jumper. She was going shopping.

It was ages since she'd bought anything for the house and once she started looking, there was so much she wanted to buy but she settled on beginning with tarting up the lounge and buying some new bedding. Everything was so bulky; she'd bought four cushions, a throw and some candles and was struggling with several huge bags. They weren't heavy and she had enjoyed indulging herself for once but at the same time, as she walked down Worcester high street, she felt like an idiot for not thinking it through.

'Lois!'

She stopped and turned around to see Oliver jogging towards her. She was so pleased to see him that she surprised herself, and not just because he might help her with her bags.

'You look like you need a hand,' he said, taking a couple of bags out of her hands.

'Thanks, that was good timing. I was just thinking that I should have paced myself.'

'Got time for a drink?' he asked with a glint in his eye.

Having been alone for almost two days, Lois couldn't think of anything she would rather do.

'Definitely. Lead the way.'

Oliver took them to The Old Rectifying House next to the river. It was fairly quiet for a Sunday afternoon, clearly they'd hit a lull between lunch and dinner. They found a table and made a pile of Lois's shopping before pulling their coats off and sitting down. Oliver went to the bar and came back with a bottle of wine and two glasses.

'A glass would have been plenty,' said Lois, even though she didn't really mind. The prospect of sitting with him long enough to share the bottle was quite nice.

'Well, you know. Once you've bought two glasses it's almost as cheap to buy a bottle.' He poured them half a glass each, then raised his glass. 'To the perfect Sunday afternoon.'

'To Sunday afternoon,' Lois said and clinked her glass against his.

'Are you redecorating or something?' Oliver asked, nodding towards Lois's bags, where the cushions were trying to make a break for it.

'I just wanted to put my mark on the house again. Freshen things up now that Alex has left.'

'Good for you. Is it strange being by yourself?'

'Not really, I've kind of got used to it. I'm quite enjoying the feeling of having my own space.' That wasn't true. Until she'd had the genius idea to come shopping, she'd been going stir-crazy.

'I know what you mean. You can have everything just how you like it and do what you want when you want. There's a lot to be said for that,' he said wistfully.

Lois wanted to ask him if he'd lived with anyone before,

but it seemed a bit nosey. 'What were you doing in town today?' she asked instead.

'I needed to get some bits and pieces,' he said vaguely and with no shopping that Lois had noticed. 'Jack usually works at the coffee house on a Sunday, so I try to get out of Croftwood at least. Have a change of scenery.'

There were more scenic places he could have gone but she knew what he meant. Working and living in the same place must be a bit claustrophobic.

'I know what you mean. I've quite enjoyed having a tiny commute for a change.'

'You live in Worcester? Of course you do, you have to be within walking distance with the amount of shopping you have.'

'Very funny.' She loved that he felt comfortable enough to gently mock her. Although it could just be the wine.

'So, Lois. Would it be too much to suggest we turn this drink into dinner?'

She wanted nothing more than to spend the rest of the day with Oliver. 'I'd love that. Here or somewhere else?'

'It's pretty comfortable here, good menu and we already have space for the shopping. We might not be so lucky elsewhere.'

'Here is fine with me.' She smiled at him and noticed the crinkles in the corner of his eyes as he smiled back at her.

'Great.' He poured them some more wine as Lois excused herself to go to the loo.

When she came out, there was someone sat at the table with Oliver. It was the Old Friend. Lois didn't even know what her name was and she felt really awkward about going back to the table.

Lois lurked at the side of the bar, but the woman didn't show any signs of leaving. She had her own drink on the table and she looked so relaxed that she could have been sat there with Oliver for hours. It seemed odd to Lois that she happened to appear during the two minutes or so that she had been in the loo, but maybe she was just being paranoid. Or maybe this woman had been spying on them.

Oliver looked over his shoulder, perhaps wondering where she'd got to and once he spotted her he stood up and came over to her under the watchful eye of the woman. Lois could feel her cheeks redden.

'I wondered where you'd got to,' he said, smiling.

'Is she joining us?' Lois asked as a joke, but her insides withered when Oliver began looking shifty and seemed to be at a loss for words.

'Um, would that be okay?'

Was he joking? Did he really think she was going to sit back down and just join in with...whatever was going on between them?

'Look, I'd better be going.'

'No, don't go, Lois. What about dinner?'

Yes, what about dinner? She wanted to be cross with him, but she didn't know him well enough to tell him how she felt.

'It's okay, another time maybe.' He still looked unsure, and she found herself reassuring him even though she was seething inside that this woman had hijacked her perfect afternoon. 'Really. I need to go and arrange my cushions anyway.'

'How will you carry all that stuff home?'

So, he wasn't going to try and talk her out of it. Or get rid of the Old Friend. Lois felt a wave of embarrassment creep down her body. She had to leave before she started crying. 'I've got my second wind now.' She forced a smile which she hoped told him that she was fine.

He looked slightly crestfallen. 'I'm glad we ran into each other today.' Why didn't he do something about it then?

'Me too. Listen, do you mind just grabbing my bags and

coat?' She hoped he would just do as she asked without making a fuss, and he did. Lois shoved the cushions further down into the bags, managed to pick everything up and stood by the door while Oliver opened it for her. She deliberately didn't look over to where they'd been sitting. The whole thing was mortifying.

'See you next week maybe?' he asked.

'Sure.' She smiled at him and headed across the bridge towards home with tears running down her face.

13

Steph pulled up in the lay-by on Hawthorn Lane and yanked the handbrake on as hard as she could. Although the road was flat and had probably been a bus stop once upon a time when there were still buses that went everywhere, there was a steep hill immediately afterwards and Steph always had visions of the mobile library rolling down the road while she was busy making a cup of tea. It was another bright autumn day which she was pleased about, especially here, because her stalwart regular, Eunice, was not that steady on her feet.

Once she'd opened the door and put the handrails up, she retrieved her tea making supplies from the bag she kept in the passenger footwell and laid it out on the table. It was never more important than for the Hawthorn Lane stop. She also took a brand-new tin of Victoria biscuits out of the cupboard behind the driver's seat.

'Good morning, Steph,' a voice called from the door. Steph smiled. It was Eunice, she was always the first customer to arrive at the Hawthorn Lane stop.

'Morning Eunice!' Steph headed for the door and retrieved Eunice's heavy bag of books and her walking stick so that she had both hands free to hold on to the rail as she climbed the three steps into the van. 'Cup of tea?' Eunice was the only one of Steph's customers who had more than one cup, sometimes more than two.

'Lovely.' Eunice unbuttoned her coat as she made her way over to the table where Steph had arranged the tea and biscuits.

Eunice had been coming to the van for as long as Steph had been visiting Hawthorn Lane. She must be in her eighties, but she was far from a little old lady. She was elegant and always looked immaculate with her perfect hair and make-up along with a hint of expensive perfume.

'How are you, Eunice? Did you get through that enormous pile of books from last month?'

'I certainly did. The Jilly Cooper one was delightful.'

Steph grinned at her. It didn't seem to matter how old someone was, they still loved a steamy romance novel. 'I'll have to see what else I can find for you if you enjoyed that.'

'I could quite easily spend all my time reading about Mr Campbell-Black, but I do need a little more variety over the course of a month.'

'Quite right, Eunice. Variety is the spice of life and all that.'

Steph loved to try and anticipate what her regular customers might like and often loaded the van with them in mind. She had chucked the Jilly Cooper in as an antidote to the regency romances and sagas that Eunice favoured, just to see what she would think.

'We're starting a book club on the mobile library,' said Steph as she poured a modest cup of tea for each of them.

'I've always thought about joining a book club but it's difficult to get out in the evenings. How wonderful to have one here.' Eunice leant towards Steph, conspiratorially. 'The only thing is, it won't be much of a club with just me, will it?'

Steph laughed. 'You're not my only customer, Eunice. I

expect Dottie will be along in a minute with little Bert. Anyway, this book club is different, so you just need to find one person who has read the same book as you and you have coffee – or tea – with them and chat about it. I'm sure you and Dottie can agree on a book together.'

'Oh, we will, Steph. What a lovely idea.'

Steph was glad that Eunice thought so. She had less faith that the idea would work on the mobile library but wanted to support Lois, however misguided she thought it was to be trying to improve a library that was about to close. But if her customers were interested enough to read the books, it was a start. Most people loved book clubs because it forced them out of their comfort zone enabling them to discover new authors and genres that they'd never have considered before. That was the main thing.

'It's Croftwood Library that's organising it.'

'I read in the newspaper that it was closing.'

'It is supposed to be, but the new librarian is trying to drag it into the twenty-first century and this is one of her ideas.'

'It's fabulous. What do I need to do to join?'

'Just choose one of these books, see what Dottie thinks too. Seeing as the two of you are my regulars at this stop it makes sense for you to do it together.' Steph thought of Bill at the Old Station Road stop and wondered how it would work for him. If he even wanted to join in, that was.

Steph put all three books in front of Eunice so that she could choose her favourite, then began emptying the books out of Eunice's shopping bag and checking them back into the system.

They heard Dottie arrive before they saw her. Two-year-old Bert was apparently not happy about something and was screaming.

'If you stop crying, we can choose some new books,' Steph heard Dottie saying to him as she let him out of his pushchair, leaving it outside.

'No!'

She appeared at the top of the stairs with an apologetic look as the quiet solace of the van filled with Bert's screams.

'Sorry. I think he'll be okay in a minute once I can distract him. Sorry,' she said again, 'I've left our books in the bottom of the pushchair.'

'No problem, I'll get them,' said Steph, grateful to nip out of the van for a few seconds of respite from the noise.

Once Bert was sat on the floor beside the picture books along with a tub of carrot sticks which Dottie produced from her bag, he was back to a normal volume and Dottie, looking highly relieved, gratefully accepted a cup of tea from Steph while keeping one eye on her son.

'How are you, Eunice?' she asked warmly.

'I'm very well, thank you, Dottie. Two is a tricky age, isn't it?' she said, with a glint in her eye.

'Oh goodness, you just don't know what you're going to come up against from one minute to the next,' she said with an exhausted sigh. 'And with Nick away so much, well it's just…challenging. And living in the village makes it difficult to meet other mums.'

Steph really felt for her. She knew that Dottie lived in a big house which had been done up when they moved to the village. It was a lovely place to live but probably too quiet for people who had upped sticks from London. And rattling around there with Bert when her husband was away so much, well, she must be lonely.

'There used to be a playgroup at the Village Hall on Friday mornings,' said Eunice. 'Does that still go on?'

'I think so,' said Dottie, 'and I know I've just complained about not meeting other mums but the idea of that scares me to death.'

'But you came here,' said Eunice, reasonably. 'Steph and I

must be more daunting than a roomful of toddlers and their mothers.'

'That would scare me off, to be honest,' said Steph.

Dottie smiled. 'I love coming to the mobile library. I mean, I can drive to an actual library, but this is special and an adventure for Bert. It never crossed my mind to worry about coming the first time.'

'That's as it should be and as a young mother it's important not to lose yourself. If this is for you more than that little man,' Eunice said, nodding towards Bert, 'then so much the better.'

Dottie looked as if she might cry which would have been awkward, so Steph was relieved when she picked up one of the book club books from the table.

'This is a good selection.'

'These are the choices for the new book club.' Eunice looked at Steph who explained it to Dottie. She was just as keen as Eunice but had similar issues.

'It's so difficult to get out in the evenings and when Nick is away it's impossible, but I'd love to join in just by reading the book. If I choose the same one as you, Eunice, at least we can have a chat about it next month.'

'That's what I was hoping,' said Eunice.

They both settled on the contemporary romance. Dottie blushed slightly when Eunice recommended Jilly Cooper to her and admitted she'd read all of them already, suggesting her favourite for Eunice's next foray into Rutshire.

As Steph drove to her next stop, she thought about the two women who'd waved her off from the pavement on Hawthorn Lane. The book club already meant something to them, Steph realised. Perhaps Lois's idea was going to work after all.

14

It was the end of the first date-with-a-book club recruitment round. Rosemary had twelve cards; twelve people who had joined in and were going to be paired up and invited to the coffee house on Wednesday evening the following week.

At the Thursday meeting, they all read through the cards and discussed how people might be paired.

'Oh my goodness,' said Rosemary, holding her hand to her chest in shock. 'The woman on this card has requested, and I quote, "Man in thirties. Tall, dark and handsome if possible." She thinks we're running some kind of dating club.'

'There are worse ways to meet a man,' said Linda. 'Finding someone who likes the same books as you is a good start. Although my Dave only reads horror so it wouldn't have worked for us,' she laughed.

'Serves us right for calling it date-with-a-book. She's taken it literally. We should try and find someone for her,' said Lois. Did any men read the same book as her?' She shuffled through the cards.

'If they did, Lois, we haven't asked them to provide their date of birth and redeeming features,' Rosemary said stiffly.

'There's one man who read the same book as her. Let's match them up. At least we'll have one satisfied customer.' Lois picked up both cards and put them together. 'Go on, Rosemary, you pick the next pair.'

They took it in turns to make pairs while Rosemary paper-clipped each pair together in preparation for arranging the meeting. They had decided to invite everyone to the coffee house and then there would be a list on the door of everyone's names with a table number.

'Has anyone had any thoughts on books for the next round?' asked Lois.

'I enjoyed reading *A Wedding in December* by Sarah Morgan,' said Linda. 'I know the next meeting isn't the last one before Christmas but it's never too soon to start reading Christmas books.'

'Do you think men would read it?'

'That's of no consequence, Lois. Despite the request on this month's cards, we are not a dating agency.'

Lois suppressed a grin. 'Quite right, Rosemary. Sorry, I got carried away for a second.'

Linda winked at her.

'Right. Linda, do you want to sort out another couple of books to add in and tweet it out?'

'Will do, Lois.'

'Great, thanks both of you. Same time next week? And we can find out how our first book dates went.'

Lois was still surprised that it had worked out having Rosemary back at the library as a volunteer, and now that they had got the measure of each other, they were well on the way to forging a great working relationship. Working at the library was rewarding and she loved it more than she had working at the Hive, which she would never have thought possible. The changes she'd made along with Rosemary and Linda were making a tangible difference and that felt amazing. So far, nothing had been said about the closure by County Libraries, but Lois felt that they were on the right track to giving the library the best chance possible.

Lois had found herself in a surprisingly good mood for the past week or so. After she'd left Oliver at the Old Rectifying House it had taken her a couple of days to absorb what had happened. One minute she was cringing again at how she'd felt forced to slink off when she wished she'd had the balls to go back to the table and brazen out the rest of the afternoon, and the next minute she was full of indignation that Oliver had let her leave when it was their date. Well, not date, but she had been there first. And he hadn't been in touch since which kind of said it all. Although, what did it say because Lois really didn't know where she stood with him now and could do with him saying something. She had hoped that their burgeoning friendship might lead to something more and she'd thought he was thinking along the same lines. He'd been so supportive about the date-with-a-book club and their other initiatives at the library, maybe she'd mistaken that for something more personal than he'd intended.

She'd felt she had no choice than to purposely avoid the coffee house but she had to go to the date-with-a-book club so she would see him then. It could be worse, at least she hadn't declared her undying love to him. It would be fine. And when she was ready to date, she could always try the date-with-a-book club for herself. Rosemary would love that.

Lois stood outside the coffee house, the glow of the lights on her face. It was the first time this winter that she had noticed her breath appear in clouds and her hands were freezing despite being deep in her pockets, but she wasn't quite ready to go in. It was the first date-with-a-book club and she had wanted to be there when it started but Rosemary and Linda were so excited that she had offered to stay behind and close the library. The relief that had washed over her knowing that she wouldn't have to confront Oliver when he was by himself at the start of the evening had surprised her but that feeling had disintegrated on the walk from the library to the coffee house.

Oliver was leaning against the customer side of the counter with a glass of wine in his hand, watching the evening unfold before him. Lois wondered whether he had finished his book yet. At least that might be something they could talk about.

She braced herself, pushed the door open and smiled at him when he looked over to see who had come in. He looked pleased to see her and despite herself, she felt the same way. Rosemary and Linda were deep in discussion, so she headed towards him.

'Wine?' he asked, waving the bottle at her, then pouring her a glass before she had a chance to answer. Okay, so they were going to pretend the humiliating non-date hadn't happened. Maybe that was for the best.

'Thanks. Are you not joining in? You must have finished that book by now.'

He grinned. 'I have as it happens but I'm not on Rosemary's official list.' He raised his eyebrows. 'Anyway, I was going to discuss it with you. Now's as good a time as any.' He headed over to a free table, taking the wine bottle with him. He had laid on wine for other guests who wanted it, Lois noticed. She gave a small wave to Linda who winked back at her.

'It seems like it's going well,' she said to Oliver. She looked around, remembering about the woman who had requested tall, dark and handsome and trying to identify her. Lois thought the most likely candidate was a blonde lady with poker straight, long hair and foundation which was a little bit too orange. Her book partner was attractive but at least ten years older than her. She was smiling though, and they looked like they were having a nice time but she couldn't see them together. Oh well, as Rosemary said, that wasn't the idea anyway.

'It's great to see something like this taking off. It's just what we need in Croftwood, something that anyone can join in with, it promotes a bit of collaboration between everyone and well, I've really enjoyed it.' He sounded melancholy and Lois couldn't tell if he was a bit tipsy or actually in that kind of mood.

'Thanks for going to so much trouble.'

'It's worth it,' he said with a shrug. 'You have to look at everything as having the potential to bring new customers in. A glass of wine from me tonight might mean they come back to have lunch sometime.'

'A glass of wine from you means they'll almost definitely come to date-with-a-book club next time too which is good for the library. Cheers.' They clinked glasses then Lois said, 'Come on then, let's join in properly. What did you think of the book and did you guess who the stalker was before the reveal?'

'I didn't!' His face lit up as talking about the book took his mind off whatever was bothering him. 'Once I got going, I finished it in no time. It was a real page-turner. In fact, I've been meaning to come to the library to swap it.'

'Good, another convert. And what did you think of the protagonist?'

'Christ, Lois,' he laughed. 'It's one thing to have a chat about the book but don't blind me with fancy vocabulary.'

'Sorry. The main character.'

'I didn't really like her. Is that awful? What did you think?'

'I didn't warm to her either, but it didn't put me off. I loved how desolate that island was. I mean, you knew they were completely cut off.' Conscious that she might be rambling, she said, 'Anyway, I'm glad you'll be back for more.'

'I haven't been in because I feel awkward about what happened last weekend.' He looked at her intently.

'Me too, although awkward is a bit of an understatement. Humiliating is more on the mark.' Might as well be honest about it, although she immediately felt awful for making him feel guilty. It was the wine making her tongue loose, as her nan would have said.

'I'm so sorry, Lois.'

He looked ashamed which took the edge off her guilt. He should be ashamed.

'I shouldn't have let it happen like that. Amy took me by surprise and I felt cornered. I couldn't ask her to leave.'

Her name was Amy. That was good to know. Lois didn't know why it made any difference to know her name, but it did.

'Are you seeing her?' Lois tried not to sound like it would matter to her if he was. He had every right to be seeing anyone he wanted. Just because she was single now and attracted to him, well that didn't mean anything.

'It's complicated. Like I said she's an old friend but...' He shrugged and didn't seem able to offer anything else by way of explanation.

'Because if you're not seeing her, then I don't really know why she ended up having a drink with you and I ended up leaving.' The wine was helping her say what she needed to. 'I felt like an idiot, Oliver,' she said quietly.

He reached his fingers across the table as if he expected her to meet them, quickly putting his hand under the table when she didn't. 'I'm sorry, so sorry that you felt like that. I do need to explain but I don't know where to start.'

She took a deep breath and despite every fibre in her willing her to fill the silence, she managed not to. Instead, she waited to see what he was going to say.

'After you left, I realised that I'd had a much better time with you than I was having with her.'

Lois smiled. 'Well, that's something, I suppose.'

'I wish Amy hadn't come to the pub, Lois.' He looked at her sincerely. 'And I wish I could tell you I would be able to ask her to go if it happened again but, to be honest, I still don't know what I could have done. I just know that I was having a great time with you, and I ruined it.'

The pleading look in his eyes won Lois over. For now. 'I was having a good time too. It's ages since I've been spontaneous like that.'

'I meant what I said. I'd love to try again sometime.'

'I'd like that.'

'Thanks for understanding.' He got up from the table and took their empty glasses over to the counter with him.

But actually, she didn't understand because he still hadn't explained properly and now she was annoyed that he thought she was okay with the whole thing. But he'd looked so forlorn that she'd had to put him out of his misery and let it go because she wasn't confident he was ever going to tell her what was going on.

Lois went over to a couple of the tables to chat to people she recognised as library customers. One of them was Jess who owned the Croftwood Haberdashery. Lois still hadn't had chance to go in there yet but she was more inclined now that she'd met Jess, who was wearing a denim jumpsuit that she'd made. It was a fabulous advert for her shop, although Lois wasn't sure she was quite up to that standard of sewing.

Once all the book-daters had left and Oliver was taking the last of the cups and glasses over to the counter to wash, Linda, Rosemary and Lois sat down together and reflected on how well the evening had gone.

'I had a wonderful conversation with that young man who had read David Cameron's autobiography. He was a staunch

Liberal Democrat supporter and it was so refreshing to talk to a young person who was interested in finding out other points of view. Fascinating. A thoroughly enjoyable evening,' said Rosemary, with a smile of satisfaction that Lois didn't think she'd ever seen before.

'The couple of ladies who'd read the Debbie Johnson book loved it. They've asked me to order the other books in the series,' said Linda. 'And I saw the woman who I think was the one who asked for a date, leaving with the man we paired her with. It could be the start of a beautiful friendship,' she added as Rosemary visibly stiffened.

'Are we agreed that it was a success?' asked Oliver, coming over to their table and sitting down, stretching out his legs and crossing them at the ankle.

'Yes, definitely,' said Lois. 'Are you okay to host again next time?'

'Of course he is,' said Rosemary. 'It's all agreed.'

Oliver nodded with a resigned smile. He had soft spot for Rosemary for some reason.

They gathered up their things and left Oliver to lock up behind them.

'I'll call in and change my book,' Oliver said to Lois, out of earshot of the others.

'Okay, see you then,' she said.

He held her gaze as he locked the door. Lois crossed the road to where she had left her bike locked to the railings outside the church, put on her helmet and fluorescent coat, stowed her bag in the basket and put the lights on ready for the ride home. When she looked back at Oliver's all the lights were out but when she looked up at the window above, she saw Oliver watching her. He looked caught out when she waved at him, but he waved back and Lois set off for home feeling sure that there was something between them but less sure that Oliver saw her as the only woman in his life. After playing second fiddle to Alex's friends for almost three years she was certain that if she got as far as having a relationship with Oliver it would have to be only the two of them in it.

15

Steph had dragged Lois to Croftwood Cinema to see the original Superman film. It was an old art-deco cinema in the park, that Lois thought Oliver might be involved with. It had just been renovated and for some reason it only showed old films but there was nothing wrong with that. Steph knew Superman wasn't Lois's kind of thing but unfortunately it wasn't her new boyfriend Max's thing either.

'I just couldn't tell him yet that I love superheroes. It seemed too soon,' said Steph, shoving a handful of popcorn into her mouth.

'But it's going okay otherwise?' asked Lois.

'Oh my god, Lois, it's amazing! I was just about at the end of my dating tether, I'd sworn it was my last Tinder date and there you go. It finally happened.'

'Really, as good as that? It's only been a couple of weeks.'

'When you know, you know. Right?'

'Yes, I guess so.'

Until recently Lois had never understood that kind of feeling at all. She certainly hadn't had it with Alex and now she knew that was what she should have held out for. The feelings she had for Oliver made her understand what Steph was on about even if nothing had really happened between them yet. There was something more than attraction, it was a connection. She wished she was sure enough to let her feelings lead the way, to take charge of the situation and go forth. But Oliver was doing a terrible job of letting her know where she stood, if indeed she stood anywhere.

'Has Alex shown his face yet?'

'No. I did text him to remind him that his stuff's still at the house, but he hasn't replied.'

'God, that's so rude. You're too soft on him, Lois. Just tell him you're chucking it away if he doesn't pick him up.'

Lois laughed. Steph always got so het up about Alex. 'Oh okay, Steph. He'll know that wasn't my idea, so he won't take it as a serious threat.'

'Well, it's hard to move on when it's still hanging over you after, hello, three months nearly four, isn't it?'

Lois shrugged. 'Not really. I've been seeing Oliver around quite a bit.' She gave Steph a look that said it was something more than that and enjoyed the reaction she got when Steph's popcorn erupted over her lap as she sat up to attention with wide eyes.

'Oliver the guy from the bar? I thought he was with that woman?'

'He was. We bumped into each other and had a drink on Sunday afternoon a couple of weeks ago, then she came in so I had to leave...'

'He made you leave?' Steph almost shouted with indignation. 'Sorry, I mean, really?' she said more quietly.

'I don't know, I decided to leave because I felt like that was what he wanted, then the next time I saw him he said that he'd not had such a nice time with her as he'd had with me.'

'Oh my god, Lois! I cannot believe you didn't tell me this immediately. The bloody film is about to start, and I have to wait two hours for the next part of the story. You're so mean.'

They both swivelled their legs to the side to let some latecomers shuffle past them.

'There's nothing to tell. He's got something going on with this woman, something that's more than that they're old friends and he's holding back telling me about it.'

'Well, be careful, because you don't want a frying pan and fire situation.' She shoved a handful of popcorn into her mouth then added in muffled tones, 'but also, if you really feel like he could be The One you shouldn't let that go.'

The lights went down and although Lois was watching the movie, she wasn't concentrating on it. She was thinking about Oliver. What if he was The One and she was just letting it pass her by because she was worried about Amy? Amy was nothing to do with her. She wouldn't even be considering Amy if she hadn't turned up at the Old Rectifying House.

'So, what's the plan, Oliver-wise?' Steph asked. They'd stayed for a drink since the cinema had a rather cool backstage bar where Patsy, the barista from the coffee house was serving.

'Well, it's tricky really because of this Amy woman.'

'Is he actually dating the Amy woman?'

'He said not. And that shouldn't stop me anyway. He said he likes me and there's definitely something between us so she's not really my concern.'

'Right, that does make sense. But can you tell me what you've done with my friend Lois?'

'Shut up. I can be ballsy when I want to be.'

'You can be, as evidenced once in a blue moon at work but honestly, I've never seen you stand up for what you want. That's not a bad thing, Lois, you're a nice person, that's what nice people do but it means you're not always very nice to yourself.'

'I don't know whether being nice is good or not now,' she

said, thinking that Steph's advice was even more brutal than usual tonight. She shushed Steph as Patsy came over to serve them.

'What can I get you?'

'Two pints of the IPA please,' said Steph.

'Sure.' Patsy started pulling the pints. 'You're Lois, the new library manager, right? I've seen you in Oliver's.'

'That's me. You must be Patsy.'

'Nice to meet you. Oliver's really enjoying the book club. Well, not the reading part,' she said with a grin, 'but the organising part. He loves having something to keep him busy.'

'He's been brilliant letting us use the coffee house.'

'He loves being involved in everything, that's how we ended up with this place.'

'It's very cool,' said Steph. 'It's the first time I've manager to buy a good pint of beer in a cinema.'

'Well, enjoy yourselves.'

They sat on stools at a tall bistro table and carried on the conversation where they'd left off.

'Being in Croftwood has been amazing,' said Lois. 'It's the first time I've worked in a place where I can make decisions that really make a difference. Seeing the book club and the new things we've done in the library take off, it's made me think that I need to sprinkle a bit of that Lois into the rest of my life.'

'Christ. That's deep but I think you're onto something. Cheers.'

They clinked glasses.

'Cheers. I think Alex leaving at almost the same time as the Croftwood job came up was fate or something. If he'd still been here, he'd have talked me out of it for sure and not having anyone to justify myself to makes it quite a liberating experience.'

'So maybe meeting Oliver is fate then,' said Steph matter-of-factly.

'Shhh,' said Lois, glancing at Patsy who was leaning over the bar talking to a blonde-haired guy who was nursing a pint. 'I'd like to think if it was fate it'd be a lot more straightforward than it seems at the moment. Fate would be making Oliver sort himself out so he tells that Amy to get lost and then sweeps me off my feet.' She sighed. 'It seems unlikely at the moment.'

'Well, maybe these things take time. There's some wise saying about that which I can't remember but good things come to those who wait. That'll do.'

Lois hoped Steph was right although she felt like she'd been waiting for years, albeit unknowingly, for the right man. If she knew she'd have Oliver in the end by waiting, then that would be okay but waiting without any certainty was pointless. She felt that she'd been as honest with Oliver as she could be about how she felt after the disastrous episode in Worcester. The ball was definitely in his court.

'Anyway, my turn,' she said, wanting something to talk about something that would take her mind of Oliver. 'So Max, what makes him a catch?'

'He matched his profile picture for a start. You can't underestimate the advantage that gives him.'

'But he's a nice person too?' Lois worried that Steph was fixating on the qualities that she thought made him her ideal man because the qualities he actually ought to have would make Steph label him boring.

'He has a motorbike and leathers which is pretty sexy and he's quite rugged and, I don't know, he's my type.'

'Right.' It was just as she feared but she had told Steph so many times before and her advice was never received with the spirit it was intended.

'Honestly, Lo, I think you'll like him.'

'I'm really glad you've found someone, Steph. Just, while we're dishing out advice, don't fall too hard until you know for sure.'

'You could do with remembering that too,' said Steph with a pointed look.

It was true. She had feelings for Oliver which she ought to try and curb until she knew what his feelings were. The last thing she needed after managing to pick herself up after Alex had left was to launch into something too fast without being sure her heart was going to be safe.

16

The next day Lois left home early. She had decided to call into the coffee house on her way to work. She propped her bike up against the window frame, took her helmet off and went inside. It was quite busy, lots of people were having breakfast. Oliver wasn't behind the counter though, it was his colleague, Patsy.

'Hi, is Oliver around?'

'He hasn't surfaced yet. He usually has a lie-in on his day off. Shall I say you came in?'

'Yes, please. It's Lois.'

Patsy smiled knowingly. 'I'll tell him. Do you want a coffee for the road?'

'Thanks, but I'm on my bike. It'd literally end up on the road, but thanks anyway.'

'No problem, see you again.'

Lois arrived at the library first and opened up. It was Linda's day off, but Rosemary was due in to do some admin on the book club.

By the time Lois had done her usual morning chores, it was eleven o'clock and she was craving the coffee that she'd turned down earlier. Rosemary hadn't arrived though so she had to settle for a cup of tea that she could nip into the office to make.

'Anybody here?'

Lois bolted out of the office to see Oliver standing at the desk with a coffee in his hand.

'For you,' he said, placing it in her hand. 'And a gingerbread muffin.' He presented her with a brown bag, the top folded over neatly.

'Thanks, you're a mind reader.'

'Pats said you came in this morning. I usually have a lie-in on my day off.'

'She said. I don't blame you.'

There was no-one else in the library, so Lois led him over to the reading table nearest the desk.

He opened his black wool coat, reached inside, and pulled out the CL Taylor book he'd read, placing it on the table between them.

'I'm returning this for the next one. But it has to be something you've read. I'm only doing   book dates with you.'

'I'm flattered,' said Lois. 'The pressure's on then.'

'I'm open to anything,' he said, shrugging with his palms upwards. 'How hard can it be?'

'Okay. I'll have to think about it while I eat this delicious muffin.' Lois pulled the muffin top off and ate that first, savouring the first taste of Christmas that had passed her lips that year.

'I was thinking that we should arrange to go out for that drink.'

Lois looked at him. Did he mean it in the way she hoped he did? She was pretty sure that was the only way he could mean and the look in his eyes told her so.

'I've been thinking too.' It felt like now or never. She was going to lay her cards on the table, tell him what she wanted and he would have to decide if he wanted it too. It came out as, 'I like you and I think we should make it an actual date,' which was a little more high school than she'd intended but she was a novice with things like this.

'Oh really,' he said with amusement in his eyes. 'An actual date?' He got up from his seat opposite her and moved to the one next to her.

Lois's heart began to thud and she willed herself not to blush. She'd never been as close to him as this. Before now there had always been a table or a counter between them.

His eyes flicked briefly over to the door, then he laid his hand on her thigh. The warmth of his palm radiated through the denim of her jeans into her skin and concentrated all the feelings she was having into a rush of energy so that when he leaned towards her and kissed her briefly but tenderly on the lips, she felt like fireworks were going off inside her.

It was so long since she'd had a kiss like that. Maybe she'd never had a kiss like that. She closed her eyes and lost herself in the moment, making the seconds of perfection imprint on her memory. She'd definitely made the right decision.

'Good grief, what is going on here?'

Oliver pulled away and shot out of his seat as if he'd been scalded by Lois's lips.

'Rosemary!'

'Oliver, this is hardly appropriate.'

'No, of course not. Apologies Rosemary.' Oliver didn't seem to be humouring Rosemary, he seemed genuinely remorseful.

'There's no need to apologise, Oliver. It was just a kiss, Rosemary, and there's no-one else here,' said Lois. She knew Rosemary was uptight but this was a bit of an over-reaction given that the library was empty.

'I'm here, Lois.'

Oliver buttoned his coat and left, flustered, not even saying goodbye to Lois.

She was stunned. How could the most perfect kiss that ended less than a minute ago have now led to him leaving in such a bizarre fashion? Almost equally bizarre was how thrown Rosemary seemed to be after witnessing an extremely brief kiss. It was a chaste kiss, thought Lois, indignantly. And despite what had just happened, she felt amazing.

'Rosemary...'

'I do not wish to discuss it, Lois.' She held her hand up.

What should she do? Go after Oliver? Make sure he was okay, because since when did a public display of affection merit such behaviour, especially when only one person had seen it? Unless there was something else about Croftwood Library that she didn't know. Perhaps there was a 'No Heavy Petting' sign somewhere.

The atmosphere lasted all afternoon as she and Rosemary worked together, in silence. Working together was an exaggeration because Lois was pretty sure Rosemary had been actively avoiding her by hiding within the shelves on the pretence of researching possible suggestions for the Christmas book club.

When Rosemary left with a curt goodbye at lunchtime, Lois breathed a sigh of relief. She would go to the coffee house after work and find out what was going on.

Oliver had gone straight back to the coffee house and asked Patsy to work the rest of the day for him. He wasn't in the mood for conversation and working to take his mind off things wasn't going to help because he needed to think about what had happened.

The effort he'd gone to, wearing his best jeans and sweater suddenly seemed ridiculous so he changed into his lounging around clothes. Now, he sat on the sofa, running his fingers through his hair in despair. What must Lois think of him?

In the moments before Rosemary had caught him and Lois kissing, he had felt like it was the most natural thing in the world. More than that, he felt like he'd found himself for the first time in a long time. The friendship he had with Lois, their easy conversations and light banter had become something he looked forward to every time he saw her. The kiss was a natural progression of that and he could hardly believe the way he'd reacted when Rosemary came in. It wasn't anything he'd consciously decided to do, to walk out and leave Lois who must be wondering what on earth was the matter with him, it had just happened.

He stood at the window, looking out over the high street as the streetlights began to flicker on. Should he go back to the library and explain? He wasn't sure yet what he could say that would make his behaviour seem normal when only a spineless idiot would run out on the woman he'd just kissed. The woman he'd wanted to kiss for ages. He should have stood up to Rosemary, he knew that. But it wasn't so easy when she was in front of him radiating disapproval.

As he watched, he saw Lois on her bike. Her neon pink jacket made him smile because he knew it wasn't what she would choose to wear, she was forced into it because no-one had made quirky safety jackets to match the kind of people who rode quirky bikes. She had stopped across the road from the coffee house and was busy locking her bike up before she took off her helmet and went inside.

By the time he realised she was probably coming in to see him it was too late to think about changing because she was already knocking on the door.

'Hey,' he said, wishing he hadn't got undressed and wishing he hadn't been running his hands through his hair all afternoon in despair.

'Patsy said it was okay,' she said hesitantly.

'Come in.'

He went over to the sofa and gestured for Lois to sit down while he stood there awkwardly before beginning to pace in front of the windows. It was a million miles away from how things had been before Rosemary walked into the library that morning.

'I owe you an explanation, Lois. There's something I should have told you before...what happened today.'

'Okay...'

'My ex, Amy, is Rosemary's god-daughter.' He waited to see what she thought of that. It went some way to explaining Rosemary's reaction at least.

'Oh, I see. How long ago did you break up?'

'It was about six months ago.'

'Six months?' Lois looked astounded. 'Are you joking? You broke up with her months ago and you and Rosemary both have some sort of meltdown when she sees you kissing someone else. That's beyond weird, Oliver.'

'For Christ's sake, Lois,' he said crossly, as he hoped she'd be more understanding, 'there's more to it than that.' He absentmindedly raked his hands through his hair.

'Go on then, enlighten me,' she said angrily.

'I left her. She had a breakdown, really bad depression and I left her.'

He could see that Lois immediately understood that he'd felt guilty.

'I didn't know how bad it was at the time. I'd just bought the cinema and was preoccupied with that. She was angry because I'd gone ahead with the project without asking her what she thought about it, at least I thought that was why she was angry. I think we'd already started growing apart, she was pushing me away, withdrawing from the life we'd had together because she was depressed. And I didn't notice. I walked away from her when she was at her absolute lowest, thinking that she wasn't supporting me.'

Lois nodded her head and her expression had softened which he took as a good sign.

'In some ways, it was the right thing to do because after I left she hit rock bottom and got some help. I think she's in a better place now but I still feel responsible for her, Lois. I don't want to, I don't think I even need to now but it's been hard to get to this point.'

He relaxed slightly and came to sit next to her on the sofa.

'And now?' asked Lois, gently.

'I hadn't heard from her at all until she contacted me a few weeks ago and we met up. When I saw you at the bar with your friend.'

'So that was why you felt you couldn't push her to leave us at The Old Rectifying House?'

He nodded. 'She's keen for us to see more of each other. I think she needs some closure or something.' Then he took her hand and stared down at it as he spoke. 'What happened today... it was the first time I'd kissed anyone since Amy, anyone who mattered to me, Lois. I think Rosemary was upset at seeing evidence that I have moved on and her reaction... I was shocked and then I felt so guilty. It just brought back all those feelings like I was letting Amy down. I'm so sorry.' He took both of her hands in his.

'Oh, Oliver. I can see how you must have felt. Maybe you should talk to Rosemary. Clear the air.'

That was the last thing he wanted to do. It was not Rosemary's business. What he needed was to draw a line under things with Amy.

'I should have talked to you and explained instead of walking out. I thought that'd be it, Lois. All day I've been thinking about how I've finally found someone who makes me feel...happy. And I messed it up straight away.'

'It's not messed up, it's fine.' Lois put her hands on his cheeks and gave him a gentle kiss. He kissed her back and they sat there, kissing for a while until he pulled away.

'The thing is Lois, things are complicated with Amy. She's a lot better now and wants us to see more of each other. But she's been so fragile, if she thought there was anything between us, well I'm not sure she'd be ready for that. At all.'

'You should have told me, Oliver.'

'I know. But once I decided to end things with her, I tried not to think about it. I had to put it behind me and move on and I'd just started to do that. And then I met you and it's the first time I've even thought about being with someone else.' He gave her a worried smile. 'I'm finding it difficult to navigate being friends with her because I'm worried she wants more than that.' He pulled away and stood up. 'I'm sorry, I shouldn't be landing all of this on you.'

Lois stood up and went to him. 'Oliver, maybe it's not the right time for us yet. We can wait, be friends,' she said with a smile, taking the tips of his fingers in hers.

He leant down to kiss her. Being just friends wasn't what he wanted but it wasn't fair to Lois for him to commit to anything until he had properly sorted things out with Amy. And he would. 'Thanks, Lois.'

There was no need to launch themselves into a torrid love affair. They were both old enough to know that if it was meant to be they could take their time to make sure it started on the right foot. And if that meant reining in their emotions for a little while until they were free of the past and free to move on together, then that was fine.

'God, I look like shit,' he smiled. 'The first time you come here and it's – '

'It's perfect.'

Oliver stood up and ran his fingers through his hair again, this time attempting to tame it. 'Look, let me get changed and then why don't we go out for something to eat?'

He could see her walking around the flat through the gap in the bedroom door while she waited for him. The flat was a bit of an extension of the coffee house in that there was lots of wood. The floor was oak boards as were the windowsills and there was a huge hunk of an oak mantlepiece above the fireplace which he'd picked up from a salvage yard. He watched Lois rub the wool tweed curtains between her fingers which he took as a sign of approval.

'Right,' he said, emerging from the bedroom, looking back to his usual self. 'Shall we go to the Rose and Crown?'

'I have no idea, you choose. I'm a Worcester girl, remember.'

'The Rose and Crown it is then.' He held the door open for her and she headed down the stairs as he turned the lights off behind them.

Patsy had closed the coffee house and was doing her last bits of tidying up.

'Thanks for today, Pats. See you on Saturday?'

'Sure thing, Ollie.' She winked at them both as they left.

'I'll come back for my bike afterwards,' said Lois.

'You could leave it here and get a cab home. I'd worry about you cycling home in the dark.'

'It's fine,' said Lois. 'I bike home in the dark every day now since the clocks changed. I've got a very bright coat and very good lights.'

'We'll see,' said Oliver looking down at her. Then he took her hand which made him feel almost as great as when they'd kissed. Tiny electric shocks seemed to pass between their fingers as he linked his in between hers and wrapped them together.

The pub was just around the corner and looked inviting from the outside. Inside was no disappointment, especially when they managed to get a table next to the log fire. It was

Italian night so they both ordered Spaghetti Bolognese with buttery garlic bread and a bottle of red wine to share.

'Does Amy live in Croftwood?' asked Lois.

'She lives in Malvern.' He paused. 'It wasn't a straightforward break-up, you know?'

Lois nodded.

'You know. You've only just been through it yourself.'

'It's nowhere near the same,' Lois said, shaking her head. 'I've realised that Alex did me a favour. And not just because of this,' she said waving her fork between the two of them. She laughed as Oliver raised his eyebrows suggestively. 'We weren't happy and I don't know how long he'd known that but it took me too long to notice.'

'All's well that ends well, then. To new beginnings.' He raised his glass to Lois and she did the same.

'To us.'

17

Robert had asked Lois to pop in to see him at the Hive so that he could catch up on how things were going in Croftwood. He was going to an important County Libraries meeting where Lois hoped he would pass on how well the improvements were going.

'Lois, lovely to see you,' he said as she made her way into his office.

'Hi, Robert. It's nice to be back, briefly.' She picked up a couple of books which had been left on the chair and added them to the nearest pile before she sat down.

'I hear from Andrew that you have built quite a Twitter presence for Croftwood Library. Wonderful, Lois.' He turned to his computer screen. 'And I've been having a look at the borrowing rates since you took over and I know that you've got lots of initiatives going on but you know how it is Lois, that's the only statistic we have that indicates actual footfall.'

Lois had been checking the rates herself every week and they had been creeping up week on week which she was very proud of but she was interested to know what Robert would conclude.

He peered at the screen. 'Thirty-one per cent, Lois. It's a very nice uplift but possibly not spectacular enough to cause a change of heart over the closure at the moment, sadly.'

'Well, no but it's only been a few weeks and new members are joining all the time. I'm sure that will improve quite quickly.' She tried to sound upbeat.

'I'm quite sure you're right but as you know, time is short.'

'They're not deciding now though, are they? How much time do we have, Robert?'

'The final decision will be made on 23rd January. That's… another ten weeks or so,' he said, consulting his wall planner.

'What kind of rate do you think would make the difference?' asked Lois.

'It's going to be a tall order, Lois. I would say it needs to be comfortably seventy per cent.'

'Seventy?!' That was insane. Completely impossible.

'When you think about it in terms of numbers rather than per cent, it is achievable. The actual number of books borrowed at Croftwood was so low, it's eminently possible.' He took his glasses off and fiddled with the arms as he carried on. 'I can see you've taken to the place but it would be a miracle for it to be saved now, Lois. I know I've just said the decision won't be made until January but we both know it's been made already.' He gave her a sympathetic look.

'It's such a fantastic place, Robert. It's an amazing little time warp that we're dragging into the twenty-first century but it's not kicking and screaming, it's flourishing and people are starting to see that. I mean, the book club has really caught people's imaginations. I'd love you to tell them about that at the meeting.'

'Ah, yes, the book club. The dating book club,' he said, smiling and raising his eyebrows. 'That certainly has got people talking and I will make sure the powers that be hear about it.'

'Thanks, Robert.'

'And I know you're putting your all into this, Lois. It's wonderful to see you flourishing as well.'

Lois walked down the staircase in a slight daze. She probably should have had this talk with Robert before she took over at Croftwood. But it hadn't mattered as much in the beginning as it did now. Everything he'd said suggested that at best they had ten weeks to prove that Croftwood Library was a valuable member of the county's libraries and at worst, there was nothing they could do. But Lois knew in her heart that they were already making the difference and she was going to carry on. She was not going to sit back and do nothing for the next ten weeks because that would be a travesty and it felt like working at Croftwood Library had given her everything that had been missing from her life.

Andrew was at the desk when she got to the ground floor.

'Hey, Lois! Nice to see you back in the Hive. How's it going out in the sticks?'

She managed a smile. 'It's really good. Much better than I expected. Totally different to here.'

'But you miss us.'

'Of course I do!' said Lois giving him a playful shove.

'And how's life without Alex?'

Lois forgot that he'd have found out from Steph. 'It's okay. I've started seeing someone else.'

'Good lord, Lois. That's quick work, especially for you.'

'Ah, Andrew. I've missed your put-downs disguised as compliments.'

'You know I'm just joshing with you. Really, that's great. Alex was not good enough for you.'

'Why is it that people think it's great to point that out afterwards? You should have told me. Even Steph thought that and didn't say.'

'We said it to each other if that helps.'

'Oh, yes. That helps, thank you.'

Lois forgot how much she'd enjoyed the banter with Andrew. It was completely different with Linda and Rosemary but she liked working with them in a different way. She could talk about work with them and they were more enthusiastic about it than her colleagues at the Hive but she shuddered at the thought of them sharing anything more personal than what they ate for dinner or watched on television.

'Night out soon then? We could have a six-some with Steph and her new chap.'

'Sounds great. I'll see what Steph says.'

Lois had the rest of the day off. She texted Oliver as she left to see if he wanted to meet once he'd closed the coffee house. They arranged to meet in the city centre.

'What did your boss think of what you've done then?' Oliver asked as soon as he'd kissed her, keen to hear how her day had gone. It was such a contrast to Alex who had been completely disinterested most of the time.

'He thinks it's a good start but we've got to ramp up the borrowing rates over the next few weeks if we're going to have a chance of saving the library.'

'Surely that's doable? I've spoken to so many people who have started coming in there. And the date-with-a-book club must be making a difference.' He was so optimistic, it made Lois smile.

'It's all making a difference, it's just not happening quite as quickly as it needs to.'

'Maybe we need to do some more publicity for the book club. The more people we can get on board with that, well it has to help.'

'It will but we need something else. I'll talk to Linda and Rosemary about it. We haven't tapped into the children's library yet. I mean, when I was a kid I used to get six books every Saturday without fail. We're missing a trick there. We get lots of little kids in but we need the kind of teenagers who just inhale books. And there are so many amazing YA books out there. That's what we need.'

'You've lost me with your library jargon now,' said Oliver, jolting her out of her thought process.

'Sorry. Young Adult books. Now that it's occurred to me, I really want to get going on it.'

'I know what you mean. I sometimes get that feeling when I come up with some new marketing angle for the coffee house. I love how you just have the idea and go for it, Lois. It must feel good to have the freedom to make changes like that.' He looked as excited as she was.

'It does, but we're restricted to doing things which cost us nothing and because the library's meant to be closing no-one's taking much notice of what we're doing as long as we don't cause any trouble. I can get the books we need transferred from other libraries but we need some other things too. I'd love to buy a few of those massive beanbag cushions to make a reading corner for older children. It needs to be cool and separate from the rest of the children's library.'

'Why don't we do some fundraising? Are you allowed to do that? And it would raise the profile of the library at the same time. If it helps to save the library, I bet we could get some of the local businesses involved. A thriving library would help all of us.'

'It's a really good idea, I probably just need to check with Robert to make sure. We wouldn't need very much to buy a few beanbags anyway.'

'I'm happy to help you get something set up and get the Croftwood Traders' Association on board.'

Lois marvelled at how great it was to be with someone who was behind her and more than that, he believed in what she was trying to do. Although she'd felt daunted by the task ahead of her, now that she had thought of her next plan, she was relishing the challenge even more. And having Oliver cheering her on every step of the way was going to make all the difference.

18

'Seventy per cent?' said Linda when Lois explained about the meeting. 'And we've only done thirty?'

'Thirty-one. It's not as impossible as it seems. I've got an idea. We'll get a load of YA books in and make a separate bit of the library for them. The teenagers will go for that, I'm sure. Unfortunately, it's probably not massively appealing to boys but we'll see what we can come up with to encourage them.'

'I don't know much about books for teenagers, Lois,' Linda admitted, 'and I doubt Rosemary will be much use with it either.'

'Leave it to me. I can speak to my colleagues at the Hive and see what they suggest. As long as you can help us get it out there on Twitter, that's the main thing. And we might need to start Instagram too if we're targeting teenagers.'

Linda retreated into the fiction section with a worried look on her face. She didn't need to worry, Lois knew she'd get to grips with Instagram just as quickly as she'd taken to Twitter and that would help them reach a younger audience.

Lois wandered into the children's section of the library. It was well stocked with picture books for little ones as well as plenty of reading books for primary school children but the teenage section was sadly lacking with just two shelves of dedicated books. Lois could remember when she was that age and managed to read almost everything her local library, which was much the same size as Croftwood, had to offer. What was on their side now was the sheer volume of amazing books available for that age range, she just needed to source some and find space for them.

After work, Lois headed straight home. She was looking forward to the evening ahead because she'd invited Oliver around for dinner. He hadn't been round to her house before and she was keen to get home, light some candles, light the fire and start the dinner before he arrived.

Deciding what to cook had been somewhat tricky. Aside from it being a while since Lois had made a proper meal – she was existing on salads and pasta – she wasn't sure yet what Oliver liked. So far, they had only eaten one meal together at the pub so she knew he ate meat and didn't mind garlic. In the end, she'd chosen a recipe that her mum always used for dinner parties; chicken breast stuffed with garlic Philadelphia cheese and wrapped in Parma ham. To save herself too much hassle, she bought some ready-made Parmenter potatoes to go with it and some green vegetables to steam.

Lois prepared the chicken, then went into the lounge to light the fire. It lit easily with some kindling which she'd cut from an errant hazel tree in the garden the previous autumn and bundled with some dried lavender. It smelled delicious.

As the doorbell rang, Lois hastily lit a couple of candles on the mantelpiece before answering it.

She opened the door and Oliver was standing there looking wretched. He leaned in to kiss her and she was bathed in the scent of his gorgeous woody aftershave but her heart sank when he made no move to come in.

'Come in, it's freezing!' she said, trying to sound more upbeat than she felt. There was something wrong. She could feel the cold on him as he squeezed past her into the hall where he stayed, making no move to follow her into the kitchen. 'What is it?'

'I can't stay.'

'Okay...' She paused, letting him know that she was waiting for an explanation.

'Amy came to see me after work today. She wants us to try again.'

Lois wasn't sure what exactly had changed. Amy had already told Oliver she wanted them to see more of each other.

'And you said?'

'I said I would. I feel I owe her that,' he said. 'She thinks that we called things off without really knowing why we'd grown apart and now that we do, and she's feeling better, we can pick up where we left off.'

'And you're going along with that?'

He nodded sadly.

'I don't get what's changed.' Lois was struggling to stay calm. 'Are you suddenly in love with her again?'

'No, not really but I feel like I have to give it a chance. For her.'

'But you'd moved on, you said it yourself. She just needs time to come to terms with that. Is it the right thing to be trying to get back something that can probably never be the same as it was before?'

'Try to understand.' He was pleading with her. 'I can't let her down again. I can't be the reason she gets depressed again. I'm willing to see what happens. I'm so sorry, Lois. I didn't see this coming and I wish things were different. I should never have started anything between us until I'd sorted out my life properly.'

She'd known things weren't straightforward. He'd told her, eventually, so she should have seen this coming too. But she was sad. Sad for losing someone who had become her friend as well as sad at losing the possibility of what might have been.

'We knew it wasn't the best timing for either of us.' She wondered why she was blurting out a cliché to make him feel better, then quickly realised she was trying to make herself feel better.

'That shouldn't matter when something's right, Lois.'

'Well, now you're just making it worse.' She attempted a smile.

'Can we still be friends?'

That would be the hardest thing in the world. 'Of course we can.'

Oliver took her in his arms and hugged her while she forced herself not to start sobbing into his chest while she drank in the feeling of being held by him. It was probably the last time, after all.

'I wish things were different. Amy's been through so much…'

'It's the right thing to do,' she said. She had to tell him that, let him leave her with a clear conscience. After all, they had agreed to take it slowly precisely because things were complicated for him. She hadn't thought it might end things between them though.

She pulled away from him, wiping her sleeve across her face.

'Thanks, Lois. I'm sorry I can't stay but Amy wants to move her stuff in tonight.'

Lois almost staggered with the impact of realising that Oliver was about to be in a full-on relationship with Amy again. They weren't taking it slow, they were picking up almost exactly where they'd left off.

'Oh, great, well I'd better let you go then.'

Oliver opened the door, then turned and took a long look at Lois. There was something in his eyes, maybe regret, maybe he just felt sorry for hurting her, but Lois thought he was feeling the loss just as much as she was.

'Bye.'

Gulping down a sob, she walked into the kitchen and took a long sip of wine. She should have expected something like this. He had said it was complicated all along and she had heard him but she had carried on, letting her feelings run away with her regardless. She had thought it would all work out. Now she was going to have to try and be friends. It sounded easy enough but it wouldn't be, especially not with Amy at his side.

19

Lois felt sluggish the next morning. She'd drunk too much wine and her eyes still felt puffy from crying so she'd had to put extra make-up on in a vain attempt to make herself look semi-normal.

'Morning, Lois. Where's your bike today?' asked Linda as soon as she walked in.

The bike ride would have made her feel better, and blown the cobwebs away, but she felt so drained that she couldn't face the thought of it. 'I got the bus this morning. How are you, Linda?'

'Good, thank you. I've just had a look at the book club cards for this month and we've already got double the number of people that we had last month and that's not even including the mobile library and there's still a week left until the meeting.'

'That's great news. Hopefully, we'll find out from Steph later how the initiative's working out on the road. I'm not sure it'll necessarily help our cause but it's important to get people involved even if they can't come and visit us.'

'Oh, definitely Lois. Anyway, I'll get on with the re-shelving until Rosemary comes in.'

Lois hadn't seen Rosemary since the kiss she'd interrupted and as far as she knew, Oliver hadn't spoken to her yet. Having been on the wrong side of Rosemary before, Lois was slightly nervous about how it would be when she came in. She hoped Rosemary would be able to remain professional. They'd made such progress since Lois had started at Croftwood that it would be a shame to take a backward step.

When Rosemary arrived, she was carrying a takeout coffee from Oliver's. He'd have known she was on her way to the library so perhaps he had managed to talk to her first. From her expression, there was no way to tell.

'Morning Rosemary.'

'Good morning, Lois. What time are we expecting Stephanie?'

'I think she's coming in around midday so we can meet during her lunch break.'

'Wonderful. I shall spend the morning changing some of the displays. Have you read any books we can have a review of Lois? We could do with refreshing them.'

'Oh, yes. The new Marian Keyes book?'

'Are you asking me or telling me.' Rosemary glared at Lois and now she was sure that Oliver had not had a chance to speak to her.

'I'll write it for you now,' said Lois and retreated to her spot behind the desk. Perhaps she should make it clear to Rosemary that Oliver and Amy were back together and that she was no longer in the picture but that was their business. It was up to Amy and Oliver to tell people if they were back together and Rosemary would find out soon enough. Lois just had to bear the cold shoulder for a little while longer.

The rest of the morning flew by with no more stand-offs and Lois was only slightly nervous about how their meeting with Steph was going to go.

'Lois!' Steph called from the door. 'Give us a hand!'

Outside, Steph was hauling a couple of boxes out of the mobile library van.

'I've bought some books over from the Hive for you, courtesy of Andrew.'

'Brilliant, thanks,' said Lois, peering in the first box and finding a treasure trove of YA books. 'This is perfect.'

'You're welcome. Are you putting the kettle on?'

'Yes, give me a chance,' laughed Lois. They took the boxes of books inside and left them in Lois's office where she made everyone a cup of tea.

'I haven't seen you for ages,' said Steph, perched on the edge of the desk.

'That's because you've been all loved up with your man.'

'True. How are things with you?'

'It's not great. Oliver is back with his ex.' Lois smiled, knowing what was coming.

'What?' said Steph, leaping to her feet. 'How did that happen, I thought it was all go with him. I know you were taking it slowly but I didn't realise he might get back with the ex.'

'Neither did I. He came round last night to tell me. He feels he has to give it another chance.'

'Bloody hell.'

'I know. And we're not talking about it anymore because I'll start crying.' She looked up at the ceiling trying to get rid of the tears that were already threatening to spill. 'And this isn't waterproof mascara. No!' she said when Steph made a move to hug her. 'You're trying to make me cry!' She half laughed, half cried and went to stand behind the chair, using it as a barrier.

'Why would I do that?' Steph was smiling but her eyes were full of sadness for Lois.

'Anyway, don't say anything in front of Rosemary, she

doesn't know.' Lois pulled a tissue out of her pocket and dabbed at her eyes.

'What's it got to do with Rosemary?' Steph looked puzzled and who could blame her.

'It's a long story.'

'Are you joking?' Patsy slammed the bag of coffee beans down so hard that Oliver was surprised it hadn't split.

He sighed. 'Come on, Pats. You know how hard it's been for her to get herself back on track. We're just seeing how it goes, picking up where we left off.'

Patsy harrumphed. 'I know how hard it was for you. How you kept going all summer, with her demanding you pay her share of the coffee house to her while we were stretched trying to get the cinema finished.'

'It was bad timing, but we know now that she was in a dark place, Pats. We called it a day based on things which in hindsight were not a true presentation of the facts.'

'She made your life a misery, Ollie, even before you bought the cinema. You weren't happy.'

'I know you're looking out for me, Pats and I know you helped me out to pay Amy her share of the coffee house. I'm grateful for, you know I am.' He didn't need reminding of those days which had been the darkest of his life.

Her expression softened slightly. 'Look, I just think the past is the past and trying to start up again with her when it wasn't so great last time is a massive mistake.'

Oliver couldn't help smiling at how incapable Patsy was at hiding her opinion from him, managing just half a sentence before she lapsed from sympathy into telling him what to do.

'And honestly, did you have to move her in here? She'll be giving me the evils all the time.'

He smothered a laugh. 'She won't. She likes you.' What

else could he say?

'She bloody doesn't. I think we both know exactly how we feel about each other.' She grinned despite herself.

'See? It'll be fine.' Oliver pulled her into a hug which she tried to get away from.

'You can't win me over like that. Get off! I'm not your friend yet!' But she was laughing and Oliver knew she'd forgiven him.

'I'm just popping upstairs,' he said, letting her go.

'Oh, and so it begins. She's got you wrapped around her little finger already.'

'Pats, give it a rest. I get it.' He made eye contact with her to make sure she knew that he was serious. He owed it to Amy to try again and Patsy had to get on board with that if only because now that Lois was probably never going to speak to him again, he needed someone to be on his side

'I know,' she said, rolling her eyes as she ripped open the bag of coffee beans and emptied them into the grinder. 'And I won't say another word about it. It's only because I love you anyway.'

He shoved her gently. 'Love you too.'

Amy was still asleep when he went up to the flat. She had bought with her what she said were the basics but the lounge was full of her things. She'd unpacked but not put anything away yet. Seeing all these unfamiliar things in his flat made Oliver realise that the place wasn't his own anymore, something he hadn't considered until this minute. When they'd been together before they'd lived at Amy's and he had kept the flat just for convenience so he could stay in Croftwood on the odd occasion that it was more convenient for work. He'd never shared it with anyone before and suddenly it seemed a lot smaller.

He moved a pile of clothes from one end of the sofa and sat down to check his emails. Just as he'd relaxed into reading the latest newsletter from the Croftwood Traders' Association, she came out of the bedroom wearing his favourite sweatshirt over her pyjamas. It felt too intimate for something that was still new to him.

'Morning,' she said, smiling. 'I hope you don't mind.' She pulled at the hem of the sweatshirt. 'I haven't unpacked yet and this was on the chair.'

'It's fine.' It had to be fine. People who lived together, that was what happened. He was just a bit rusty. And at least she'd said something. Christ, it was just a sweatshirt. It didn't matter.

'I thought you might have bought me a coffee up?'

'You don't drink coffee at breakfast. You always have tea.'

She shrugged. 'I do now.'

'Sorry…' he got up, thinking that Patsy was going to be thinking that he was already running around after Amy but feeling that he'd somehow started things off on the wrong foot.

'It's okay, you didn't know. Sit down, I'll make a cup of tea. Do you want one?'

'Thanks that'd be great.' She disappeared into the kitchen leaving him sitting on the sofa running his hands through his hair, wondering how he'd got here.

20

Bill was waiting in the Red Lion Inn car park for Steph as she pulled up. She waved and grinned at him, pleased as ever to see one of her regulars.

She opened the door and dropped the steps down.

'Morning Bill, got time for a cup of tea today?'

'All the time in the world, Steph. How are you?' He steadily made his way up the steps, leaning on the handrail.

'It's been a busy morning,' she said as she pulled her tea-making supplies out of the cupboard, laying them out on the table. 'I've been on my normal round and then high-tailed it over to Croftwood to drop some books off to them and have a quick meeting about the new book club.'

'A book club? That sounds interesting.' Bill took a biscuit and dunked it into his tea. Steph loved little signs like that which showed how comfortable people were when they visited the van.

'The idea is that you have a date-with-a-book where you and another person who has read the same book get together to have a chat about it. It's a bit easier than a whole group discussion and good for us on the mobile library because we can join in more easily.' Although not at this stop, Steph realised, as Bill was the only regular. Still, as word spread about the book club it might encourage more people to visit the mobile library.

'I think you'll have to count me out then, Steph unless you're reading the same book as me,' he said.

'That could be arranged,' she winked at him. 'You know, I wonder whether we can get some of my other regulars involved and a group of us could go to the main book club evening in Croftwood? It's organised by the library but they hold the meeting at a really cool coffee house.'

'It's years since I've been to Croftwood,' said Bill. 'I expect it's changed a lot since then. I can't remember there being anywhere cool.'

'I can tell you now, the library hasn't changed since at least 1970 although my friend Lois is managing it at the moment and she's breathing a bit of life into the old place.'

Bill chuckled. 'If she's anything like you, Steph, I can quite believe that.'

'I'll take that as a compliment.'

'As it was intended.' Bill was such a gentleman.

'So do you think you'd be up for a night out in Croftwood, Bill? I bet Eunice and Dottie from Hawthorn Lane would be up for it too.'

'Well it's been a while since I've had a night out but it sounds like a wonderful idea. I'm sure I can arrange a taxi if you let me know when it is.'

'You know what, Bill? I might try and borrow the Dial-A-Ride minibus for the evening. That would save anyone from having to sort out taxis and it'd be more fun to go together.' It was a great idea. She'd run it past Lois first but she felt sure it would be fine.

'That would be even better. What a good idea.' He dunked another biscuit. 'I hope the refreshments at this 'cool' coffee shop are going to match up to yours, Steph,' he said, completely seriously.

'I think we'll be alright but I'll put a packet of custard creams in my bag just in case.'

On the way to her next stop, Steph thought back to Lois. She'd been shocked to see her in such an emotional state. Even when Alex broke things off out of the blue, she hadn't been as upset as that and unless she'd missed something, Lois hadn't even been seeing Oliver. Not properly anyway. That evening at the cinema, Lois had said something about Alex not being The One. Did that mean she'd started to think Oliver was The One? That would explain things.

When she pulled into her next stop, she opened up then took out her phone and rang Lois. It went to her voicemail.

'Hey, I just wanted to make sure you're alright. I feel like an idiot for not realising how much you liked Oliver. Sorry, I wasn't being very helpful earlier. If you want to get together later, ring me back. We can drown your sorrows over some gin and tonics or something.'

She had a text from Max asking her if she wanted to go out for a drink on Saturday night. Maybe she would see if Lois wanted to go too. It was about time she introduced them and it might cheer her up to see that things were going well in someone's love life at least.

21

'The Christmas lights switch-on is next Saturday,' Oliver said to Lois while he steamed the milk for her morning latte. It was the first time she'd seen him since the night at her house when he'd decided to give things another go with Amy.

Now that they were collaborating with the book club and he was helping out with fundraising for the beanbags, avoiding him altogether wasn't an option she could afford to take. Not without jeopardising the momentum they were creating and that was more important than a bit of personal humiliation at the moment, however hard it might be to walk into the coffee house as if nothing had happened.

'Oh, yes. Someone came in and asked what we were doing. I've got no idea what the library normally does.'

'Nothing,' he said. 'It closes at five like any other Saturday.'

'Not this year, we're going to join in. I love Christmas and the build-up is more fun than the actual thing when you're a grown-up.'

'A grown-up,' Oliver teased, smiling at her in a way that made her heart ache.

'You know what I mean. Don't you feel like that?'

He shrugged. 'I suppose so. It's good for business at least.'

'That's not very Christmassy.'

He laughed, 'I haven't got time to be Christmassy.' He handed her the coffee along with a muffin. 'On the house,' he said softly.

Lois sighed in relief as she left the coffee house. As sorry as she was that things hadn't worked out with Oliver, she was glad things weren't weird between them. Now she just needed to turn her feelings off as quickly as Oliver seemed to have done.

'Hey, Lois!'

She turned to see Patsy heading towards the coffee house. She was wearing a red duffel coat which clashed spectacularly with her hair in the most fabulous way.

'Hi, Patsy. You on your way in?'

'Yep, Ollie's off to the wholesaler this morning. How are you doing?'

Lois was surprised by the question. Had Oliver told Patsy what had happened?

'Sorry, I don't mean to be nosey. I was as shocked as anyone to see him back with Amy. Honestly, I don't know what he's thinking.' She put a hand on Lois's arm. 'He's an idiot.'

Lois sighed. 'He's just trying to do the right thing.' Even now she felt she had to defend him.

'He's an idiot,' Patsy said again, softly. 'Take care, Lois.'

So Patsy, who seemed like the most amiable person in the world, didn't approve. Lois would go so far as to guess that Patsy didn't like Amy and for some reason that ignited the tiniest spark of joy amidst the peaty lump of darkness which had settled inside Lois when it had all ended.

That evening she headed into town. She'd been persuaded to meet Steph and her new chap, Max. The picture of him on Tinder, which Steph had insisted proudly was a true representation, was not all that flattering or attractive so she was quite curious to see what he was actually like. Lois wished they'd invited Andrew so that she didn't have to be a gooseberry but Steph had wanted to introduce him to her friends in stages. Admittedly Andrew had very little diplomacy and might not have been able to keep his thoughts to himself so for Steph's sake it was probably better that Lois was the advance party.

Steph and Max were already in the bar when Lois arrived. She went over to the table and Steph made the introductions then insisted on going to the bar to get a drink for her.

'So, what do you do, Max?' asked Lois, wishing that she had insisted more firmly on getting her own drink so that she wouldn't have to make small talk with this man who looked like a cross between a Hell's Angel and the Hulk.

'I'm a motorbike mechanic.'

Of course he was. Steph handed Lois a glass of wine, then sat down next to him, grinning like a loon, gazing at her thick-necked tattooed monster of a boyfriend with love-hearts for eyes. Lois knew she had a habit of being very judgy when she met new people and more often than not changed her mind about them completely once she got to know them. And after all, he was going out with Steph, a librarian, so he couldn't be that bad but poor Steph was a terrible judge of character when it came to her boyfriends. Still, she shouldn't stereotype him. Even if all of Steph's other boyfriends had turned out to be dicks, it didn't mean he was.

'Have you lived in Worcester long?'

'Nah. Moved here with me ex. I'm from London way.'

'He has five motorbikes, Lois,' said Steph proudly.

'They're Harleys darlin'. You gotta start rememberin' the difference.' He brought his fist down on the table to emphasise his point.

Nice.

'Sorry, I'll get to grips with the jargon.' Steph grinned at Lois, seemingly oblivious to the fact that this boyfriend might be the biggest dick of them all.

'Lois.'

She turned to look at someone who had said her name. Someone she hadn't heard utter her name for a few months.

'Alex, what are you doing here?'

'I'm back for the weekend.' He looked past her at Steph, who raised her hand solemnly in greeting, his eyes landing on Max with a slightly startled look.

'Are you coming to pick your stuff up?'

'No, I hadn't planned to. I didn't think I'd see...' He trailed off as he realised how that sounded. 'I mean, I was going to call you...'

'There's no need to be weird about it,' Lois said. 'If you don't want to talk to me that's fine but at least have the decency to pick up your stuff and move out properly.'

Alex's friends, Rich and Marc appeared with pints in their hands while he looked at Lois in surprise. She was pleased. He'd messed her around a lot and she was fed up with it. It was about time she stood her ground with him.

'Alright, Lois?' asked Rich enthusiastically, completely unaware of the atmosphere.

'I'll be out on Sunday,' she said, ignoring Rich. 'Pick your stuff up and leave the key behind when you go.' It had only just occurred to Lois that he still had his key and now she wanted it back but she also didn't want to be there when he came round. 'I'll be getting the locks changed on Monday either way.'

'There's no need to be like that Lois,' he said, looking like a wounded puppy.

'Alex, come on. I've been waiting for you to be ready to sort this out for weeks and now you're here and you weren't even going to bother getting in touch. I've put everything ready in the spare room. Sort it out on Sunday, please. You owe me that.'

He turned and walked away with his mates.

'Christ, Lois. I bet he never knew you had it in you,' said Steph, looking impressed.

Lois felt pleased with herself. The shock of seeing Alex unexpectedly would have floored her a few weeks ago but now she was almost indifferent to it.

'Are you alright?'

'Yes, I'm fine.'

'Bloody hell, it's like EastEnders in here,' said Max. 'Brightened things up, didn't he?'

22

On Monday morning, Lois left the house resolving to sort out the Alex problem once and for all. Perhaps unsurprisingly he hadn't turned up to collect his things on Sunday. The whole time they'd been together it was a very rare occasion that he did anything for her, especially if she'd asked him to, so she shouldn't have expected anything else.

Despite that, she felt positive and in a good mood now that she'd decided to get the closure she deserved from that relationship, so she decided not to risk ruining her buzz by going into Oliver's for coffee. She had yet to come across Amy since she'd moved in with him and was now officially Oliver's girlfriend, and the longer she could postpone that moment, the better.

'Morning Lois. I've got something really exciting to show you.'

Lois was taken aback by Linda's early morning enthusiasm but pulled off her coat and joined her at the computer.

'Look, it's a competition for the Library of the Year Award! There's a category for initiatives which enhance the local community, I think we should enter with the book club.'

Lois hated to burst Linda's bubble but there were loads of book clubs and she wasn't sure that theirs was different enough. 'It's a good idea, we can look into it.'

'We'll need to get people to vote online for us so we will have to do some campaigning. We can use Twitter and Instagram,' she said proudly, having been to see Claudia again at the Hive to learn the next steps in her social media journey.

'It would raise our profile, I suppose. Okay, come up with the pitch or whatever it is we have to do to enter and we'll discuss it at the meeting in the morning. It's the book club on Wednesday so I guess we could mention it to some of the customers and see if they'll vote for us.'

The more she thought about it, the more Linda's enthusiasm rubbed off on her. This competition could be the boost they needed to get the library into a position where people would start to care whether it was there or not.

When Lois checked the emails there was one from Robert to say that they were officially allowed to fundraise for the things she wanted to put into the children's library. She tried not to think about the fact that Oliver had come up with that idea. It was good news, perhaps they could launch it at the Christmas lights switch-on event. Which reminded her, she needed to think about what they were going to do to entice people to visit them on the night. Once she'd jotted down some ideas for a competition they could run, she googled the Library of the Year awards and was engrossed in making some notes she thought they could use in their application when she realised someone was waiting at the desk.

'Sorry, what can I do for you?' She hurriedly logged off the computer, looked up and saw Amy. A feeling of dread settled in Lois's stomach. Her being in the library, literally having to face her, was so much worse than the prospect of seeing her in the coffee shop.

'Hi, I'm interested in joining the book club.'

Did Amy know about her and Oliver? She must know that they were friends at least if he'd told her about the book club. But her biggest worry was whether Amy knew about the kiss.

'Great,' said Lois, trying to sound friendly without coming across as a weirdo. It was going to be a struggle. 'I'll show you the books you can choose from this month. There's not much time left until the meeting but come along anyway as long as you don't mind spoilers if you haven't managed to finish it.'

'Oh, I don't mind. I'm just keen to join in. Since I've moved in with Oliver I thought I ought to.'

'He's been brilliant helping us to get the club started. Rosemary seems to be able to get him to do anything,' she smiled.

'Yep, she certainly does have some power over him but he's genuinely looking forward to the meeting anyway. Maybe I should pick the same book as him but that seems a bit dull, doesn't it? I mean we can talk to each other whenever we like. The whole point is to meet new people.'

'He's reading *The First Time I Saw You* by Emma Cooper.' She probably knew that, Lois realised after she'd said it, so added, 'Isn't he?' as an afterthought.

'Yes, I was quite surprised, especially now that I see he could have chosen this,' she said, picking up the latest Jo Nesbo book, *The Thirst*.

'Some people use book clubs to widen their reading outside their usual favourite genres.' Lois hoped that Oliver didn't tell Amy that he had asked Lois to choose a book for him so that they could talk about it at the date-with-a-book club. He probably wouldn't want to do that now anyway.

'Well, that makes sense. I think I'll take this one. A thriller is bound to elicit some interesting conversation.'

'Quite right.'

'I'm surprised Oliver has time to host and join in.' It wasn't a question, yet Lois could feel Amy's eyes boring into her, waiting for a response.

'Well, we're all there to help out and there weren't that many people at the first meeting but who knows what will happen this time!' Her tone was far too jovial. 'We've had a lot more people registering for the next meeting,' she added more calmly.

'Great, I'm looking forward to it.'

'Mmm, me too.'

'And what book are you reading?'

Lois could feel her cheeks reddening in betrayal because clearly, lying was her only option. 'I'm reading the biography.' Telling Amy she was reading the same book as Oliver seemed tantamount to admitting they'd been on the brink of a relationship. If he chose to tell her, that was one thing but Lois didn't want to be drawn into any kind of competition with Amy and she seemed to be trying to get some kind of reaction.

Lois asked Amy to fill in one of the book club cards while she busied herself with issuing her a new membership card and checked the book out, all the time hoping that the conversation was over.

As Amy turned to leave, Lois gave her what she hoped was a friendly smile and felt the most enormous relief that she'd managed to navigate the whole thing without making a fool of herself.

'Oliver told me what happened between you. I just wanted to say no hard feelings, I hope we can be friends.' And she turned and left, thankfully not giving Lois the chance to respond. In that minute she might not have known what to say to Amy but she was sure of something. They definitely weren't going to be friends.

The encounter with Amy had shaken Lois but at the same time, it had underlined the fact that it was over with Oliver. She had to move on. So, to take control of at least one element of her life, she decided that the time had come to gain closure with Alex. Given how things were between them, some drastic action was called for.

'Linda, I think I might take the day off tomorrow. Are you okay to cover for me?'

'Of course, Lois. What are you up to?'

'I'm going to London for the day.'

'Lovely! There's nothing like London for a bit of shopping.'

The following morning, Lois was sat on the train to London. She hadn't told anyone what she was doing; she was beyond the point of needing advice from anyone.

While she had time to spare on the train journey, she designed an entry form and a poster for the children's treasure hunt she'd decided to have in the library to coincide with the Christmas lights switch-on in Croftwood. It was a distraction from where she was going and what was going to happen when she got there, as well as a job which had to be done. Despite the single-mindedness that had gripped her when she'd decided to confront Alex, her nerve was deserting her in direct proportion to how close she was getting to London.

It wasn't in her nature to take a stand against anything or to stand up for herself. Especially that. But seeing Amy sweep in and take Oliver, getting exactly what she wanted, and then coming to the library to flaunt it, that was where her drive had finally come from. She had spent too long letting her life meander wherever it may, being manipulated and shifted in different directions by other people when the only person who had the right to do that was her.

When the train pulled into Paddington, Lois caught the

Tube to Bank and walked the short distance to Alex's offices, on a side road off Fenchurch Street. As she'd never been there before, she'd done some googling to work out where she needed to go. Luckily his company occupied the whole building so Lois was able to go straight to the reception and ask to talk to him.

'Is he expecting you?' asked the receptionist, picking up a phone to call him but stopping midway, holding it away from her ear to demonstrate the power she held for that particular moment.

'No, it's a surprise,' said Lois, smiling in what she hoped was a conspiratorial manner.

'Lovely,' she said, sounding like it was anything but. 'Take a seat.'

Lois sat down opposite the desk and watched as the woman called Alex. Everyone was dressed for business but rather than feeling out of place Lois was grateful that she got to express herself however she liked every day and she secretly hoped it would embarrass the hell out of Alex when he saw her in her dungarees and docs.

A couple of minutes later, he emerged from the lift wearing his overcoat. He looked so smart that Lois momentarily felt a little thrill run through her before remembering very quickly that the image he portrayed didn't meet the reality.

He marched towards her, grabbed her hand as she stood up to greet him and said in a low, urgent voice, 'Leave it until we get out of here.'

She'd known he would be surprised but she was quite taken aback at his brusque tone. He knew her better than to think she was going to make a scene. Maybe he really was embarrassed by her. They walked out of the building and he didn't speak again until they reached the end of the street.

'What are you doing here, Lois? You can't just turn up like this.' He was pacing around in front of her. It was quite an overreaction.

'We need to talk, Alex. Face to face. You don't reply to my texts and when I saw you in Worcester you hadn't told me you'd be back and then even though I arranged to stay out for the whole day you still didn't collect your stuff.'

His shoulders slumped and he stopped pacing. 'I've got half an hour. Come on, let's grab a drink.'

They crossed the road and Alex led them down the side of the Walkie-Talkie building, going inside a door at the back. He flashed a card at a security person on the door and they were waved over to a lift.

'I thought you meant a coffee,' said Lois.

'This is a bit nicer than Costa,' Alex said, as he concentrated on the light display above the lift doors.

The lift was extremely fast and when it opened on the 32nd floor, Lois hadn't expected that they would be that high so quickly. They were in what was effectively a huge, curved greenhouse which covered the top of the building. There was a cafe, a pricey-looking restaurant and a cocktail bar nestled amongst plants and trees galore. Alex bought them both a coffee and led the way outside onto the terrace where they could enjoy the panoramic view of the City of London and the River Thames.

They stood side by side in silence for a few minutes.

'I'm sorry if I shocked you by coming here, Alex but I just need things to be finished between us. You need to get your stuff and leave properly.'

He leant on the balustrade, his coffee hovering over the heads of unknowing people below. 'I know.' He sighed and bowed his head. 'I know it was me that called it off and I still think it was the right thing to do but I suppose part of me thought maybe this London thing wouldn't work out and I could come back.'

'You wouldn't be coming back for me though. I'm not just

a convenient backup plan, a place to come to when there's no other option. We're over, Alex and everything that goes with it is over too. Did you really think that I'd have you back after all of this?'

He looked at her and she could tell that he did think that she was his backup option. And what was worse, she knew that a few months ago when he'd first left, she probably would have considered it if he'd wanted to come back, but not anymore. Even if she never found anyone else, that was better than being with Alex who didn't love her.

'I'm doing this for us, Alex. I'm pretty sure you know that, and avoiding me, avoiding what needs to be done, it's not fair on either of us. Get your stuff, Alex. Make a new life for yourself here, if that's what you want. This is your chance to start afresh, do what you want to do with no ties or anything.'

'And what are you doing, Lois? Are you okay?' It was the first time she could remember him ever really asking her if she was okay.

'I'm great. Work is the best challenge I've ever had in my life and I'm happy.'

'Good. It's been hard to let go. I thought I'd come to London and work in the week then come home to you at the weekends and that everything would stay the same.'

'That was never going to happen and it's good that you realised that because I'm not sure I would have. I was so used to how things were that I didn't stop to think about whether we were happy. And I don't think we were, or at least not happy enough, not like we both deserve.' She was being kind including him in her assessment of how things had been between them. She was fairly sure he'd been quite happy having her to hang around with whenever his mates weren't around. He'd probably accepted that he hadn't been madly in love with her and he was fine with that. But since she'd met

Oliver, her idea of what a relationship should be, and what she was going to hold out for, had completely changed.

'I felt like I was living the worst part of both lives and that I needed to choose and I chose this.'

'You didn't tell me any of that, Alex. We never talked about it properly. Why?'

'Would it have made any difference if we'd talked about it?'

'Maybe not in the end but we should have done it anyway. I don't think I'd be stalking you around London if we had.'

'I'm so sorry, Lo.' He turned to her and took her hand. 'I'll come back at the weekend and move my stuff out. I've sorted out a proper place to live, sharing a flat with a bloke I work with.'

'Great. I'll be working on Saturday and at home on Sunday. Come whichever day you like. I haven't changed the locks.' She smiled and squeezed his hand.

'Thanks,' he grinned. 'I didn't think you would have.'

Then she wished more than anything that she had, just so that she could keep surprising him.

They travelled back down in the lift together and lingered outside the door.

'You didn't come all this way just to see me?' Alex said.

'Of course not,' lied Lois. 'I have a meeting at the British Library this afternoon.' She wasn't going to give him an ego boost by telling him the truth.

'Maybe see you at the weekend then.' He gave her a quick peck on the cheek.

'Thanks for the coffee.'

'You're welcome. It was nice to see you.' He looked like he meant it, giving her a lop-sided smile that reminded her of why she'd fallen for his limited charms in the first place.

She headed back to the Tube with a spring in her step. She had taken control of the situation and managed to get it resolved. Obviously, he hadn't moved his things out yet but this time, she knew he would.

23

The coffee house was full. More than full, it was heaving. Somehow, there were far more people who had turned up for the date-with-a-book club meeting than had filled in forms. The careful pairings and list that Rosemary had prepared was being massacred by Lois as she tried to welcome and seat as many people as they could fit. In the end, they'd had to abandon the idea of pairing people and instead had dedicated an area for each book and were sending people off to find someone to discuss the book with. As a result, it quickly morphed into a more usual kind of book club where it could be difficult to join in if you were not feeling at your most confident.

Oliver was run off his feet. Patsy was working at the cinema and their other barista, Jack, had been working all day so Oliver had sent him home. He resorted to calling Amy over from chatting with her group to help him make drinks. Linda had gone to the supermarket to buy some extra bottles of wine for him and staggered through the door just as the last people had arrived. Or who Lois hoped were the last people.

'Lois, can you pour some wine for that table over there?' asked Oliver as he made what seemed like twenty coffees all at the same time.

'No problem. Just let me know what else you need. I'm all yours now they're inside.'

Even though there wasn't room to swing a cat in the place and some people were having to sit on chairs which Amy had fetched from the flat upstairs, as Lois walked around delivering drinks to various tables she was thrilled to overhear enthusiastic conversations about the books going on all around her.

'Good grief, Lois. I didn't expect this,' said Linda leaning against the counter once she'd finished waitressing as well.

'I know. And I don't want to sound ungrateful but a lot of these people aren't Croftwood Library customers.'

'That's what I thought. There are more people in here than we get through the library doors in a month, but I don't know what we can do about it.'

'Well, we need to do something because this is just the kind of thing we were trying to avoid. I'd be terrified if I walked through the door tonight expecting a date with a book and one other person.'

'Me too,' agreed Linda, flicking her eyes over to a woman with a very loud voice who was expressing her disappointment with the book she'd read and not allowing anyone to disagree with her.

'Hmm. I do have an idea but I need to talk to Oliver and see if he can help.'

Linda looked exhausted so Lois sent her off to perch on the end of a bench to join in the discussion of the book she'd read.

'Hey, Oliver,' Lois said, once he was wiping down the coffee machine and looking slightly less manic. 'Do you think anywhere else in town would be up for hosting the book club like this?'

'Fed up of us already?' he joked.

'We need somewhere quieter.' She missed that the most, having a conversation like this with him but she was relieved that she was managing to behave normally around him. His tack of pretending nothing had happened was easier to go along with than she'd thought and now that they'd not spoken about it for a couple of weeks, the moment had passed to start hashing things out.

'If we could just have got rid of this book club thing tonight it would have been fine,' he said with a grin that made Lois forget for a second that she should be trying harder not to find him attractive anymore.

'I've been talking to Linda about how we've never seen most of these people in the library and I love that so many people are enjoying it, but if even one or two more people had turned up, some of our lovely customers might not have got in. I thought if we could get another venue on the same night, we could have this as the actual date-with-a-book club where we stick to the plan and pair people up from the cards they fill in at the library and anyone else who wants to join in goes to the other place.'

'Well it's either spreading the joy or people will be offended but I take your point. If it carries on like this we'll be turning people away and that's not good for either of us. I'd love to offer you the cinema but we've got bookings every evening for the event spaces even when we're not showing a film that night. I'll have a word with Jen at the Courtyard Café and see if she'd be up for helping. It's the closest place to here as well which would help.'

'Brilliant, thanks. But I'm worried now that people will think we're being snobby or something.'

'Nah, it'll be fine,' he said confidently. 'All they have to do to be in the club is come into the library. It's not that hard,

Amy managed it.' He suddenly looked awkward and turned away briefly.

'And we're assuming that they'll prefer coming here to going to the Courtyard Café,' said Lois, trying to get the conversation back to light-hearted.

'Lois!' He turned back and his grin told her that he was fine.

'Sorry, you know I don't mean it.'

'I know. You're one of the few people who understand the vast difference between a coffee house and a café.'

As Oliver began another round of coffee making, Lois turned back towards the throng to look for Linda but instead saw Amy watching her and Oliver. She flashed a tight smile at Lois, then turned her attention back to the person she was talking to although her eyes kept flicking back to them.

Even if Oliver hadn't been too busy to join in, Lois knew there was no way either of them would have suggested sitting down together to discuss their book, it would have been a step too far. Lois had been hoping she might be able to join in with one of the groups but there was nowhere to sit down and after seeing Amy's face, she felt a bit awkward standing at the counter and chatting to Oliver again. Instead, she began making her way around the room collecting empty cups and glasses.

She clustered all the empties she could find on the counter and then went behind and began washing up. She knew Oliver had a dishwasher but it would take umpteen loads and would make it late for him locking up if he had all this to do before he went upstairs.

'Lois, you shouldn't be doing that,' he said, as he came out of the store cupboard with a fresh bag of coffee beans.

'There's nothing else I can do. It's fine.'

'I hear you went to London yesterday?'

She didn't know whether to be annoyed that he knew that

from the grapevine or touched that she had settled into Croftwood so well that she was the subject of town gossip.

'I did. I went to see Alex. I was getting nowhere with asking him to move his things out of the house so I thought confronting him when he was sober was the best bet.'

'And did it work?'

'Well, we'll see at the weekend. I've got high hopes though, we had a really good talk. It cleared the air so I think the game playing's over.'

'I'm glad. You don't deserve to be messed around.' He looked at her for a bit longer than felt normal and Lois was sure she could feel Amy's eyes boring into the back of her head.

'Thanks. I'll go and clear some more tables now that people are starting to leave,' she said, drying her hands on some paper towel.

'What's up with you tonight? You seem on edge.' He stood in the way of her exit from behind the counter.

'Nothing's up,' said Lois, pasting what she hoped was a relaxed smile on her face. 'It's just so busy and I didn't expect it, that's all.' It said something that it hadn't occurred to him that Amy being at the book club might be weird for her. Did he think she would just take it in her stride? If he did, he had more confidence in her than she had in herself. It was taking everything she had to try and act normally while being highly aware of how everything she did would look from Amy's perspective. And Amy clearly felt that Lois was a threat, judging by the number of times Lois had caught her looking over at her.

But Oliver seemed satisfied with the answer and moved aside.

When people began to leave, Amy sidled over to the counter and stood next to Oliver, snuggling into his side until he bent down to kiss her. It seemed like a very clear sign to

Lois that Amy was staking her territory as well as being something she didn't want to have to watch, so she went and stood by the door instead and thanked people as they left, assuring the people who she knew had signed up to the club that the following month would be back to the promised format.

Once she left the coffee house and the adrenaline had worn off, Lois had a nauseous feeling come over her as she thought back on the evening. She wasn't sure she could cope with that level of scrutiny from Amy. It was going to make life in Croftwood, and especially the book club, very tricky indeed.

24

When Lois arrived at the library the next morning, Linda was waiting in the doorway.

'We've had an email!' she blurted out before Lois had even taken her cycling helmet off.

'About what?' Lois wandered into the office to dump her bag and coat with Linda following her, clearly desperate to impart whatever news she was so excited about.

'The Library of the Year competition! We're through to the next round!'

'Are we? I didn't realise we were even in it yet. I thought people had to vote for us?'

'They do, that's the round we're in now. Then if we get enough votes we're in the final,' explained Linda patiently.

'Right. So we're actually up for Library of the Year, across the whole country?' As much as she had come to love Croftwood Library it certainly wasn't of the calibre she suspected was necessary to compete for being Library of the Year.

'Well, yes and no. I entered us into the Community Spirit category for the date-with-a-book club. If we end up the winner of that category we get automatically through to the Library of the Year Award. There's a posh dinner for the final where they announce the category winner and then all the category winners compete for being the Library of the Year.'

'Blimey. That sounds amazing. So how many other libraries are we up against in our category?'

'Five, there's six of us altogether and it's all on votes. I'm going to tweet my socks off about it.'

'That's a great plan, but we need to find out how people can vote so we can put a link in the tweet or whatever. I assume it's online voting?'

'Yes, but they'll send us some postcards to give out to people who aren't online. I suppose there are still some people out there living in the dark ages,' sighed Linda, forgetting that she had been one of them until very recently.

'We ought to let the Gazette know, that would be great publicity and I'll tell Robert at the Hive in case there's anything they can do to help us out. Maybe they'd put up a poster or something.'

'There are some official posters attached to the email which we can print off to display. I'll run some off this morning. I gave Rosemary a ring to see if she'd pop in a bit earlier today. Maybe we can ask her to put some up around the town and with the Christmas lights switch-on coming up, it's great timing.'

'Good idea. She's doing a great job of getting businesses to donate prizes for the children's competition.'

Later that day, Lois rang Robert to tell him the good news.

'Hmm.' He sounded less than pleased. 'I'm not sure you should have gone ahead with entering given the situation with Croftwood. It could be rather embarrassing for the council if you were to get any further in the competition only for the library to close.'

'But don't you think it could save the library if we won?'

She could hear Robert suck in a breath. 'Well, it's not for me to say, it's a decision that's bigger than me or you.'

'It's a great library, Robert. I think we're proving that it's a valuable part of Croftwood.'

'I don't think that's in dispute, Lois. These decisions are purely financial, you know that, and however much you can improve the library, the powers that be have decided that it's not worth the money it takes to keep it open.' He paused. 'Having said that, passion can go a long way. Let me gently spread the word about this competition before you tell the world, Lois. Give me a couple of days and I'll let you know how the land lies.'

'Okay, thanks. We need to get public votes for the next round so we need to get on with the word-spreading.'

'Leave it with me. I understand how you feel, Lois. It's dreadful to have to see a library close and we both know how easy it is to fall in love with the places.'

After the phone call, she briefed Linda not to do any tweeting until Robert gave them the go-ahead.

'Does that count for the posters too?' said Linda, looking sheepish. 'Because I sent Rosemary off with fifty while you were on the phone.'

'It does. Don't worry, I'll try and catch her up.' Lois grabbed her coat from the office and hurriedly left the library, ran to the road and looked both ways to see if she could spot Rosemary. The high street was the most likely direction she'd gone in so Lois headed off at a brisk pace. Not able to see Rosemary ahead of her, she took a shortcut through the churchyard.

As she walked through, she could hear a noise coming from behind one of the tombs and crept off the path to have a look. It was Amy, sitting on a bench, crying.

It went against Lois's instincts to carry on without going over to see if she was okay. After all, she wasn't a stranger. On the other hand, she was most likely crying about something to do with Oliver and that made things a bit tricky.

'Are you alright?' Lois stood in front of her, feeling like it was too forward to sit down.

Amy looked up and wiped her eyes quickly. 'I'm fine, thanks.'

'Okay, well take care.' Lois managed a tight smile, feeling relieved that she'd done her duty and stepped away.

'You and Oliver are friends, right? I mean, aside from whatever else went on.'

Lois nodded. 'We've not known each other long, just a couple of months since I started working at the library.'

'Did he tell you about me, about what happened?'

Lois nodded again, worried that she was somehow being disloyal to Oliver by admitting it.

'I'm not sure he ever expected me to come back to him. He hasn't said that to me, he said he hoped we'd be able to pick up where we left off...'

'Have you spoken to him about it?' she asked.

Amy's watery eyes looked up at the sky as she sighed. 'I've tried, he just won't open up to me.'

Lois sat on the edge of the bench. 'I'm sure it's hard for both of you.'

'I didn't think it would be like this. I hadn't stopped loving him, but I think he'd given up a long time ago and he's moved on without me.'

'Maybe it seems like that but I think he's trying his best to make it work.' Lois didn't doubt that was true.

'Do you think so? I find it so hard seeing him being friends with you. Sometimes I wonder if he'd rather be with you.'

Lois hoped she hadn't blushed. 'We're just friends, Amy. There's nothing to worry about.' It surprised her that Amy was so frank, though she seemed much softer than she had when she'd come to the library.

'It's just, the book club seems so out of character for him. I know it's been a while since I've been involved enough to know what he's up to but honestly, books are not him at all.'

Lois tried not to take that as a personal insult. As if there was ever anything wrong with anyone liking books. 'I think it's the benefit it brings to the coffee house more than anything else,' she said tactfully.

'Hmm. Or maybe he's changed more than I realised.'

Lois thought that was probably true. 'Try to talk to him again, Amy. Tell him what you've told me, I'm sure he'll understand how you feel.'

'Thanks, Lois.' Amy stood up and smiled. 'Pop in for a coffee sometime.'

'Will do.' She almost definitely wouldn't.

Lois watched Amy walk back towards the coffee house, wondering whether she would talk to Oliver about how she felt. He was so easy to talk to, she could imagine them sitting down together and him earnestly listening to Amy's worries. But it was an image that was too painful to think about. Too close to how it had been that night after the kiss when she'd gone round to his flat and he'd told her everything. She closed her eyes and took a deep breath, pushing Oliver from her mind as she suddenly remembered that she was supposed to be looking for Rosemary. She headed towards the Post Office which would be on Rosemary's way home and glancing at the window, saw a poster. 'Vote for Croftwood Library!' it said, with the details underneath about how to vote.

Lois's heart sank momentarily until she thought, what's the worst that could happen? Nothing that would be worse than the library closing. It might ruffle a few feathers but if the County Library bosses disapproved, it would be more embarrassing for them to pull them out of the competition. They might as well go along with it and see what happened.

Chances were that Croftwood wouldn't make the cut but they had to try.

There didn't seem much point in trying to find Rosemary now so she turned back, walking down the high street. As she passed the coffee house she could see Oliver and Amy sitting at a table talking. Being honest with each other was the best thing they could do although she couldn't stop herself from hoping that might not be enough to save their relationship. It went against the grain to wish the worst for anyone but for once, Lois was going to look out for herself and anyway, she thought that if they were honest with each other they'd probably realise they were trying to resurrect something which had died long ago.

Thankfully it was a quiet morning in the coffee house. Oliver was sitting on the stairs to the flat, looking at his phone and listening for the door. He was so tired, he didn't think he would make it through the whole day. Why couldn't Amy have picked a fight the night before one of Patsy's shifts?

He needed an espresso so stood up, stretched and pushed his phone into his apron pocket. He hadn't heard the door so was surprised to see Lois waiting at the counter.

'Oh, hi Lois. What can I do for you,' he said, failing to sound as upbeat as he'd intended to.

'Are you all right, Oliver?' Her brow was furrowed with concern.

He knew he looked terrible. His eyes were puffy, giving away the fact that he hadn't slept at all and he hadn't had the time or energy to sort his bedhead out.

'Yeah, yeah, fine.' He raked his hand through his hair, making it stick up in all directions. 'Well, you know...' He could just tell Lois what had happened. He needed a friend but it was hardly fair to start moaning to her about the problems he and Amy were having.

Nevertheless, she said, 'If you want to talk…if now's not a good time, you know where I am.'

He looked at her intently for a second, wondering whether he could. It might make him feel better. He thought better of it, shook his head briefly and said, 'Breakfast is it?'

'Yes, please. A latte and an egg and avocado bagel to go.'

'Coming up.'

He busied himself with preparing her order and managed not to make eye contact or conversation again.

When Lois left, instead of his spot on the stairs, he went and sat on one of the stools at the window bar, just in case he didn't hear someone else come in.

He watched her walk down the road, seeing her turn and glance back at the coffee house, with a worried expression on her face.

Amy had left. For how long, he didn't know. She'd walked out, taking her car keys at the height of their row the night before and hadn't been in touch since. He hadn't slept at all, wondering where she was, where she had gone…what she had done. Because he knew she was still fragile he worried that any disagreement that made her as upset as she was last night could be what sent her over the edge. There was an edge, he could see that as soon as they had got back together. He didn't think it had ever been there before and now, he could see her teetering on it, and yet he seemed to have very little influence over how close she got to it because he couldn't seem to do anything right. He was failing to anticipate what he might be doing wrong at every turn because there seemed to be no logic behind any of the issues that Amy had with him.

It was never going to be plain sailing being back together again when so much time had passed and if he was honest, it hadn't been when they were together before and they had both forgotten that. But he didn't feel like a man who was having a second chance with the love of his life, so what was he doing it for?

He sent yet another text to Amy begging her to call him or come home then left his phone on the side while he made himself the espresso he'd been promising himself since before Lois came in.

25

The usual Thursday morning meeting had been postponed until Friday as Rosemary had been so keen to distribute the posters, that she hadn't made it back to the library the day before. She hadn't heard about the book club and was incredulous when Linda and Lois related the tale of how busy it had been.

'Full? But we only had twenty-two cards handed in. That's more than last time, I grant you but they surely didn't fill Oliver's.'

'I think the word has spread, probably thanks to Linda, which is great but has sort of eclipsed our original intention of increasing footfall here at the library.'

Lois went on to explain her plan to split the evening between the two venues. 'And the best thing is that the next meeting will be just before Christmas so we can make it extra special anyway.'

'When I was at the Hive over the weekend I saw they have a wonderful display of Christmas books. Could we do that and have one of the book club choices be from that selection?' asked Linda.

'That's a great idea. The other thing we need to organise is the treasure hunt for the Christmas light switch-on evening. I've made an entry form and a poster. Rosemary, would you be able to take them on your travels, see if you can get people to put one up here and there for us?'

'Of course. I assume you will need extra help on that day?'

'If you don't mind, that would be brilliant,' said Lois, silently hoping that Rosemary would be able to stop herself from telling off any exuberant children.

'I'll be in that day too,' said Linda. 'I'm looking forward to it.'

'Thanks, guys. It'll be a chance to launch our fundraising for the teenagers' area of the library so I hope we can get loads of people in that day.'

'Do we have enough prizes, Lois? I can ask some more of the local businesses if needs be,' Rosemary offered. Sometimes it flummoxed Lois how Rosemary could have left Croftwood Library in the dark ages for so long when she was so proactive with everything Lois introduced.

'Thanks, Rosemary, we're probably okay for prizes with what you've already managed to collect. I'd love to drum up some enthusiasm for the fundraising, I think that needs to be our next focus. Right, let's get to work.'

That evening Lois was glad to be able to go home, get her pyjamas on and binge the new season of Jack Ryan. After being in London on Tuesday and the crazy book club on Wednesday, it felt like the first minute she'd had to relax for days. It would almost be time to watch Christmas movies, her absolute favourite thing about the run-up to the big day. Depending on which day Alex came to clear out his things, if she had Sunday afternoon free, she would be tuned into the cheesy Christmas movies on Channel Five which had already started.

Her phone pinged with a text notification.

Can we have dinner tomorrow night? I'm staying at Rich's this weekend. Alex

Lois rummaged for the remote control and paused Jack Ryan. She was wary of reading too much into Alex's invitation, it would be easy to overthink it. They'd said all there was to say and she couldn't understand what could be gained by any more discussion. She needed a second opinion.

'Hey, Steph.'

'Lois! Good to hear from you. What's up?'

Lois sighed. 'Alex wants to have dinner on Friday and I'm worried that…well, I don't know exactly what. But it doesn't seem like a good idea.'

'What's the harm? He's coming to clear his stuff out which is what you wanted, maybe he's just trying to have a nice ending.'

If Steph wasn't still in her loved-up bubble she would not be saying that. Since when did Alex ever suggest doing anything like eating out, unless it was dinner at the pub with his mates? Lois could count on her thumbs the number of times they'd been out for dinner somewhere nice, alone. She had rung Steph for reassurance that she was right to be suspicious about Alex's motives, and she wasn't going to get it.

'Maybe you're right,' she said, purely to satisfy Steph that nothing else needed to be said on the subject. She wasn't about to start trying to convince Steph to be on her side instead of Alex's. 'And how's it going with you and Max?'

'Really good. He's taking me out with his motorbike friends on Saturday. We're going to Weston-Super-Mare in a big convoy.'

'Oh, brilliant,' said Lois, trying to sound enthusiastic. 'Well, have a good time and maybe we can catch up next week.'

'Okay and let me know how it goes with Alex.'

Lois pressed play but had lost concentration on Jack Ryan.

What was Alex up to? And why did it bother her anyway? A dinner to say goodbye was a nice idea if that's what it was, and she should probably go along with it.

Dinner sounds great. Let me know when and where. L x

On Saturday evening, she cycled home with butterflies in her stomach. It was only Alex, she kept telling herself. If it was Oliver she was lucky enough to be going to dinner with maybe she would understand it. She pushed the thought out of her mind before she could think any more about how much she would like that.

Alex had texted to say he would meet her in The Friar Street Kitchen, a cool place in Worcester that did sharing platters and cocktails. Lois was pleased that it was a restauranty place rather than a pub. That was an improvement from Alex, verging on being out of character but she was happy to embrace it. Perhaps living the high life in London was starting to rub off on him.

It was cold and crisp and thankfully not raining, so once she'd changed out of her work clothes into a comfortable dress that nonetheless felt like she'd made an effort, Lois enjoyed the short walk over the bridge into town. Fairy lights were twinkling everywhere, making her feel Christmassy. Croftwood would be just as festive the following week, she thought, looking forward to the light switch-on which she had heard so much about.

Alex was waiting outside the restaurant, hands in his pockets and the collar of his coat turned up against the biting cold. He held her arms gently as he leaned forward to kiss her on the cheek. It was a touching gesture that took Lois by surprise.

'You look great,' he said, smiling as he looked at her.

'Thanks, so do you.' He was wearing a suit underneath his

smart coat. He would never normally go out in town dressed like that. All these tiny things were adding up and making Lois wonder whether something was afoot.

They sat at a table in the window that it turned out Alex had booked – also out of character. They made small talk about their working weeks then when the drinks arrived Alex made a toast.

'To us, Lois.'

'To us.' It was an odd toast, drinking in celebration of the end of the life they'd shared but Lois was glad that Alex seemed to be more at peace with things than when they'd seen each other in London. She'd been worried that he was finding it hard to move on but tonight he seemed happy and together. It was good. A relief.

'After you came to London, Lois, I started thinking about what had made me decide to take the job in London given that it meant leaving you behind.'

'I think you just wanted a new start, from what you said the other day,' she said helpfully, in a bid to keep Alex on topic.

'In a way.' He paused to sip his drink. 'But I don't think I made the right decision. I miss you.'

She stared at him. 'You're not moving back in, are you?' It came out of her mouth before she'd had chance to phrase it more tactfully. There was no way she would let him move back in now, too much had happened. And more to the point, it wasn't what she wanted anymore.

'No, of course not,' he said. 'I want you to move to London with me. I never asked you properly before because I thought I wanted out of everything. Us, my life here, everything. But, when you came to see me the other day, it made me realise that I love you. I think that's why I didn't move my stuff out sooner because I wasn't ready to leave the idea of us behind.'

'But you said it was just that you were afraid to let go of

everything here, not because of me.' Lois began to wonder if she'd completely misinterpreted their conversation in London as well as the way things had been between them for so long. 'I think you're forgetting how things were, Alex. We hadn't been happy for a long time. It was the right thing to do to break up.'

'But since I've been away, I've realised that I don't think that it was a problem with us, Lois. I think I just needed to be in a different place to see how things should be between us. In Worcester, I feel like I'm still a teenager, hanging out with the lads just the same as it's always been. Since I moved to London, especially since we broke up and I stopped coming back every weekend, I've changed.'

'But I don't want to move to London, Alex.' There was more to it than that and he deserved to hear the truth. There had been little enough of that in their relationship and Lois was determined for there to be no misunderstanding. 'It's hard for me to say this to you, but I've been happy since you left. It made me realise that we'd been stuck in a rut together and it wasn't until you put an end to that that I'd even realised that's what had happened and neither of us had noticed. We let ourselves down by compromising and we both deserve better.' She looked him in the eye and gathered all the bravery she could muster. She had to tell him. 'I don't feel like we made a mistake by splitting up.'

He looked at her with a sorrowful expression. He didn't say anything else. Lois was relieved that he'd taken in what she said and seemed to have accepted it.

'I'm sorry, Alex.'

'I'll come to the house tomorrow and get my things.'

They ate their food in silence. There was nothing left to say. Lois felt bad for him, but she knew he would see she had made the right call for them both, eventually.

At the end of the meal, Alex wasted no time in requesting

the bill. He wouldn't let Lois pay for her share.

'Let me get it, Lois. I should have done more of this when we were together.'

'Alex…'

'I'm sorry I let you down, Lo. I didn't know when I had a good thing going and I think I'll always regret letting you go.'

'Alex…'

'You okay getting home?'

'Of course. I—'

'Bye Lois.' He kissed her on the cheek and walked away before she could say anything else.

When the doorbell rang the next morning, Lois ran down the stairs wondering why he didn't just use his key.

'Hi… oh, hi.' It wasn't Alex. Instead, Rich stood awkwardly on the doorstep holding Alex's key out to Lois.

'He couldn't face it. Are you okay if I pick his stuff up?'

'Yes, of course. Come in.'

Together they carried Alex's things out to Rich's car. Lois was upset at how badly Alex was taking her decision not to get back together.

'Is he alright?' she asked Rich once he was ready to leave.

Rich shrugged. 'I don't know. He hasn't said much but I think he's only just realised what he did by moving to London. You don't know what you've got 'til it's gone, and all that.'

'Right. Thanks for doing this, Rich. I think it's for the best, for both of us.'

He nodded, gave an awkward wave and got into the car.

Lois sat on the sofa and was momentarily surprised when she began crying. The whole thing was overwhelming. She hadn't cried when Alex had broken up with her, at the time it had even felt like a relief. But now, she was sad for him that he had finally realised what a grown-up relationship might look like, and it was too late. At least now she knew what she wanted even if she couldn't have it. What she'd had so briefly with Oliver had made her sure that she and Alex weren't right for each other and in time Alex would realise that too.

26

Rosemary had done a fabulous job of spreading the word about the library's Christmas light switch-on competition. The lights were officially going to be switched on at 5 pm but all day there had been a steady stream of people coming into the library, not just children taking part in the competition.

Linda had made what seemed like several hundred gingerbread reindeer biscuits which they had put on festive paper plates and dotted around the tables and Lois had bought a flask of mulled wine with her for them to share later in the day to make it feel like they were part of the festivities even if they couldn't all leave the library to go and join in properly.

There were plenty of children taking part in the competition and so far, it was going very well. Lois had hidden fifteen children's books on different shelves throughout the library. The children had to find them and write down the name of the book they'd found. To make it fair, Lois had three age categories. The under-fives had to find five books, the under-tens ten books and fifteen for anyone ten and over.

The books had been hidden high and low within the shelves of the library and Lois had made a careful note of the position of each to make it easy to retrieve them afterwards. A couple of them were very tricky to find and Lois privately thought she would give an extra prize to anyone who found those particular books. Rosemary had amassed prizes from local businesses who had donated selection boxes to book tokens to cinema vouchers and Lois was thrilled that they had been able to pull off an event which had captured people's interest.

The donation bucket on the top of the information desk was visible to people as they came in and Linda said she'd seen someone drop a five-pound note in there which was thrilling for all of them. They had an identical bucket at Oliver's and another at the Tourist Information Centre, and the Library of the Year competition flyers had been dropped to lots of places around the town too.

Lois hadn't seen Oliver since the day after she'd come across Amy crying. She had been thinking about him and wondering if he was okay. When there was a lull in visitors to the library after lunch, Lois decided to pop into the coffee house to see how he was. She took coffee orders from Rosemary and Linda to make herself feel better about leaving.

The high street was closed off to traffic for the day and people were milling around, enjoying the festive feel of the town. There was a craft market along one side of the street, in front of the church where there was a gap in shopfronts. Stalls were selling high-end hot dogs and burgers and the delicious smell of them, mingled with the aroma of mulled wine drifted towards Lois making her determined to sample something from them later on.

Oliver had decorated the coffee house with tiny white fairy lights, filling large jars with bundles of them as well as having them strung around in between the plants and other paraphernalia on the shelves and walls. It looked so pretty. Lois looked through the window and could see Oliver and Patsy behind the counter, chatting to each other as they worked.

She walked in and was greeted straight away by an exuberant Patsy. 'Lois! What can we get you?'

'A skinny latte and two cappuccinos to take out, please.'

'Coming up,' said Patsy as she busied herself with making all three drinks at once, waving Oliver away with a flap of her hand.

'How's it going at the library?' he asked.

Lois was pleased to see he was his normal smiling self. 'It's been quite busy. The competition seems to have been a hit and we've seen a few people donate money into the bucket so yes, we're having a good day. How about you? The place looks great, by the way. I love all the lights.'

'Thanks, got to make an effort to be festive,' he said, sounding as if perhaps it had been quite an effort. 'It's been really busy, and we've seen plenty of pound coins going into your bucket.'

'Great. And are you okay?' She hoped she was conveying her concern as she looked at him.

Panic flashed across his eyes, but he said, 'I'm great, thanks.'

'He's been under my feet all day,' said Patsy as she placed Lois's drinks in a holder and handed them to her. 'Take him with you, he needs some fresh air. Go on!' She gave Oliver a playful shove to which he rolled his eyes and grabbed his coat from the back of the door which led up to the flat.

'Come on then, I'll treat us both to a mulled wine. I've been tempted by the smell every time the door opened today. One for you, Pats?'

'No, me and Matt are going later,' she said, nodding

towards a table where the blond man Lois remembered from the backstage bar at the cinema, was chatting to one of the coffee house regulars, Toby.

They went outside and wandered to the mulled wine stall where Oliver ordered two then they walked into the churchyard and found an empty bench to sit on.

'Where's Amy today?'

He sighed. 'She's gone to her mum and dad's for a few days. We had a bit of a humdinger the other day and she said she needed a break,' he explained.

'Oh.' Lois didn't know what to say to that. If she asked him about it, he might tell her, and she wasn't sure she was ready to hear any more about the intricacies of their relationship. 'Are you okay?' she said in the end.

'I don't know. It's been really hard, Lois. I've tried to get things back to how they were before…you know. We've both been on a different journey for at least a year and to be honest, I never thought she'd want me back. Even before we split up, we'd grown so far apart. I can see that now. As soon as we split, I thought I wanted her back, until recently when I'd finally got over it all and then when she turned up wanting exactly that…it feels too late.'

'Have you told her that?' asked Lois gently.

'No, how can I after all she's been through.' He was looking down at the floor as he spoke.

'You've been through it too.'

'She doesn't think it was hard for me like it was for her. She thinks I left her at the time she needed me most, at least that's what she says when she's upset. There are other times when she admits it was the best thing I could have done but,' he shrugged sadly, 'it's hard to know what she really thinks, whether she blames me for how hard it's been for her.' He turned to look at Lois, tears threatening to spill from his eyes.

She took his drink and set it on the floor with her own then put her arms around him and held him. He buried his face in her shoulder for a minute then pulled away, wiped his eyes with a finger and thumb and smiled.

'God. Sorry about that. It doesn't seem fair to be dumping on you, of all people.'

'Don't apologise.' She handed his drink back to him, her heart aching briefly at his reference to what might have been if not for Amy. 'It's good to let it out once in a while. If it makes you feel better, I had my own moment last weekend when Alex's stuff finally went. I honestly thought I was fine with it, and I am, but I did have a good cry on the sofa afterwards.'

He smiled at her. 'A bit of Christmas is just what you need.'

'Ditto. Who knew you loved Christmas so much?'

'Who says I do?' he teased.

'The fairy lights speak volumes. I think it's been proven that there's a direct correlation between the number of sets of fairy lights a person owns and how much they love Christmas.'

'Is that right? So, I should expect to see quite a few at the library?'

'Well, you know, the ceilings are very high, and I don't want to be pushy because not everyone loves Christmas but my house will be a different story.'

'I'd expect nothing less.'

The way he was looking at her made her heart feel as if it was going to inflate like a balloon and soar out of her chest.

She took a deep breath. 'You know where I am whenever you need to talk. Honestly, I mean it.'

'Thanks. Likewise.'

They walked back to the coffee house in companionable silence then Lois said goodbye and went back to the library with the lukewarm coffees in her hand hoping that she could manage to be good friends with Oliver without wanting to subconsciously sabotage his relationship with Amy. That wasn't her intention at all, but it was hard to see someone she cared about being thrown around on an emotional rollercoaster when he thought he'd got off it months before.

'Sorry the coffees aren't very hot,' apologised Lois as she handed them out. 'I ended up chatting to Oliver on the way back. The coffee house looks amazing, it's full of fairy lights.'

'Amy's doing, no doubt,' said Rosemary with a hint of pride which Lois chose to ignore, holding back from pointing out that Amy was nowhere to be seen.

'Has it started to get busy yet?' asked Linda. 'I'd love to have a mooch around the craft stalls once it's dark. They'll all be lit with fairy lights as well.'

'Go whenever you want to, Linda. You too, Rosemary. I'm happy to hold the fort here.'

'You should go and see the light switch-on, Lois as it's your first Christmas in Croftwood. I can look after things here later on,' said Rosemary.

Lois was touched. She had wanted to watch the lights going on but as it was her regular day to work, hadn't thought she'd be able to.

At quarter to five, Lois and Linda left the library and headed to the top of the high street where everyone was gathering around the Christmas tree. There was a choir singing carols and children were holding lanterns that lit up their little faces, full of the joy of Christmas. The mayor gave a short speech and then all the streetlights were switched off.

Lois stood there in the dark as a hush swept over everyone.

'This is it!' whispered Linda.

'Ten...nine...eight...'

Lois and Linda joined in with the countdown and as everyone cheered after they reached 'one!' the Christmas lights sprang into life, bathing Croftwood in a warm glow of twinkling, starry lights that made the town look picture perfect and beautifully Christmassy.

Lois thought how amazing it would be if it was snowing, and right on cue snow began to gently fall as the choir sang 'Oh, Christmas Tree.' It was completely perfect. She and Linda hugged each other briefly then Linda left to look at the market leaving Lois to soak up the Christmas magic, letting the fake snow catch in her hair and on her coat, imagining that it was the real thing.

'Magical, isn't it?' Oliver said softly as he came to stand next to her.

'It really is,' grinned Lois, knowing she looked like a loon but not able to help herself. 'I love Christmas, this kind of Christmas. You know, the traditional parts.'

'I do know and luckily Pats knows that I need this more than she does, especially this year.' He was looking up at the Christmas tree, the lights reflecting in his eyes and making them sparkle.

'Merry Christmas, Oliver.'

'It's a bit early for that, Lois,' he said breaking the spell. 'You can't go around saying that until at least the week before Christmas.'

'Sorry, I thought we were in a Christmas movie for a second there. Right, I'd better get back to the library or Rosemary will be sending out a search party.'

As she turned away, Oliver gave her the briefest of touches on her shoulder making her stop and look around at him.

'Merry Christmas, Lois,' he said sincerely, then turned away and headed towards the coffee house.

How she had wanted to take him in her arms at that moment and stand in the fake snow and pretend they were in a Christmas movie. She closed her eyes for a second and allowed herself to wonder but then firmly put it out of her mind. She seriously needed to get a grip where Oliver was concerned otherwise she was going to end up miserable, and after getting her life nicely on track in the wake of Alex leaving, she wasn't going to let that happen.

Now that the Christmas spirit had got her, Lois was happy to immerse herself in Christmas preparations. She spent Sunday in her pyjamas with Spotify playing Christmas songs to her while she made and decorated a gingerbread house, prepared a batch of blackberry vodka from some blackberries she had frozen in the summer and printed some Christmas cards with a kit she had bought at the craft market the day before.

When she'd finally exhausted herself, she sat on the sofa with half of the roof from her gingerbread house, having posted a picture of it on Instagram before it was demolished and watched three terribly cheesy Christmas movies back-to-back with a glass of wine in her hand. It had been the perfect Sunday. She was just settling down to watch the *Strictly* results show when her phone rang.

'Lois?' It was Alex. She hadn't heard from him at all since the dinner they'd had when she'd felt as if she'd broken his heart.

'Alex, how are you?'

'I'm really good. Look, I just wanted to tell you, for closure or whatever, that you were right about us. We did the right thing, and we should both move on.'

It was such a relief to hear him say that and she was glad that it had only taken him a week to get over the fact that she didn't want to get back together.

'That's great to hear. Thanks for ringing.' There was nothing else to say.

'Maybe we can go for a drink next time I'm in Worcester so you can meet her.'

So that was how he had brought himself around, with a new girlfriend. Lois smiled. 'Great, I'll look forward to that. Take care.'

'Bye, Lois and thanks for setting me straight. You did me a favour.'

It was only ever going to be a matter of time before Alex found someone new and Lois was glad. She'd half suspected that he'd started seeing other people once he'd moved to London and that that was really at the heart of his decision to end their relationship, but it didn't matter now. She was glad that it was done and dusted. She topped up her wine, poked at the fire to perk it up a bit and sat on the edge of her seat to see who was going to make it into the quarterfinals.

27

Robert had been in touch a couple of days later as he'd promised. He'd arranged a meeting with the head of County Libraries for himself and Lois, so she was heading to the Hive. She was nervous because she'd not told Robert about the posters going out. That had been over a week ago and she still hadn't had a formal go-ahead, but she knew that people had started voting for them. The huge pile of voting cards that they'd had on the desk for people to pick up had all disappeared on the day of the light switch-on. She just hoped that the head of County Libraries hadn't been in the vicinity of Croftwood over the past week.

Andrew was at the information desk when she arrived.

'Lois! You didn't waste any time getting your new pad a nomination for Library of the Year.'

'How do you know about that?' she asked, knowing that Andrew would not have ventured to Croftwood to see the posters.

'Luke had to pick his niece up from school and there was a poster on the noticeboard by the gate. He sent me a photo.' He pulled out his phone and showed Lois a selfie that his partner had taken with the poster.

'Right. Well, we were a bit previous putting the posters up. Robert thinks the bosses will be upset that we've put ourselves in for the competition when they want to close the library.'

'I think it's brilliant. They're mad if they don't let you go for it, it'd be amazing publicity for all the county libraries as well as Croftwood.'

'Hopefully, they'll share your enthusiasm. I'd better go up to Robert. Will you have time for a coffee afterwards?'

'Yeah, for sure. Come and find me.'

Lois climbed the stairs up to the top floor where Robert's office was. She hoped she'd arrived before the boss but when she knocked on the door and was called in, he was already sat there.

'Ah, Lois, this is David Hunter. Head of County Libraries.'

David stood up and leaned forward to shake her hand. He looked pleasant enough. He had dark hair, was about six feet tall and was probably in his mid-forties. 'Good to meet you, Lois.'

'Nice to meet you.'

'Right, so David, as you know, I asked Lois to stand in at Croftwood after Rosemary retired. Obviously, due to the planned closure, it was a caretaker position, but Lois has implemented some improvements, at no cost to the library I should add, and it seems to have revitalised things at Croftwood somewhat.'

'Thank you for the overview, Robert.' He turned to Lois. 'I understand that you used to work here at the Hive.'

'Yes, I loved my job here, but Croftwood Library is somewhere that has become very special to me. It had been well looked after before I arrived but hadn't been brought into the 21st century and no-one had tried to make that happen because I'm sure there would have been some resistance. Anyway, I just made some very simple changes but the main thing we've done is to start a book club.'

'Book clubs are fairly common in libraries,' said David directing a conspiratorial smile towards Robert.

'Ours is different,' said Lois, undeterred. 'We don't meet as a huge group; we try to match people with someone else who has read the same book then one evening a month we host an evening at a local coffee house where everyone comes to meet their book buddy. We call it date-with-a-book-club. We've tried to roll it out to the mobile library too, but Steph would be in a better position to tell you about that. Our club has been so successful that we're looking to expand to a second venue.'

'And that's reflected in the borrowing rates, is it?' he addressed the question to Robert who looked awkwardly at Lois.

'We are starting to see an uplift,' she began. 'We've also added an exclusivity element to the book club to make it more attractive for people to contact us in the library as part of it. And we've successfully fundraised to make part of the children's library into a teenage reading space.'

'I think whatever way we look at it, the fact that you have reached the voting stage of the national competition is good for Worcestershire County Libraries and to pull your entry now would be a shame. I do think you should have run it by us before you entered but I can see that you're passionate about Croftwood and that has perhaps been lacking there for some time, leading to us overlooking its potential.'

'Thank you, David. I appreciate your support. We'll make every effort to fly the flag for County Libraries, not only Croftwood.'

'And in that vein, I'm sure the Hive would assist in spreading the word, Robert?'

'Absolutely.' Robert looked relieved that he seemed to be

off the hook for somehow letting this go under the radar until now.

'So, does that mean Croftwood has a reprieve from closure?' asked Lois, hopefully.

'It does not, I'm afraid,' said David. 'Unfortunately, the savings to the budget are already part of the plan for the next financial year so there's nothing we can do.'

'But there is a final decision to be made in January?'

'Yes,' he said uncertainly, 'but it's more of a formality.'

Lois thought that's what he would say but it was worth asking and she still held out hope that things could change depending on how successful they were.

'Fair enough. Thanks for your time today, David, Robert.' She stood up and shook each of their hands in turn.

Once she'd left the office and closed the door, she breathed a huge sigh of relief. Thank goodness neither of them had realised that they'd already publicised the voting for the next round. Linda would be excited to have the official go-ahead and she would ask Andrew if he could start publicising through the Hive as well. He was loitering at the information desk when she got to the ground floor.

'Come on,' she said. 'My treat, they gave us the go-ahead.'

'Brilliant, can you stretch to a Christmas cookie as well as a coffee?'

They sat at a table which overlooked the river.

'How are things with you? Alex finally moved his stuff out, did he?'

'Yes, but not before he decided he'd made a mistake by breaking up with me and asked me to move to London.'

'He didn't!'

'He did and he was pretty gutted when I turned him down but a week later, he rang to tell me he had got over it and he has a new girlfriend.'

'Christ, Lois. Are you okay with that? It's pretty quick.'

'It's fine. I'd come to terms with the whole thing and not even a tiny bit of me was tempted to give it another go aside from the fact I don't want to move to London.'

'Steph said you'd met a guy at the book dating club.' He looked eagerly at Lois for more information.

'Okay, first, it's not a date with a person it's a date with a book.' Although she loved the idea of meeting someone with a shared love of books. 'And second, she's talking about Oliver who hosts the book club meetings in his coffee house and is with someone else.'

'He's not. Bloody hell, Lois that's unlucky. Steph thought that was a goer with you two.'

'No, it never got past the first date then his ex turned up and that was that. We're still friends though.'

'Anyone else on the scene?' He was giving her the third degree. She'd forgotten what it was like working here with the massive scrutiny that everyone gave every part of each other's lives. She quite liked that about Croftwood. No-one was into interrogating her on a daily basis about her love life which suited her fine.

'You'll be the first to know, Andrew. Anyway, tell me how things are with you and Luke.'

The next half an hour was spent with Andrew telling her about what felt like every night out he'd had since she had started working at Croftwood Library, but it was nice to hear about someone else's love life instead of obsessing about her own.

'And I can't believe Steph's still going out with that numpty motorbike bloke.'

'I know. It can't be long before she sees the light now,' agreed Lois.

'I think you're right. She was pretty cheesed off about that trip to Weston. She said he was off chatting to his mates too much. The beginning of the end, hopefully. Well, I'd better get back to stacking the shelves.' He rolled his eyes. 'It's been good to catch up.' He hugged her as they stood up to leave.

'Come to me next time you have a day off. I'll show you around Croftwood.'

'Lois, have you ever seen me outside the city limits of Worcester?' he grinned. 'But I might make an exception for you.'

28

Oliver had three Christmas trees, one on either side of the coffee house door and another one inside. They had appeared since the light switch-on and were festooned with fairy lights the same as the rest of the shop.

'Nice trees,' Lois commented as she waited for a lunchtime toasted sandwich and latte.

'Thanks, I wasn't quick enough to organise them for the light switch-on but better late than never. Have you got your tree yet?'

'I just need to get it out of the attic.'

Oliver put the milk jug down and turned to look at her. 'You of all people don't get a real tree?'

'What do you mean, 'me of all people'?' she asked laughing.

'You forget that I saw you having a moment by the Christmas tree last weekend. You love Christmas, you have to have a real tree.'

'It's tricky to carry a tree on a bike,' she pointed out.

'Okay, when's your next day off?'

'I don't need a real tree.' It hardly seemed worth it when

she was by herself, although she did love the smell of the real ones.

'Come on, tell me. Thursday, is it? Saturday?'

'It's Friday. I'm working on Saturday.'

'Great, Jack's in on Friday, so it's a date. Well, not a date, you know what I mean,' he said blushing slightly.

'Okay, if you insist. Bring Amy if you want,' suggested Lois, hoping that deliberately acknowledging Amy would define it as a harmless outing and if Amy questioned them going out, he could tell her that Lois had suggested she come too. Oh, god. She was overthinking this.

'She won't want to come. She's not keen on traipsing through a muddy field to find the perfect tree.' Oliver handed her the latte. 'I'll bring the toastie over in a minute.'

Lois sat in her usual seat. She was already looking forward to going to pick out a tree with Oliver. It used to be her favourite thing to do as a child. She used to go with her dad and brother to choose a tree and if they didn't find the perfect one in the first place they tried, they would go somewhere else. Once, it took until the fourth place to find their tree and Lois thought that was probably the last time her brother had gone with them after losing his patience with the whole thing. After that, it was her and her dad, both happy to search endlessly for Christmas perfection.

But she would try and rein in her need for the perfect tree and choose one that was a perfectly acceptable tree. Otherwise, Oliver might not realise what he'd let himself in for.

He delivered her toastie to the table and sat down opposite her. 'Amy said she spoke to you the other day. I just wanted to say thanks. She hasn't got anyone to talk to around here and she said you were nice to her.'

'I told her she should talk to you, that's all.'

'We did talk. I think she's had so much therapy, it comes

easier to her whereas for me…it feels weird to talk about how I feel to her. It feels like a criticism or something.'

'Is she okay now? Are you?' she asked softly.

'Things are a bit better. I'm still not sure we're on the right track but I'm giving it a go.'

At the risk of being disloyal to Amy, Lois said, 'I think she senses you're holding back.'

'I am. I don't know how I'll know when it's okay…I don't know.'

'You'll figure it out,' she said, 'but you probably need to keep talking to each other.'

'Yeah, well. If it was like talking to you, I think it'd be okay.'

One of the regulars to the coffee house, Toby, came in and greeted them, gesturing for Oliver to stay where he was. 'No rush, Oliver,' he said with a smile. He headed straight for a table in the window, giving Lois a valuable minute away from Oliver's attention to tell herself not to read anything into his last comment.

But the Christmas tree outing seemed like even less of a good idea now.

When Patsy arrived to help with the lunch shift, Oliver asked her if she'd be able to work on Friday lunchtime to help Jack. It was always busy on a Friday.

She raised an eyebrow. 'Why? You went to the wholesaler yesterday. You never ask me to work extra shifts unless it's something really important.'

'I know you're working on Friday night at the cinema, but I need to help Lois get a Christmas tree.' He deliberately avoided Patsy's eye line and busied himself with grating some cheese.

'You need to help her?' She shoved his arm, making him

drop a chunk of cheese on the floor.

'Patsy!'

'Ollie!'

He picked up the cheese and threw it in the bin. 'Look, she loves Christmas and she's got this crappy tree in her attic and no car to go and buy an actual tree. It's not right.'

'Maybe it's her tradition. Not everyone has a real tree, including yours truly.'

'I know you don't normally bother but I bet Matt does.'

Patsy rolled her eyes. 'It's for the kids. If it was down to me...'

'Yeah, right. That house is begging for the biggest tree you can buy.'

She grinned at him. 'It will look amazing. Imagine the fire roaring and the stocking hung along the massive mantelpiece. We'll be living in a Christmas film.'

Patsy had a tiny attic flat which she kept despite spending almost all of her time at her boyfriend Matt's. Unsurprisingly, as an architect he had an amazing house that would be more at home in a snowy American ski resort.

'You should have seen her face, Pats, when we were watching the light switch-on.' As he thought back to it, he realised that he'd been watching Lois more than he'd noticed the lights themselves.

'You could give her one of the hundreds of trees that keep sprouting up in here,' she said gesturing with her bread knife.

'There are three, and two of them are outside. Come on, where's your Christmas spirit, Pats?'

'Oh, alright I'll cover for you, but you owe me.'

'Will wages do, like normal?'

'Yeah, course,' she said with a grin. 'And seeing you smile for a change is a nice bonus.'

'Sorry, I know it's been a bit tough around here lately.'

'It's not been tough, just that there's some dark energy

force near here that's sucking the joy out of everything.'

He didn't know what to say to that. It was true that since Amy had got back from her parent's place she had been going around as if a dark cloud was over her head all the time and Oliver was terrified that it was a sign she was having some kind of relapse.

'Sorry Pats.' It was one thing to be having relationship problems, but it wasn't fair to Patsy or anyone else for it to be seeping into the coffee house. And Oliver didn't want that anyway. It was important to keep some separation between work and home when both were almost in the same place.

'You've got nothing to apologise for, Ollie. Everything was fine until she turned up.'

'Pats…'

'You've known me for long enough to know I'm terrible at keeping my thoughts to myself,' she said, pointing the bread knife at him. 'I don't know what you think is happening between you two but from an outsider's perspective, this isn't what it should be like. If going to buy a tree with Lois helps, then I'm all for it.'

It probably wouldn't help, especially if Amy found out but he knew he could trust Patsy and it was just a favour for a friend. A favour he'd suggested and despite it seeming to be a risk he didn't need to take, he was looking forward to it.

'So, we'll just keep it on the down-low,' he said, giving Patsy a meaningful look, that they'd been friends long enough for her to be able to interpret.

'Sure thing, boss.'

29

'Now I'm joined by Lois Morgan from Croftwood Library which has been shortlisted for the Community Spirit award in the Library of the Year Competition. Welcome, Lois.'

'Thanks for having me, Fiona.' Lois said, feeling apprehensive at being on live radio for the first time, even if it was BBC Hereford and Worcester which she wasn't sure anyone she knew listened to anyway.

'Lois, I believe this is the first time a Worcestershire library has been shortlisted for this award since the Hive was in the running for the Innovation award when it first opened in 2012. What made you decide to enter Croftwood Library which is destined for closure?'

Awkward. Lois wasn't sure how widely known it was that the library was facing closure and now she had to comment on it.

'Well, Fiona, the date-with-a-book club that we started at Croftwood Library has been so successful that it has made a difference not just to the library but we are collaborating with local businesses who host our book club meetings and have rolled out the club to people who can only access library services via the mobile library. My colleague, Linda, felt that it was something that brought the community together unlike many other book clubs or indeed, many libraries.'

'There will be people who will think it seems a shame to go to all this effort only to see it wasted when the library closes. What's your response to them, Lois?'

'I think whatever happens to Croftwood Library in the future, right now we are making a difference to people's lives. A difference that will stay with them, hopefully, whether the library is there or not. It's sad to think that Croftwood Library might close but that's what can happen when people take wonderful resources like libraries for granted. And I think in this age of digital books, which has hit us hard, we have to find new ways to interact with the community apart from the traditional ones. That's what we're trying to do at Croftwood.'

'And will you fight to keep Croftwood from closure?'

'My team and I will do our best for Croftwood Library whatever happens.' Lois was aware that Fiona was trying to draw her into making a comment that could easily end with Lois pitting herself against the County Libraries team, but she wasn't going to do that.

'Details of how to vote for Croftwood Library are on our website—'

'Please vote for us,' interrupted Lois. 'And if you don't have access to a computer, we have postcards in the Hive and at Croftwood Library and lots of shops in the town so that you can vote by post or pop in anyway and we can show you how to vote online.'

'Thank you, Lois. Best of luck with the competition. And now, the new Christmas single from Robbie Williams.'

Fiona removed her headphones. 'Sorry if I came on a bit strong but people will get behind you if they think it could save the library. Even if they never set foot in the place, you'd be surprised how people rally to a cause.'

'Thanks for having me on,' said Lois, still not sure if Fiona had done them a favour or not.

'No problem and come back if you win!' she said with a wink that said she didn't think they would.

Lois walked home along the riverside. She made a cup of tea and opened the boxes of decorations she'd hauled out of the attic the night before. When she'd left home, her mum had made her a beautiful parcel of all the baubles which she had ever chosen for the family Christmas tree and every year since, Lois made a point of buying one more to add to her collection. It was an eclectic mix. There was one from a trip to Disneyland, a glass one which she had blown herself at a workshop she went to with her mum and a revolting one she had made out of salt dough at school that really ought to be thrown away but it was part of the collection so it survived. Alex had thought it was insane and had lobbied every year for a themed tree like you saw in home interiors magazines, but Lois had resisted and because he didn't care about Christmas as much as she did, he always gave in first. She suspected that Oliver, with his tasteful fairy lights at the coffee house, may also be in favour of themes and might think her stash of mismatched decorations was horrendous but the fact that he was so insistent that she have a real tree gave her a glimmer of hope that he may love Christmas just as much as she did.

The following morning was foggy but cold and dry. Lois dressed for the cold and decided that wellies were essential in case they did end up trudging around a field.

Oliver was right on time and as she'd been looking out for him, she waved from the window to save him from parking up.

'Morning,' he said brightly.

'Morning.' She settled herself into the Mini and wondered whether they would even fit a tree into the relatively small car. 'There's no way you picked your trees up in this car.'

'No, I had them delivered,' he said sheepishly. 'But it's a Clubman, you know, with the doors on the back,' he explained as Lois looked blank. 'It'll be fine. Anyway, how big a tree do you need?'

'It needs to be taller than me, that's the rule,' said Lois without thinking.

'The rule? I've never heard of that.'

'It's a family rule,' she admitted, wishing she'd never mentioned it.

'Oh, that's important then,' said Oliver smiling.

They hadn't even got there yet, and he already thought she was a tree-buying lunatic.

'Isn't your tree taller than you?'

'Actually, it is. You're right, maybe it's a thing.'

'It definitely is.'

'Where are we going to try?'

'We'll go to Coddington.' As he said this, they passed the huge local Christmas tree farm.

'Not there?'

'No, it's not the right place.'

Lois wondered why Oliver wouldn't have just chosen the nearest place.

Twenty minutes later, he pulled off a small country lane in Herefordshire into Coddington Christmas tree farm. There were fields with a wonderful mix of different types of trees, all in different sizes, nothing like the well-ordered larger farm they'd passed. This was a special place, Lois could tell. As well as the fields of trees, they also had a stock of freshly cut ones ready to take away.

'I think it's better if we go and choose one from the field,' said Oliver as they got out of the car.

'Okay, whatever you think.' Lois was thrilled. She had seen places like this in the cheesy Christmas films she loved but never realised they existed in real life and were so close by.

They wandered in between the trees, inspecting them carefully before Oliver shouted over that he'd found a good one.

Lois stood and looked at it. It was a good shape, bushy enough at the base, symmetrical and the right height but there weren't many branches near the top. It wasn't perfect. As it was the first tree they'd seen, Lois felt it was reasonable enough to discount it without seeming like a nutter. They carried on looking.

'Hey, Oliver! Over here!' The tree that Lois had found did look pretty perfect. 'I think this one is it,' she said as he came over.

He looked at it thoughtfully. 'It's a touch shorter than you.'

'I think that's okay.'

'Rules are rules, Lois,' he said, then turned and walked away, leaving Lois astounded next to her tree. Well, she could humour him, keep looking for a while and come back to this one. She made a mental note of where it was and carried on looking.

The next time Oliver called her over, it was the absolute perfect tree. It was beautiful and when she leaned towards it and inhaled, she smelt Christmas.

Oliver reached into his pocket, pulled out a piece of red string and tied it onto the top branch of the tree. 'So they know which one we want.'

Which one we want. Lois was momentarily sad that it wasn't their tree, it was hers. Hers alone. But it certainly felt like their tree as they stood there.

'Haven't you got an axe with you?' The thought of him manfully chopping the tree down was all she could think about.

'I left it in the car,' he grinned. 'I think we'll have to walk back and find someone. They won't see us through the fog,' said Oliver. 'Come on.' He took her hand.

In the same instant, she pulled it out of his grasp.

'What's the matter? Do you want to pick a different one?' he asked, oblivious to what had just happened.

'No, this tree's fine,' she said and walked past him towards the farmhouse.

'Are you alright, Lois?' He caught up with her. She could see his look of concern from the corner of her eye as she willed him to realise what he'd done.

They paid for the tree and waited while the farmer went to cut it down. Oliver was looking at her like a wounded puppy.

'We're friends, Oliver.'

He nodded, looking puzzled.

'Friends wouldn't hold hands.' Especially friends who had almost become more than friends.

He shrugged. 'I didn't mean anything by it. I would have done the same with Patsy if it helps.'

If he didn't see the flush of embarrassment that washed over her, she would be amazed. 'Okay, so I may have overreacted. Being friends is harder than it sounds, that's all.'

'I'm sorry, it was spontaneous. I didn't think about how it would make you feel,' he said gently. 'That it might mean something,'

It meant everything. 'Sorry.' She felt like an idiot for making something of it. She should have embraced the moment and taken his hand, enjoyed the closeness without overthinking it.

'It's fine.' He smiled at her.

The farmer appeared like a vision out of the fog with the tree trailing behind him.

'Lovely tree, that one. Think you've got the best of the

season there! You going to get that in your car?'

'Sure will,' said Oliver, although they could all see that the tree was much taller than the size of the boot.

'Righto then. Merry Christmas!'

The tree was too tall to fit in the car unless it went through the back doors and into the front passenger seat, so Lois ended up sitting behind Oliver on the way home, silently berating herself for ruining the outing.

At her house, she stood aside while Oliver began to pull the tree out of the car then once it was almost there, she grabbed the other end of it to help carry it inside.

'Where do you want it?'

'In the living room, please.'

Oliver walked backwards into the room and put the tree down in front of the window, helping Lois to push it upright.

'Steady, you almost touched my hand then,' he said.

'Oh, sod off.' But she grinned at him, glad that he thought it was funny. She wanted to tell him that it wasn't even about the handholding. It was about the fact that when they were together, they fell into this comfortableness that made it so easy to forget that they could only be friends. And Lois was just trying to protect herself, to have it not be any harder than it already was by Oliver doing something that she longed for. Like holding her hand.

He stood with his hands in his pockets, watching as she cut the string which was holding the branches closed.

'The farmer was right. It is the best tree.'

'Yes, the best at completely filling the room,' he said, stepping backwards as the branches pinged outwards and hit his shins. 'But it is taller than you, so I guess it ticks all the boxes.'

'It does. I love it. Thanks for taking me, Oliver. It's much better than my fake one.'

'No problem. Well, I'd better get off. See you.'

The most natural thing in the world would be to kiss him on the cheek but after making such a fuss about the handholding it would be weird. She wished more than anything that she'd just kept hold of his hand at the Christmas tree farm. It would have been worth the inevitable heartache when they'd have let go and she'd have to try and be happy with that being all she could have. All he was going to give her. And these little things he gave her all the time; the odd look, the odd comment, his hand today, they meant everything and were devastating at the same time and Lois wasn't sure how much longer she could carry on like this. Somehow, she had to forget that he had ever been a possibility.

30

By the time Oliver got back to the coffee house, it was the lunch rush and Patsy and Jack were run off their feet.

'Sorry, Pats. Where do you want me?'

'Can you start on that wadge of food orders, and we'll keep going on the drinks. Oh, and Amy was looking for you.'

Amy was going to have to wait.

He enjoyed the repetition of making toastie, after panini, after sandwich. Being with Lois had done wonders for his mood even if her little freak out when he'd grabbed her hand had almost ruined the whole thing. He hadn't been to Coddington since he was a kid and it brought back great memories. That was probably why he'd got a bit carried away, kind of forgotten who he was there with for a minute.

There were still a couple of orders to finish when Amy came down from the flat.

'Oh, you're back. I came down earlier looking for you. I didn't know you were going out this morning. I asked Patsy to tell you to come upstairs when you got back.'

'Patsy and Jack were run off their feet when I came back so I haven't had the chance.' It might have been nice if Amy had thought to lend a hand.

'Where were you, anyway?'

'Wholesaler.'

'Oh right. Well, come up when you can.' She disappeared back upstairs.

'Don't worry, you get off,' Oliver said in response to Patsy's side-eye glare at where Amy had just been stood.

'Stick up for yourself, Ollie,' she mumbled.

Oliver smiled and shook his head. There was no-one like Pats for telling him what was what. And no-one else who could get away with calling him Ollie after being scarred for life by being labelled Ollie-the-Wally at school.

'Ignore her. I can look after myself.'

'Sure you can. Why don't you just tell her where you were? Let nature take its course.'

He sighed. 'You know why. I'm not going to stop being friends with Lois because Amy says so. We're not in primary school. It's just easier not to have the conversation at all.'

'You chicken.'

'I'm not scared of her. I just want an easy life.'

'Understandable, you're a man after all. Just watch yourself.' She pointed a spoon at him. 'And watch Lois, she's lovely and she deserves better than what you're offering her.'

'I'm not offering her anything, Pats.'

'Exactly.'

It was only once Jack had left, he'd closed up and finished cleaning that Oliver finally went upstairs to the flat where he found Amy lying on the sofa watching television. She didn't look up when he walked in, and he could tell by the expression on her face that she was not happy. He could and maybe should have come up earlier, but he had a feeling that this would have greeted him whenever it had been.

'Do you fancy a takeaway?'

'I'm not hungry.' Her eyes stayed glued to the screen.

'Okay. I'm going to order a Chinese. Sure you don't want anything?'

'I'm fine.'

He rang his order through, adding on a couple of the vegetable pancake rolls he knew she liked and a tray of chips and curry sauce because it was that kind of evening, then he sat on the opposite end of the sofa and picked up his book. Amy's stare left the television and settled on him instead. He could feel it and it made him uncomfortable.

'You're obsessed with that book club.'

'It's a good book, you'd enjoy it.' He kept his tone deliberately light-hearted.

'Not the book, all of it. Is that where you were today? Sorting something out with Lois?' She sounded spiteful and he hated her for it.

Even though Amy thought the book club was the worst thing he could have been doing, if he told her about the Christmas tree farm it would bring a whole new level of wrath which he couldn't face.

'I was at the wholesalers. I thought I told you that when you came down.' Well, they did wholesale Christmas trees. He kept his eyes on his book.

'Patsy didn't say that when I'd asked her.'

'She was so busy, she probably forgot.'

Was that going to be it?

'I hardly see you, Oliver. You're either working or you just go off without saying and leave me up here by myself.'

She needed to get a job, something to get her out of the flat. No wonder she was on at him all the time. She must be bored out of her mind but she'd had no luck finding anything. Committing a few hours to the coffee house or the cinema would be a start but that didn't seem to be an option. He hadn't gone as far as to say he thought it would be a good idea because she would think he was criticising her. It was better to say nothing.

The food arrived and when he sat at the table, Amy came over and sat down too.

'Can I have a spring roll?'

'Go ahead, I got them for you.'

'Thanks, that's really thoughtful.' She sounded surprised. Was it that unusual for him to think of her?

'Look, Ames, I'm sorry about today. I should have asked you if you wanted to come with me.' Not a total lie, Lois had suggested it. 'I forget it's not just me anymore and I'm used to getting on with things by myself.'

'I don't want to come to the bloody wholesalers, Oliver.' He heard the smile in her voice and looked up from his food. 'I just want you to tell me you're going. I want to be part of your life, all of it.'

It sounded slightly sinister. There was no need for them to keep tabs on each other to that extent. They never had before. So it was for some other reason. Maybe Amy was jealous of Lois.

'There's nothing weird going on. You know everything there is to know.'

'I just want things to be how they were before.'

'I'm not sure that can happen,' Oliver said gently, reaching for her hand. 'A lot's happened to both of us since then. We can't try and make things the same. We have to see if we can start a new life together and it might be different from the old one, but it might still be great.'

'You don't think it will be?'

'I think it's too soon to know, to be honest. We need to be brave enough to admit if it's not working but brave enough to move on together and leave the past behind if that feels right.'

Amy looked thoughtfully at him but didn't say anything. The fact was, it didn't feel to him that things were going to work out between them and knowing how fragile Amy was and how much she wanted to pick up where they'd left off, being honest with her about how he felt seemed like the best thing to do.

'I know it's hard starting again. It feels a bit like we're strangers but we have to try, Oliver. We have to.'

The desperation in her voice left him feeling uneasy.

31

Lois had invited Oliver to the Thursday morning meeting so that he could help with the logistics for the next date-with-a-book club meeting. He'd offered to talk to Jen, the owner of the Courtyard Café so that they would have extra capacity for the next one.

He arrived right on time with a tray of coffees and a bag of muffins.

'You know how to endear yourself, Oliver,' said Rosemary as they all sat down around one of the big tables.

'Least I can do. The book club has done wonders for my business. Probably made a difference to quite a few Croftwood businesses one way or another.' He grinned and sat down next to Rosemary. Right opposite Lois.

'Lois, Stephanie has managed to secure the Dial-A-Ride minibus for the evening of the next meeting,' Rosemary announced. 'She's planning to bring about six of her regular mobile library customers, so we need to make sure we account for them in our numbers.'

'That's brilliant. So how many proper sign-ups do we have for next week?' Lois crossed her fingers that there wouldn't be too many to fit into Oliver's.

'We have thirty-four plus Stephanie's, so forty,' said Rosemary as she shuffled through the sign-up cards.

'That's okay for you, right?' Lois asked Oliver.

'Yeah, that's perfect.' He leaned back in his chair and crossed his ankle over his knee. 'Are we doing it the same as before, offering wine as well as tea and coffee?'

'If that's alright. How about the Courtyard Café? Will they do the same?'

'No, they don't have a licence, so they'll stick to tea, coffee and soft drinks. It's okay if it's different, right? We wanted to make it attractive enough for them to want to register with you guys.'

'Exactly.' Lois inexplicably loved that he said 'we'. 'Not that we're trying to tempt people with alcohol.'

'Of course not,' said Rosemary. 'The atmosphere at Oliver's is what sets it apart.'

'No offence to the Courtyard Café, hey?' Oliver grinned at Lois, and she smiled back as his comment went unheard by Rosemary.

'So, we'll need to split ourselves between the two places?' asked Linda.

'Yes, I will be at the Courtyard Café to make sure they are up to speed with the way we run things,' said Rosemary.

Oliver raised his eyebrows at Lois.

'I'll start off there with you, Rosemary,' said Lois, picking up what she knew was Oliver's concern that Rosemary might rub them up the wrong way.

'No, Lois,' said Linda. 'You should be at Oliver's to be the face of Croftwood Library for the mobile library visitors. Rosemary and I can manage the Courtyard café together.'

Lois was constantly surprised by Linda at the moment. She embraced every new step they made and became more confident all the time. She was strong enough to keep

Rosemary in line, having moved far beyond being cowed by her when Rosemary was still her boss. It did make sense for her to be at Oliver's. It was going to be tricky having to turn people away and at least all that awkwardness would be dealt with by the time anyone was greeted by Rosemary at the Courtyard Café.

'Are you happy to organise the pairings for the customers who have registered with us, Rosemary?'

'Yes, of course. Do you want me to mix Stephanie's in with ours?'

'That's a good point. I think she has some ideas about that, so I'll get her to email you. Right, so if that's all...'

'Have you got time for a quick chat, Lois?' Oliver asked.

'Um, yes of course.'

Oliver's hair was looking particularly finely quiffed today which didn't help Lois in her efforts to put him out of her mind. She'd been imagining running her hands through it for most of the meeting.

They stayed at the table as everyone else went off to do whatever else they had to do. Lois picked the top off a muffin as she waited until Oliver seemed ready to talk.

'I just wanted to say, in case you see Amy... well she's had enough of me going on about the book club so I could do with keeping it on the down-low that I'm doing anything aside from just being there on the night.' He suddenly seemed different from his usual laid-back self and had a slightly manic edge to him.

'Okay...'

'I feel weird having to say anything, but things are a bit tricky. You know.'

She didn't know. It was one thing having to deal with tricky things like Alex arranging to meet her for a date and then turning up with all of his mates but it was a whole new level of tricky for Oliver to have to prep her as to what the 'party line' was that she needed to stick to with his girlfriend.

'It's fine. I won't say anything.' She waited to see what he was going to say next but when he didn't, she decided to say what she was thinking for a change. 'What's the problem? Is it taking up too much of your time?'

'Not exactly.' He pushed his hands into his hair and let out a deep sigh. 'She's a bit paranoid. She's started going on about needing to know where I am all the time. It's a bit suffocating to think that someone is kind of watching my every move.'

'I suppose that's natural,' said Lois, reasonably. 'If you live with someone you do want to know that kind of thing.'

'It's more than that, she doesn't believe me when I tell her. Admittedly I did lie about being at the wholesalers when actually I was buying a Christmas tree with you but if I'd told her where I was, she would have gone mad. Do you think that's normal?'

'It's normal to be suspicious if your boyfriend is lying and you know it.'

'I don't think it's that, I think she's jealous of you.'

What could she say to that? Oliver was talking to the wrong person. If Amy was jealous perhaps it was because she could see that there was something between them, something that Oliver seemed able to ignore with much more success than she was having.

'You should probably just be honest with her. She's not being paranoid, Oliver. She has a feeling you're lying to her and she's right. That's not her fault.'

Amy's jealousy was playing into Lois's hands. If she wanted to ruthlessly pursue Oliver, now was her chance to manipulate this to her advantage. But that wasn't her style and whatever her feelings for Oliver, she found herself feeling sorry for Amy.

'You make it sound like we're up to something.'

'Well, she might think that and that's not good for either of us.' She took the remainder of the muffin and stood up. 'Thanks for coming to the meeting and for bringing coffee. I'd better get on.'

'Okay. And Lois, thanks for the talk. I'll sort something out so it's not a problem.'

The problem was that Oliver wasn't thinking straight and it was probably better if Lois took the matter in hand rather than leaving it to become a festering mess of a problem. She went behind the desk where Linda was scheduling some tweets.

'Linda, I know we just decided that you'd help out at the Courtyard Café, but I think it'd be better if we switched.'

'Oh, okay, if that's what you want.'

'To be honest I need to put a bit of space between me and Oliver for a while.' It was definitely better if she wasn't at Oliver's for the book club.

Linda squeezed Lois's arm. 'Don't worry. Whatever you want to do is fine with me.'

Now all she had to do was wait for him to wonder why she wasn't at the coffee house on book club night. And she was sure he would.

32

Steph was running late, and it was raining. She fought against the urge to put her foot down. The mobile library van didn't respond well to being forced into doing anything out of the ordinary and she didn't fancy the idea of ending up in a ditch buried under a pile of books if she lost control of it.

The lay-by on Hawthorn Lane came into view and she could see Eunice standing there under a clear plastic umbrella, the same kind the late Queen used.

She pulled up, leaned over, and flung open the passenger door.

'Eunice, get in here before you catch your death!' she called.

Eunice managed to climb gracefully into the passenger seat while simultaneously putting the umbrella down.

'Oh, Steph, thank you. What a dreary day.'

'It certainly is. Stay put while I get the van sorted and then I'll pour us a lovely cuppa. Oh, and I've got a surprise for you.'

Steph opened the main door and put down the steps then pulled out the extra chairs and her flasks just as Dottie arrived. Eunice moved from the front seat to sit in her usual spot around the little table.

'Good morning, Dottie, good morning young man.'

'Morning Eunice, hi Steph,' said Dottie as Bert waved at them before going to sit on the rug next to the children's books. 'Do you mind if I bring the buggy in?'

'Go for it. Ready for a nice cuppa?'

'Lovely, thanks.' Dottie expertly folded the buggy, picked out a board book for Bert and sat down next to Eunice.

'Did you enjoy the Lady Glenconner book?' asked Eunice as Steph poured the tea for them all. It had been their book club choice.

'Oh my goodness, I loved it. What a life she's had,' began Dottie.

'Hold your horses.'

They both looked at Steph in astonishment.

'What are you both doing next Wednesday evening?' They both continued to look blank. 'It's the Croftwood Library book club and I've wangled a minibus so I can pick everyone up. You two are at the top of my list. Are you in?'

'I have no plans on Wednesday, I'd love to come. What a wonderful idea, Steph.' Eunice looked at Dottie expectantly.

'Actually, I think I can make it. Nick's working from home next week. Are you sure about the bus Steph because I can drive Eunice and myself if it's easier?'

'No way! It's more of a night out for you if I do the driving and the bus ride will be half the fun. Plus, I have it on good authority that there's mulled wine on offer if you want it.'

'How exciting. So, we shouldn't talk about the book today, is that right Steph?' Eunice asked. 'We should wait until Wednesday.'

'Exactly. I think you'll enjoy it, I'm so glad you can both come.'

'Are any of your other customers going?' asked Dottie, as

she took a biscuit, broke it in half and shared it with Bert.

'Yes, there are another four of my regulars and one of them has read the same book as you.'

'It'll be lovely to meet some other mobile library customers, more of your regulars like us.'

'Ah, they're not all like you, Eunice,' said Steph. 'I've only invited my favourites.'

'Oh, go on with you,' said Eunice looking as pleased as anything.

'I'm just so glad you get the chance to join in with the book club properly.'

'Should we meet you here?'

'God, no. You don't want to be wandering around here in the dark. Let me know your addresses and I'll pick you up from the door.'

'Gosh, that's wonderful, Steph. Thank you.' Eunice had tears in her eyes.

'Right, another biccie anyone?'

It had been hard deciding how to bring the book club to her customers. The fact was that at some stops there just weren't enough people to make a mini-club. Eunice and Dottie were pretty lucky and would have been happy to have their book club meeting today, but Steph knew they'd both love the proper meeting at Oliver's and if she hadn't suggested it they wouldn't have thought to go by themselves. In the end, Steph picked the people who were really into the idea and who had been supportive of the mobile library. As well as Eunice and Dottie, she was taking Bill from the Red Lion Inn car park, Flora and Jerry who lived on a smallholding near her Grove Hill stop and had no car and Audrey who was partially sighted and came to the Wells Green stop. Steph always made sure to have a good selection of regency romances in large print for her. Zoe from Old Hollow was keen to join in but was going to make her own way since she couldn't commit to going on the bus with everyone else in case she was late finishing work.

Lois had said that she should let Rosemary know whether any of her customers would need pairing up. She thought Eunice and Dottie would want to be together as they'd planned to discuss the book with each other anyway. It would be more fun for them to do that at Oliver's, but the others would probably enjoy meeting new people so once she'd made her last stop of the day Steph emailed Rosemary with their names and which books they'd read so she could add them into her pool of people.

She pulled out her phone and dialled Max. It went to his answerphone, so she left a message.

'Hi, it's me. I'm really sorry but I have to work late tonight. I'll call you tomorrow.'

They had planned to meet for dinner, but Steph was starting to feel cornered. Whether Max would believe that someone who ran the mobile library van would have to work late was debatable, but Steph was sure he would get over any disappointment pretty quickly. She tried not to think about how this relationship was following the same path as all the others she'd had and how once again she'd thought things were different with this one. But they weren't.

The rose-tinted glasses had fallen off the night before when she'd gone round to his and he'd answered the door wearing a pair of Y-fronts from circa 1980 even though she'd arrived at the time they'd arranged. Was it too much to ask that if he had to be semi-naked, he at least wore his best pants? Perhaps they were his best pants. It felt like it was all going to be downhill from there.

33

Lois and Linda had decided to tackle organising the teenage library after work that day. The beanbags had been delivered and were stacked, still in their boxes in the corner of the children's library.

'Okay, let's empty these shelves and we'll move them to make a kind of wall around this area,' said Lois, gesturing with her arms. 'It needs to feel like a secret corner, I think.'

'Yes, absolutely,' said Linda, beginning to pull books off one of the shelves and making piles of them against the wall. 'I hope it works, Lois. I'd love to see some older children bring a bit of life to the place.'

They'd also managed to find some posters of past YA hits like *The Hunger Games* and *Harry Potter* which might not seem teenage, but Lois would bet that every single teenager who was likely to come to Croftwood Library and hang out on the beanbags would have read and loved at least one Harry Potter book. With the fundraising money they'd had left after the beanbags had been purchased, Lois had bought several charging sockets which were essential when teenagers were involved. The library already had WiFi, they just didn't use it, but Lois had asked Linda to make a few posters with the WiFi password on to advertise the service to everyone.

'When we've finished, we'll take some pictures and put them on Instagram. I wonder if we can rope some teenagers into following us and sharing it to get the word spread.'

'I could ask my niece, she's fifteen,' said Linda. 'She might be able to help. And could we ask Oliver if he could put something up in the cinema? I know a lot of the kids go there at the weekends. And the swimming pool might be a good place to advertise too.'

'Brilliant, those are great ideas. We could get Rosemary on the case with taking posters around, she seems to enjoy doing that kind of thing.'

'She does like to get out,' said Linda. 'She's like a completely different person these days. It's hard to remember how things were before you came, Lois. She was so cross all the time, rude and brusque to customers and yet now, she's happy as Larry about all the changes, relishing them even.'

'Maybe she was just stuck in a bit of a rut and then having to retire forced her out of it.'

'Hmm. I think she regrets that she didn't move with the times. She can see how it's bringing the place to life.'

'It's easy to see in hindsight,' said Lois, thinking of how easy it was now for her to see how things had been between her and Alex compared to when she'd been living it every day and had no idea. 'It's taken this place to make me realise that I was stuck in a rut as well. I loved working at the Hive, but this is a whole different level of job fulfilment that I never even knew existed.'

Linda nodded. 'I know, there's something about this place. The past few years it has been so quiet, but it holds a special place in my heart and even when my Dave was telling me to jack it in, I just couldn't. And now I know I made the right decision to stick it out because you've brought a spark of something with you, Lois and whatever happens I wouldn't have missed this for the world.'

'Thanks, Linda.' Lois was touched.

'And I know things have been difficult for you with Oliver but don't let it put you off your stride. You're doing great things.'

'We're doing great things, Linda. We're a team, I definitely couldn't have done any of this by myself.'

'It's lovely of you to say.'

'Right, let's move this shelf then.'

The reading nook looked amazing by the time they'd finished. The shelves which were facing into it were filled with the YA books that Steph had delivered, and they had written a couple of recommendations to put on the shelves. Where it had seemed a little bit dark, Lois had hooked some strings of fairy lights that she'd found in the office along the tops of the shelves. The beanbags covered most of the floor but standing them on their side and then dropping yourself on the top made them into a comfy chair, they discovered, so they spent some time at the end arranging them into seats like that to clear a bit of floor space.

'Thanks, Linda, it looks great, doesn't it?'

'It does. I'd have loved it when I was a teenager.' Linda lowered herself onto a beanbag and Lois thought she might as well join her.

'Wow, I could spend an afternoon reading on one of these.'

'Or we could have a little nap when we have a lull,' Linda laughed.

'Chance would be a fine thing at the moment, not that I'm complaining.'

'I know, there's nothing worse than being bored at work. Although, I did have time to sit and read when we were quiet, back in the old days. It was a brainwave you coming up with this.' Linda had her eyes closed and her hands clasped together on her chest.

Lois smothered a giggle and followed suit, relaxing right into the warmth of the beanbag, putting thoughts of the cycle ride home she still had to do, out of her mind.

'How are you... and Oliver?' Linda asked tentatively. 'I was rooting for you two until Amy came back on the scene. That's why you want to swap places on the book club night, isn't it?'

'Yes,' said Lois, finding it easier to talk now that they were both lying there with their eyes closed. 'Amy's not that keen on him being involved in the book club and last month's meeting was awkward enough and that was before I knew what she thought about it. You don't mind, do you?'

'No, of course I don't mind. I'm happy to go along with whatever you want. And I can see what you're up against there. The thing is, he might not realise it, Lois but you're the one he wants, not Amy. He doesn't keep coming in for the books, believe me. He'd barely set foot in the place before you arrived.'

'Thanks, Linda.' She turned to find Linda smiling at her.

'Don't you worry. It'll all turn out in the end.'

They locked up the library and went their separate ways. Lois climbed onto her bike, wishing that she didn't still have the twenty-minute journey home in the dark because she was exhausted.

She wanted to take what Linda said and believe it was true more than anything. She had believed the same thing until she saw the lengths that Oliver was willing to go to make things work with Amy. He was willing to sacrifice quite a lot, including, it seemed to Lois, his happiness. That was one thing she did find sad. They had been on the journey of the date-with-a-book club together and he'd been so interested and supportive of the fundraising for the teenage library and now it was difficult for him to be involved with any of it in the way he wanted to be because of Amy. Lois would have loved to involve him in her and Linda's after-hours adventure that evening but nothing like that was going to be possible anymore.

34

In a supreme act of selflessness, Lois had agreed to go out on a date with Tom Reeves, the teacher she had met briefly when she'd been out with Steph on the mobile library. Steph was apparently having doubts about Max, what a surprise, and wanted Lois to be there as reinforcement for their next date.

'I'm not coming by myself,' Lois had said when Steph suggested it during a brief pit stop at Croftwood Library to collect a reservation for one of her regulars. 'It was a nightmare last time.'

'Well bring someone then.'

If only it was that easy. Until her last conversation with Oliver, she might have considered asking him to go with her as a friend but that was out of the question now. A night out together was probably right at the top of the list of things Amy would disapprove of, and Lois didn't blame her. If she was with Oliver, she'd feel the same way.

'I don't have anyone to ask,' she admitted.

'No problem,' said Steph, 'I can find someone.'

'No way. That would be worse than coming by myself.'

'How do you know? It might be the man of your dreams.'

'Steph, I'm not sure I trust you to know who the man of my dreams might be, you have enough trouble identifying your own.'

Lois ducked to avoid a chunk of muffin that Steph aimed at her head.

'What about Tom?' asked Steph.

'Tom?'

'You know, Mr Reeves from St. Hilda's.'

Lois mulled it over for a second.

'Okay. I'm not saying that he's the man of my dreams, but I can get through a night out with him.'

'Great. I'll set it up. A match made in heaven.'

On Friday night, Lois made sure to arrive at the restaurant five minutes later than she'd arranged with Steph so that she wouldn't be there first. She was walking towards it when she spotted Tom coming towards her, looking anxious. He'd obviously been as reluctant as she had about agreeing to what was almost a blind date.

'Hey, Tom.' He looked at her blankly for a couple of seconds before he registered who it was.

'Lois.' He leaned in to kiss her cheek and looked a lot more relieved.

She wasn't sure whether to make a joke about having been roped into it by Steph or whether that might come out sounding offensive, so she decided against it. He was wearing jeans and a worn black leather biker jacket. Somehow, she'd imagined he would turn up dressed as a teacher. He looked cooler and younger than she remembered.

'Nice to see you again,' she said, deciding to gloss over the being set-up aspect.

'You too. Shall we?' He held his arm out, gesturing for her to go in first.

Steph and Max were sat on opposite sides of a table for four meaning that Lois had to sit next to Max. Lois had no idea why they wouldn't have sat next to each other. It wasn't like Steph to go by rules of etiquette, and it certainly hadn't stopped her last time they'd been out together when they could barely keep their hands off each other.

'Alright, Lois? Got a bloke in tow this time. Nice one.' Ah. She'd forgotten quite what a charmer Max was.

'Hi Max, this is Tom. Tom, Max and obviously you know Steph.'

Tom leant over and kissed Steph on the cheek.

'Mate, steady there,' said Max without a hint of humour. 'Got your own missus for that.'

'Oh, shut up, Max,' said Steph sharply. 'Take no notice.' She rolled her eyes at Lois.

They all sat down and studied the menu.

'Is anyone else drinking wine?' asked Tom.

'I'd love a glass of red,' said Lois. 'Shall we get a bottle?'

'Not for me and Steph. We're on the brew.' Max raised his pint to Tom.

'Thanks, Tom, I will have wine actually,' said Steph, throwing Max a dirty look that he didn't see.

Lois knew something was up. Steph never drank wine; she was a beer and spirits person so she was sharing the wine purely to be argumentative. Maybe it was over between Steph and Max, but Steph hadn't got around to telling him and maybe hadn't realised herself yet.

'I like your jacket, Tom,' said Steph leaning towards him as she spoke. 'It looks vintage.'

'I picked it up from a flea market in Germany.'

'Not a biker though, are you mate?' Max chipped in.

'I don't have a bike at the moment, no. I think I'm going to have the chicken fajitas. How about you, Lois?'

'That sounds good. Me too.'

Once the food arrived, Lois was relieved for the lull in conversation. Tom was having trouble saying anything without an immediate put-down from Max following even the most innocent remark and it might have been awkward, but he was oblivious to everything apart from Steph and the more Steph drank, the more she directed all of her conversation and all of her eye-contact towards Tom. They had an easiness between them, punctuated only by Tom looking guiltily at Lois now and again.

'Twos to the loos?' she asked Steph once they'd finished their main courses.

Steph looked surprised but followed Lois to the ladies.

'What's going on with you and Max?' she asked. 'You've hardly managed to be civil to him all evening.'

Steph looked sheepish. 'Is it that obvious?'

'Apparently not to him but I think everyone else at the table can probably tell. You need to tell him, Steph.'

'I know,' she sighed. 'I just...god, Lois. I think I like Tom. I know I set him up with you and I'm so sorry but when I saw him tonight, he looks hot, not like a teacher at all and I've always liked him, I just thought he was too nerdy for me.'

Lois laughed. 'I don't fancy Tom, it's fine.' If anything, it had made her realise that just going out with any nice guy wasn't going to work for her. No-one was going to match up to Oliver. 'And I agree, you two are getting on like a house on fire but one thing at a time. You need to finish it with Max. Basically, at the moment you're on a date with two men.'

Steph looked shocked for a second. 'You're right. I'm such an idiot. What am I doing? I never should have bought Max tonight. I can't stand the sight of him, to be honest, but I couldn't see a way out.'

This was typical Steph behaviour. She always carried on with relationships well beyond the point that they were over as if she was hoping she might miraculously stop thinking the guy was a total idiot and everything would be great. It never was. Lois had lost count of the times she'd pointed out to Steph that the end was nigh.

'Look, we need to call it a night. Tom and I will leave, and you need to talk to Max.'

'Okay. So, I should break up with him tonight?'

'Yes! You just said you like Tom. What are you worried about? He's not violent or anything is he?'

'No, but I think he'll be quite cross.'

'Do it somewhere in town then. Don't take him back to yours or go to his. Are you going to be okay, or do you want us to wait somewhere until you've done it?'

'Would you? Maybe you and Tom could go for a drink, and I'll meet you there once... you know.'

Lois and Steph arranged where to meet then went back to the table where Lois asked for the bill.

'Christ, I haven't finished my pint yet, love,' said Max, making Lois cringe. How her best friend could choose such uncouth men, she had no idea. Still, at least Tom seemed to be normal. If he felt the same way, Steph would at least have a fighting chance of having a good relationship for a change.

'Sorry, I have an early start tomorrow.' She looked at Tom and widened her eyes, urging him to go along with her.

'Yes, me too. Thanks for a lovely evening,' he said, standing up and pulling a couple of notes out of his wallet and leaving them on the table.

'Very generous of you, mate,' said Max. 'Joking,' he added after a glare from Steph.

'Do you fancy grabbing a drink?' asked Lois after they'd left the restaurant.

Tom shifted around uncomfortably. 'Um, thanks but I'd better not.'

'Because you like Steph?'

'I'm so sorry, Lois. You're great, but yes, I've always liked her. To be honest, I can't see it working out for her with that bloke, so I'll hang on and see how things pan out for her.' He was staring at his feet now, his hands in his jacket pockets and desperate to be able to leave.

'Steph's coming for a drink too if that makes a difference.' It wasn't her place to tell him what Steph was about to do and besides, she still may not manage to do it.

'Oh. Well, maybe for a quick one.'

They walked to Heroes, a cocktail bar on the first floor of a crooked half-timbered building on New Street. Lois and Steph had been going there for years. They sometimes worried nowadays that they might be too old, but it hadn't stopped them yet.

Tom bought drinks for them, and they managed to find a table in the corner.

'Steph said you're working at Croftwood Library?'

Lois nodded as she sipped her drink.

'One of the parents at school has rallied to your cause and asked us to put the flyers for the Library of the Year competition out with the school newsletter this week so you might get a few extra votes.'

'Wow, that's brilliant. Honestly, it's amazed me how many people have said they've voted for us.'

'Everyone loves an underdog,' he said winking.

'Well, we are that.'

Steph appeared, not five minutes behind them. That didn't bode well, there definitely hadn't been time for her to say what needed to be said.

'Sorted,' she said, with a broad grin.

'Really?' asked Lois doubtfully.

'Yep, turned out he wasn't feeling it either and, no offence, he thought my friends were boring.'

Lois gulped her drink down, pleased that she'd chosen a gin and tonic and not a glass of wine. 'I'm off then.'

Steph stood up and took her aside as Lois was putting her coat on.

'Thanks, Lois, I appreciate this.'

'No problem. Have a lovely evening. Bye,' she called to Tom over Steph's shoulder. He waved at her, grinning like the Cheshire cat.

Lois headed towards the bridge for the short walk home. If the night had taught her anything it was that she wasn't ready for any relationship that wasn't with Oliver. It was impossible to forget him and just as hard to avoid him. And she didn't want to have to avoid him, she liked being friends. But what had seemed like a good compromise was making it a lot harder for her to move on. Even the fact that he was so involved in the book club made it impossible to draw a line under their relationship in whatever form it was, and she probably needed to accept that she was going to be in this state of limbo until she left Croftwood Library. She just had to make it through until then.

35

Steph had picked up the Dial-A-Ride minibus after her shift, had already collected Flora, Jerry, Audrey and Bill and was on her way to Eunice's house for Eunice and Dottie. Tom had tagged along for company. They had seen each other almost every day since she'd finally got herself together and dumped Max on the night of the double date.

Max had been completely indifferent when Steph told him she thought maybe it wasn't going to work out between them, so it had been easy to suggest that they call it a day without either of them being upset about it.

Once Lois had left her and Tom together in Heroes, he'd admitted to her that he'd thought about asking her out before but thought she wasn't interested. She felt so comfortable with him that she was able to say that she'd always thought he was too nerdy for her but that when she'd seen him in 'real-life' she'd fancied the pants off him. They were both relieved that Lois hadn't been interested.

So, Tom sat in the front of the minibus with Steph, his hand resting over hers on the gearstick when she was on a stretch of not having to change gears. It struck her as vomit-inducingly sweet, but she loved it all the same.

'Just got to pick up Eunice and Dottie now,' said Steph as they headed for the village where the Hawthorn Lane stop was on her mobile library route. Eunice lived in the middle of the village in a Victorian semi. She pulled up outside and Tom jumped out onto the pavement.

'I'll go,' he said and jogged up the path where Eunice was already opening the front door.

Bill opened the side door of the minibus and stepped out onto the pavement ready to lend a hand.

'Ever the chivalrous gent, Bill,' said Steph with a grin.

She watched Tom offer Eunice his arm as they made their way down the path with Dottie behind them. Tom was just as chivalrous as Bill, it turned out. Steph could live with a bit more of that in her life. Maybe it was her age, but she wanted a man who was considerate and thoughtful. Like Tom.

'Good evening, ladies,' said Bill with a small bow as he held the side door open for them to climb into the minibus.

'Goodness gracious me!' exclaimed Eunice, holding her hand to her chest as she stared at Bill.

'What is it Eunice, are you feeling alright?' Dottie asked her.

'It's William Templeton!'

'Yep, it's our Bill alright,' said Steph, surprised to see that Bill was blushing. 'You two know each other then?' Might as well get the awkward reunion out of the way before they carried on to Croftwood.

'William Templeton, well I never.' Eunice was still shaking her head and smiling at Bill as he took her hand and assisted her into the bus, leaving Dottie to close the door behind them. Tom took his place next to Steph.

'Do you think they used to be an item?' he whispered to her. She shrugged and widened her eyes in amusement at Eunice's reaction then checked her mirrors and pulled away.

'It's very flattering of you to remember after so many years,' Bill was saying to Eunice.

'I loved *Where Love Lingers*. I saw it at the picture house in York with my friend, May. Twice. You were very handsome, William.'

'You're making an old man blush…'

'Eunice.'

'What a lovely name, Eunice. It's a pleasure to meet you.'

Steph glanced in the mirror and saw that they were sitting in seats across the aisle from each other, both looking at each other and smiling. It was love at first sight right there, in the minibus. She turned to Tom and could see that he had noticed it too.

When they arrived in Croftwood, Steph pulled up right outside Oliver's so that everyone could jump out while she went to park the bus nearby. Bill was out first, holding out a hand for Eunice and escorting her into Oliver's while she gazed at him, still with the same look on her face.

'Did you know he was a film star, Steph?' asked Flora.

'No idea. I do remember thinking that Templeton had a fancy ring to it though.'

'Blimey,' said Jerry. 'That'd be like me meeting Kate Winslet.'

'Oh, for god's sake Jerry,' said Flora. 'She's twenty years younger than you. Bonnie Langford, she's more your type.'

They waited for Audrey and then went inside while Dottie hung back, looking nervous.

'Tom, go in with Dottie, would you?' Steph asked him as he went to climb back onto the bus.

'Fed up with me already?' he said, grinning. 'Course. She looks terrified. See you in a minute.'

Steph drove around the corner and parked the minibus in the church car park. She was excited about the evening ahead. Aside from being thrilled that Tom had wanted to tag along – he had insisted – she was looking forward to seeing the book club in action. Hopefully, it would bring the whole thing to life for her customers and spread the word around the villages that the mobile library had something extra to offer.

The smell of mulled wine greeted her as she opened the door and she saw that Tom and Dottie had wasted no time in taking advantage of it.

'Hi Steph, grab a seat wherever you can,' said Linda who was on the door. 'Your crowd are split between the Lady Glenconnor book and the psychological thriller.'

'Thanks, Linda, is Lois around?'

'No, she's over at the Courtyard Café with Rosemary.' Linda's eyes darted over to Oliver who was busy making coffee. 'She thought it was for the best.'

Steph had been so caught up in her own love life that she hadn't had the chance to catch up with Lois about hers for ages. Did she still like Oliver? She'd assumed that once the ex-girlfriend had turned up, Lois would have moved on.

Steph went over to where Tom was sitting with Dottie, across the table from Bill and Eunice who were engrossed in conversation with each other.

'Looks like you lost your book date, Dottie.'

'Well, it's nice to see Eunice enjoying herself. I don't mind. There's bound to be someone else I can join in with.'

'There will be. I'll find out from Linda who Bill was meant to be paired up with.'

Bill's partner turned out to be someone called Laura who hadn't arrived yet. Steph primed Linda to send Laura over to sit with Dottie when she arrived then excused herself, along with Tom.

'We're not leaving already, are we?' he asked as Steph led them outside.

'No, I just need to call into the other place to see Lois.'

They strolled down the road to the Courtyard Café where Lois, wearing a Santa hat, was on the door with Rosemary and people were standing in groups outside, despite the chilly winter evening, with take-out cups in their hands, all cheerfully talking about books.

The inside was adorned with fairy lights, not as many as Oliver's had but it was a good effort and looked very festive, nevertheless.

'Hey, Lois.'

'Stephanie, there is, unfortunately, no room inside and as library staff, you are entitled to attend the evening at Oliver's,' said Rosemary in her most officious voice.

Lois gave Rosemary a tight smile. 'Can you hold the fort for a minute please, Rosemary? I just need a word with Steph.' She took Steph's arm and steered her past the crowd to a quiet corner of the courtyard.

Tom stayed behind and Steph could hear him introduce himself to one of the groups. The benefits of dating a teacher; he seemed to be able to deal with anything that was thrown at him.

'I'm loving the hat by the way,' said Steph, provoking no reaction at all from Lois. 'So, what's up? I thought you were going to be at Oliver's. Has something happened?'

'Not really.' Lois sighed. 'It's complicated. Amy has a bit of an issue with him doing the book club with me, so I thought it was easier to stay away.'

'Right…'

'He's so easy to be with, so it's weird to have to be careful so she doesn't get upset. It's less stressful for everyone if I just steer clear.'

'So that's it? You're just going to avoid him for the rest of your life?'

Lois shuffled her pieces of paper while she stared intently at them. 'Yes, if I have to.'

'And what about you? Are you happy to do that? This book club is amazing, and you did this and now you're having to be all... furtive.'

'I'm not being furtive. I just want an easy life. And anyway, it kills two birds with one stone.'

Steph raised her eyebrows to let Lois know that needed more explanation.

'Well, maybe I'm not over him. It's so stupid, I mean, nothing ever really happened but I like being with him and it just makes it worse knowing nothing can happen.'

'Oh, Lois. I didn't know you still felt like that about him.'

Lois shrugged. 'It doesn't matter. I'll be okay.' She turned back to look at the café. 'Tom seems to have found his tribe.'

'He just gets on with everything, it's great. I might not be able to drag him back to Oliver's though and I ought to get back to see how it's going. I think there's a bit of a romance blossoming between a couple of my customers.'

'At least someone's getting lucky.'

'You won't have to wait 'til you're eighty, don't worry.'

'It feels like love at eighty might be the best I can hope for at the moment,' said Lois but at least she was smiling now. 'Ring me tomorrow.'

Steph managed to extract Tom from his new group of friends who were animatedly talking about the best way to kill a person in a crime novel, and they walked back to Oliver's.

Dottie had paired up with Zoe from Steph's Old Hollow stop and they both looked like they were enjoying themselves. Zoe hadn't come on the bus because she was worried she might get stuck at work, but Steph was glad she'd come and even more pleased that she and Dottie had hit it off. Dottie could do with someone like Zoe to encourage her to let her hair down. They both waved at Steph once they spotted her.

'Coffee or wine?' asked Oliver when they walked up to the counter.

'Cup of tea for me, please. I'm the designated driver,' said Steph.

'Same for me,' said Tom.

'We've just been over to the Courtyard Café, they've got almost as many people outside as they have in,' said Steph.

'This is better than last month. We ran out of seats, and it was complete chaos. This is much more manageable.'

Steph thought the place looked rammed and there were no free seats that she could see. Lois certainly did have a hit on her hands.

'So…Lois is over at the Courtyard?' Oliver asked Steph, trying to sound casual.

'Yes, trying to keep Rosemary calm under pressure, I think.'

'Not an easy thing to do.' He paused, then attempted to say equally casually, 'I haven't seen Lois for a week or so. She alright?'

'She's fine.' He was an idiot if he didn't realise Lois was steering clear. 'She's really looking forward to Christmas.' Why did she say that? It was true but she should have come up with something that made it sound as if Lois was super busy, too busy to think about Oliver. 'And obviously, she's completely slammed with the whole awards thing.' Could being nominated for an award make a person slammed with things to do? Steph hoped Oliver would think so.

'Yeah, right, of course.' He passed their teas. 'Cheers guys, enjoy.'

'He seems like a nice bloke,' said Tom once they'd found a premium patch of floor next to a radiator to sit down. 'Friend of Lois's?'

'Kind of. I mean, he is but his wacky girlfriend thinks there's more to it, so Lois is having to avoid them both.'

'And is there more to it?'

Steph grinned. If Tom wanted to talk about stuff like this, it was going to be the best relationship ever.

36

The envelope was waiting on her desk. Lois couldn't imagine how Linda had contained herself for a whole twenty-four hours and not opened it. It was a letter from the Library of the Year Awards.

She took off her cycle jacket and hung it on the back of the door to dry. It was a dreary day and was barely daylight when Lois left home. Her hair was damp, but she twirled it up into a bun and that would have to do.

'Hey Linda,' she called as she walked to the front desk with the letter.

Linda appeared from the children's library with wide eyes. 'Have you opened it yet? What does it say?'

'Come on, you do it.' Lois handed her the letter and was glad she'd passed on the job to Linda who looked like she might burst with excitement. Hopefully, it would be good news otherwise they might both drown in a flood of Linda's tears.

'Oh gosh, I'm shaking!' She pulled out the letter and scanned it while Lois waited, patiently for a reaction. 'Yes! Yes! We've been shortlisted for the Community Spirit award which means we get to go to the awards ceremony at the London Library!'

'That's brilliant!' Lois hugged Linda and they both danced around laughing, Linda waving the letter in the air and singing 'We're simply the best!' over and over again.

'Can anyone join in?'

Lois turned around to find Oliver leaning on the front desk with an amused look on his face.

'Oh, sorry.' She pushed some stray hair behind her ears. 'Morning. What can we do for you?'

'I just came to see how you are. Bought you guys a coffee and some muffins.'

Lois sighed silently to herself. She was trying so hard, and he was so oblivious. Linda grabbed her coffee and said thanks before disappearing back to the children's library.

'Thanks. We've just found out we're on the shortlist for the Library of the Year Awards.'

'That's fantastic! Congratulations, Lois.' He leaned across the desk and kissed her on the cheek. It took her by surprise, but she tried not to show it and anyway, the gorgeous smell of him had dazed her somewhat.

'Thanks. It's been a massive joint effort and the book club definitely wouldn't have been such a success without you.'

'Lois, it's all you. But I'm happy to have helped.' He smiled, then dropped his gaze to the floor. 'I missed you on Wednesday. You haven't been around at all lately, you're not avoiding me, are you?'

Did he really not know why she'd been staying away, after what he'd told her about Amy?

'Oliver, I can't carry on as if I don't know Amy's bothered by us being friends. It's awkward and I think being around you a bit less, not coming into the coffee house, it has to help.'

He gave an exasperated sigh. 'It's not down to you to worry about Amy. We're friends and I'm not going to let that change. Christ! We're not bloody teenagers. I can have a girl who's a friend.' He shoved his hands through his hair, ruining the quiff he'd probably spent some time on that morning.

'Look, I know you think that, and I appreciate it but to be honest I could do with distancing myself a bit anyway.' She paused to gauge whether he realised what she was trying to say without her having to say it. Clearly not. 'After what happened… what almost happened. With us. It's difficult. I like you. Do you hear what I'm saying?' Because this was excruciating.

'Right. No, I get it. And I'm sorry.'

His belligerence had gone. He looked beaten as he turned and left, not saying anything else, leaving Lois with a coffee and muffin that she just wanted to cry into.

'Everything alright?' asked Linda, looking concerned as she came out of hiding.

'Yes, fine,' sighed Lois.

'You never know, it might not last with him and Amy.' Linda had adopted a conspiratorial tone. 'He's not going to put up with getting told who he can and can't be friends with, is he?'

But he might. Linda wasn't accounting for the guilt factor which seemed to be driving Oliver more than anything or that he and Amy were giving each other a second chance and that seemed to come with a higher tolerance level for what each of them were willing to take before they snapped. The stakes seemed to be higher for Oliver and he seemed willing to stick with Amy whatever that meant he had to go through. The worst part was, Lois knew he wasn't happy.

'Maybe not,' smiled Lois. 'Anyway, are you up for spreading the word about our victory?'

'Oh, definitely. I've already written the posts in my head. You'll have to get a new frock for the ceremony. It's so exciting!'

Lois hadn't thought as far ahead as the ceremony. She'd have to let the County Libraries office know in case they wanted to send some of the top people, but she hoped as they'd not been that involved with the process, they might leave the places for Lois and her colleagues at Croftwood.

It was still drizzling when she left the library that evening. Cycling in the rain never bothered her normally but after her encounter with Oliver, she had struggled to lift her mood and the rain wasn't helping. As she cycled up the high street she concentrated on the Christmas tree at the end of the road instead of torturing herself by trying to catch a glimpse of Oliver through the coffee house windows like she usually did, only to end up seeing a snapshot of him and Amy locking up the shop together or chatting at a table.

She could hardly believe it was only two weeks until Christmas. Her Christmas spirit seemed to have deserted her this year. The tree and the lights were pretty, but she wasn't excited. She'd have to go to her brother's house where everyone would be judgy about the fact she wasn't with Alex anymore. They would think it was her fault and would wonder what she had done to ruin a perfectly good relationship. That was probably what was at the bottom of her gloom. Maybe once Christmas was over, she'd feel better. This one would be a write-off but one bad one out of thirty or so wasn't the end of the world.

Oliver was cleaning the coffee machine. Rosemary had been in before he closed to say that the County Libraries people had decided that he and Lois should go to the Library of the Year Awards ceremony to represent Croftwood Library. Unfortunately, she'd picked the moment that Amy had chosen to perch at the end of the counter and now he was concentrating on cleaning the coffee machine so that he didn't have to give the impending argument his full attention. All the arguing was wearing him out.

'You can't go, not with Lois.'

'It's not like it was my idea, Amy. Come on, it's great publicity for the coffee house.' He wanted to go, and he wasn't going to let Amy talk him out of it.

'Oliver, apart from you letting them use the coffee house for the book club, it's nothing to do with you. Why do you have to get so involved with this?'

'It's great for the town.' He sighed and polished the steam wand more vigorously.

'You always say that when it's something to do with Lois as if there's nothing you can do about it and actually, I think you just like doing stuff with her.'

He already knew it was the wrong thing to say but it came out anyway. 'I do like doing stuff with her.'

Even though he wasn't looking at Amy, he could feel the vibes.

'Would you stop cleaning that bloody machine and talk to me?'

He turned around and put the cloth down on the counter. 'There's no reason for me not to go, Amy. I want things to work between us, but I won't be dictated to about who I can be friends with. It's crazy.'

'Oh, okay. So is it a coincidence that she hasn't been in here since the morning you apparently went to the wholesalers?'

'What? How would you know that? Have you been sitting there twenty-four-seven waiting for her to appear?' But she was right, it was no coincidence, but he hadn't realised that until he went to the library. How had Amy realised? Was he being stupid, and something was going on that everyone else but him could see?

'I'm pretty sure she has not been in here, Oliver. If she

doesn't turn up even for the precious book club, she hasn't been in at all!' Her voice was getting louder, a sign that she was about to blow but at least it would soon be over.

'Well, I don't know why she hasn't been in.' He hated blatantly lying but he had no choice. 'You're reading too much into stuff that's just not there.' He reached out and took her hand. 'It's just a dinner with a hundred other people, it's work.'

She looked at him and tilted her head to one side. He'd won her over.

'Okay. You'd better be planning to take me out to dinner to make it up to me.'

'You've got it.'

After he'd been to the library to see Lois, he'd felt sorry not to have realised that she was finding it hard to stay friends. It was understandable. He'd moved on with Amy which had made it easier for him to forget what might have been between him and Lois. It was different for her, and he was an idiot for literally asking her to explain herself. But now that they were going to the awards ceremony in London, was she going to be okay with that? He was pretty sure it wouldn't have been her idea and if she wasn't happy about it, he didn't know what he'd do. He was looking forward to it and determined that Lois was going to enjoy what would hopefully be a very special night.

37

Lois was loitering at the information desk in the Hive waiting until it was time for her meeting.

'What are you going to do then? Go in and tell them it's your gig and you're going to choose who gets to go.' Andrew got on his high horse so easily.

'I can't do that.' That was exactly what she wanted to do but she wasn't very good at having to stand up for herself at work. It seemed risky. All the other risky things she'd done recently were very much under the radar.

But the alternative was that she was stuck going with Oliver. That in itself wasn't bad but given how they'd left things last time she'd seen him, it was going to be awkward having to spend the evening together as well as having to cope with the rest of the group from County Libraries who she didn't know very well. She also felt bad that Linda and Rosemary had been overlooked, and she'd have taken Steph as well because it was no mean feat getting the mobile library customers involved.

'Christ Lois, you don't want to spend an evening in London living it up with that lot.' He tipped his head and looked upwards even though the only person who had an office in the Hive was Robert and Lois wasn't sure he was invited either.

'No, I don't really and if it was Robert making the decision, I might have the nerve to say something but David is a bit intimidating, to be honest.'

'Well, you're going to have to suck it up and hang out with Oliver. Why's that so bad anyway? What's wrong with him?' Andrew paused mid-scan of a book and looked at Lois with narrowed eyes.

'Nothing's wrong with him. He's really nice. But...' It would be a mistake to tell Andrew. It would invite a lot of advice that she didn't need. 'He's a bit boring, to spend a whole evening with... you know.'

'Hmm. Maybe you will end up spending the evening with that lot then.' He was scanning books like a demon again, so Lois decided to take the opportunity to cut the conversation short while she was ahead.

She climbed the stairs to Robert's office. The door was open, and she was the first to arrive.

'Lois! Lovely to see you. How is life in Croftwood?' Robert took his glasses off and made a steeple with his fingers.

'Great, thanks, Robert. Things have picked up on the borrowing front over the past couple of weeks and the new teenage library is working out well.' The beanbags had been in full-time use over the weekend, and they were starting to get people calling in after school now as well.

'Excellent. I did have a quick look at the figures, and it is certainly doing very well. Well done.'

'Robert, before David comes, do you think I've got any sway at all with trying to have some input into who gets invited to the awards ceremony?'

Robert sucked in a breath and pursed his lips. 'You could try by all means but, in my experience, the ones who do all the work rarely get the glory.'

'Morning, Robert. Lois,' said David as he strode into the office, folding his coat and laying it carefully on top of a pile of books. 'Fantastic news about being shortlisted for the award, Lois, really fantastic.'

'Thanks, David.'

'You must send our thanks and congratulations to your team.'

It was now or never. He had paved the way for her. 'I was hoping that some of the Croftwood staff could come to the awards ceremony.'

'Yes, of course, we've allocated two tickets to Croftwood. Did you not receive the email from Sue about it?' He started tapping his phone with a frown on his face.

'We did, I just wondered if there was any flexibility. More people have had a hand in this than me and Oliver, it would be nice for all of them to experience the evening.' Lois's heart was beating so loudly she was sure he'd hear it.

'No, I don't think so. Unfortunately, we have to satisfy the powers that be and that means there's not much anyone can do about it. Sorry,' he added without sounding it.

'Okay, no problem, thanks.' At least she'd asked. She'd make the best of it with Oliver. If she was honest, spending the evening with him was an attractive prospect and the thought of him in a suit or dinner jacket sent shivers down her spine. It wasn't going to do anything to help her attempts to get over him but maybe she could allow herself that night and then start again afterwards.

'Before the awards, we need to establish our party line. It would be very bad form to have to mention the fact that Croftwood Library is listed for closure so we will focus on the book club. After all, that's why we're in the Community Spirit award category.'

It annoyed Lois that he said 'we' as if it was anything to do with him or his colleagues. They were the ones trying to close the library; the very people she was trying to prove wrong.

'Well, Linda wrote the application so I think she would be well-placed to explain how we've got this far. The judges must have liked it.'

'Quite right, Lois,' said Robert. 'Linda seems to be a social media whizz these days. It's a real feather in her cap.'

'It is,' agreed Lois. 'Perhaps you could email her about it, David?'

'Yes, will do,' he blustered.

'I must say, the book club choices are in high demand right across the county,' said Robert. 'The Croftwood effect is spreading.'

David looked less than pleased to hear that which filled Lois with glee. Robert was on her side.

'Well, as I said before, there's nothing we can do about saving Croftwood Library at this stage,' David said.

'Interesting though, isn't it?' Lois was feeling braver by the second. 'That a library that was considered unworthy of existing any more can be making such a difference.'

'All to do with the vision of the management, Lois,' said Robert with a knowing look. 'It's a real tribute to you what you've managed to achieve at Croftwood, and I look forward to making more of your skills when we have you back at the Hive.'

Lois's eyes filled with tears. 'Thank you, Robert. That means a lot to hear you say that.'

'So, good luck with the awards ceremony. It's wonderful to have got this far, it's further than we got in 2012 with this place, isn't it, David?'

David nodded, his face like thunder and Lois suspected that Robert was just as pleased about that as she was.

Although the meeting didn't resolve the problem of the awards dinner for Lois, she came out of the Hive feeling that she'd had a victory. If David even thought twice about what she'd said, it had been worth speaking up.

38

It was Steph's last week on the mobile library before Christmas and her final stop was Hawthorn Lane. She hadn't seen Eunice and Dottie since the book club and was looking forward to hearing whether the friendship Eunice and Bill had struck up had progressed.

She pulled up in the lay-by and got everything ready. She'd bought some non-alcoholic mulled wine for them in one of her tea flasks along with tubs of Twiglets and Cheeselets and a brand-new box of Victoria biscuits.

'Morning Steph!' Dottie was first, minus Bert. 'Merry Christmas!'

'Merry Christmas, Dottie! On your own today?'

'My parents are visiting for Christmas, so I've left Bert with them. They love being in charge of him so it's win-win.' She took her coat off and sat down.

'Have you seen Eunice since the book club evening?' asked Steph.

'Mmm,' she nodded while she munched on a Twiglet. 'I saw her at the village shop last week and she looked very spritely. She'd been out for afternoon tea with Bill the day before. It's so funny how they hit it off, isn't it?'

'It's great. I think they're both lonely and stuck in the middle of nowhere. No offence.'

Dottie smiled. 'You're right. The village is lovely until you can't get around as easily anymore, then it's just isolating.'

'Morning, girls!' called Eunice from the door. Steph jumped up to help her but there was no need. Bill was right behind her.

'Bill! This is a surprise,' said Steph grinning.

'I don't think you're due at the Red Lion Inn until after Christmas, so I decided to tag along with Eunice.'

'Brilliant! The more the merrier. Come in, sit down.' Steph was thrilled that Eunice and Bill were still going strong.

'Is the book club carrying on over Christmas?' asked Dottie.

'Yes, here are the choices. *Christmas at Cold Comfort Farm*, a classic, although they're not all Christmas stories. *Twas the Nightshift Before Christmas* by Adam Kay and *The Christmas Secret* by Karen Swan for you romantics.'

Bill blushed and chose the Adam Kay book while Dottie and Eunice went for the romance as they tended to do.

'I love a Christmas romance,' said Dottie.

'Speaking of romance, is Tom your new chap, Steph?' Eunice was straight to the point. Steph only wished she or Dottie were as brave when it came to finding out what was going on between Eunice and Bill.

'He is,' said Steph, finding herself feeling unusually proud of her partner which made a nice change from cringing every time they opened their mouth. 'He's a teacher at St. Hilda's.'

'A teacher?' Eunice looked surprised and impressed, as well she might. She had heard Steph recount tales of bad dates and bad boyfriends often enough to know that a teacher was a very different prospect. 'Well, he's a very nice young man. I wish you all the best.'

'What are you doing over Christmas, Eunice?' asked Dottie.

'I'm spending Christmas Eve and Christmas Day with my son and his family in Bristol. He's coming to fetch me in the car and then will take me to Bill's on Boxing Day.'

'Oh, lovely,' said Dottie. She stole a glance at Steph who winked back while Eunice and Bill were busy looking at each other. They were getting along well. 'How about you, Steph?'

'I'm taking Tom to my parents in Warwickshire. Baptism of fire for him but he seems to be keen anyway.'

'That's a good sign,' laughed Bill.

They chatted and laughed together until Steph had to leave. The mobile library always got emptied and spruced up over Christmas, so she had to deliver it to the Hive before the end of the day.

'Shall we go to the book club again in the New Year?' Dottie asked Eunice and Bill. 'Nick is home for the whole of January so I can drive us and not worry about having to get a babysitter.'

'That sounds like a very good idea,' said Eunice. 'We will see you both next year.' She gave Dottie and Steph a kiss on the cheek and then Bill escorted her out of the van.

'Oh, it's so lovely, isn't it? For them to find romance at their age,' said Dottie with a whimsical look in her eye.

'It's a flipping miracle at any age.'

'Have a lovely Christmas, Steph.' Dottie hugged her, then skipped down the steps.

That was it. Another whole year over. And for once, Steph could say it was ending in a much better place than where it had started.

39

It was so cold on the platform of Foregate Street station that Lois was considering opening her case and putting some extra layers on. It had been snowing for a couple of hours now and not wanting to sit on a train for four hours freezing and wet, she had taken a taxi to the station.

'We are sorry to announce that the ten-fifty service to Birmingham New Street has been cancelled.'

Lois dragged her case along the platform to join the small crowd of passengers that had gathered around the information screen. All the trains were cancelled, not just hers.

'Anyone interested in sharing a cab to New Street?' someone called.

It was a tempting offer but as she needed to get a connection from there to York, she thought that being stranded in Birmingham with no way to get home or to York would be much worse than having to go home now. Given the weather, it probably wasn't worth the risk.

Her phone started vibrating in her pocket. It was her dad.

'Lois? Have you left yet, love?'

'My train to Birmingham's been cancelled, Dad. What's the weather like up there?'

'Blooming dreadful. Your mum and I think it's too risky for you to come. I don't think we'll get the car out to be able to meet you at the station if it keeps on like this for much longer.'

Lois's heart sank. It was Christmas Eve. Literally, the last chance to get anywhere – or not. 'I won't be able to come, Dad.' Although she'd had mixed feelings about spending Christmas at her brother's with the rest of the family, now that it wasn't an option she was devastated. 'Say sorry to Jim and Lizzie for me.'

'I will and not to worry, love. Better that you're safe. See how it goes, maybe try on Boxing Day or whenever the trains start again.'

Lois knew he was right, but the prospect of spending Christmas alone was not that appealing. Steph had gone to her parents with Tom, and Andrew and Luke had gone to St Lucia. There was nowhere else she could invite herself to apart from Linda's or Rosemary's if she didn't want to be by herself.

'Okay, Dad. I'll call you later. Love you.'

She pulled her hood up and zipped her coat right to the top then grabbed her case and headed home. The snow was a couple of inches deep and in true England-in-the-snow style, there was not a taxi to be seen outside the station. She would have to walk. It was normally only a twenty-minute walk but with her wheelie case behaving like a snowplough, she had to carry it, and then it seemed like it was going to be a very long way home.

The snow was falling steadily and when she wasn't cursing the spare pair of Doc Martens she had packed and the Le Creuset milk pan she had bought for her mum for Christmas, she enjoyed seeing how the city changed in the snow. The sounds were muffled, the traffic almost non-existent and the Christmas lights made it all magical.

She crossed the river bridge and was almost tempted to walk right in the middle of the road where there was virgin snow and no cars on a normally very busy road. She didn't hear the car pull up next to her, it was going so slowly.

'Lois?'

She turned to see Oliver in his Mini. He had a dusting of snow across his shoulders and his hair was damp.

'Get in.'

She was not about to refuse a lift. She brushed the worst of the snow off her case and heaved it into the back seat then gratefully collapsed into the front.

'Thanks. You've saved my arms from being wrenched from their sockets by that bloody suitcase.'

He grinned. 'Where are you going?'

'I was going to York to stay with my brother and the rest of my family, but the trains are cancelled so I'm going home.'

'To spend Christmas with…'

'Myself?'

He looked at her, maybe trying to gauge whether she was joking. 'Seriously?'

'Yep. But I'll be fine. I've got my beautiful tree which would have been lonely without me, and I can watch the *Strictly* Christmas special with no interruptions.'

'Come to mine.'

'What? No. That'd be weird. Amy wouldn't be up for that.'

'She's gone to her parents. I was supposed to drive down there today but that's not going to happen now.' He shrugged. 'I thought I'd take the car out to see what the roads were like. It's always worse in Croftwood but it's getting pretty bad everywhere.

Lois noticed now how slowly he was having to drive to keep traction on the snow. Could she spend Christmas with him?

'Look, I know you've been trying to stay away from me because... well, you know. But it's Christmas, Lois. It makes no sense for two people who have had their plans thwarted by the weather to both be alone for no good reason. It's Christmas,' he said again with a beseeching look for good measure.

It was a solid argument. It seemed silly for both of them, people who were at the very least friends, to be alone when they didn't have to be. It was Christmas. And with Amy away Lois didn't have to worry about what she was going to think because she'd never know.

'We can't tell anyone. I mean, we can't let Amy find out, it'd be awful.' She paused, waiting for him to enthusiastically agree. 'Wouldn't it?'

'It would. I accept your terms.'

It was the craziest thing in the world to be considering this. Spending Christmas together. Snowed in together.

'Okay. But why don't we do it at mine? I have a very nice tree and a spare room.' She knew she wouldn't be able to enjoy herself at Oliver's amidst all the evidence of his and Amy's life together.

'Deal. But I'm bringing the food.'

Oliver drove them to Croftwood where he spent less than five minutes getting everything that he needed for a couple of days while Lois waited in the car wondering whether she'd made the right decision.

Lois opened the be-wreathed front door and Oliver followed her into the house. The wreath on the outside was a mere hint at the amount of Christmas inside. The hall was decked with actual boughs of holly and ivy which wound their way up the banister. The whole place smelled like Christmas and after a few seconds Lois flipped a switch somewhere and hundreds of tiny fairy lights fluttered on around the edge of the ceiling.

'Ah, I see you are the one who proved the correlation between fairy lights and Christmas spirit.'

She was beaming at him even though her socks and jeans were wet from tramping through the snow and her hair was in damp curls around her forehead. He was so glad he'd suggested this and that she'd said yes.

Oliver left his overnight bag in the hall while he took the food and drink he'd bought with him into the kitchen. He was surprised at how empty Lois's fridge was before he remembered that she hadn't planned on being here. Luckily, even though he'd been going away with Amy, he'd stocked up with all the essentials to make a Christmas lunch for them both when they got back because he couldn't miss out on his annual bubble and squeak fry-up with the leftovers. He'd also grabbed a bottle of Prosecco, essential for Christmas morning, and a couple of bottles of red wine which he might mull if Lois fancied it.

'We're not going to starve, then,' said Lois, walking into the kitchen wearing leggings, an oversized jumper and woolly socks. 'Do you want a cup of tea?'

'Yes, thanks. You can never have too much food at Christmas.'

'That's true.'

He watched her as she made the tea with her back to him, her curly hair tied on top of her head in a bunch.

'Do you want to light the fire?' she asked.

'Definitely. It's the law when it's snowing outside. Oh, I should have bought marshmallows.'

She smiled at him. 'Never mind. You've thought of everything else by the looks of it.'

He followed her into the lounge where she sat down in the corner of the sofa with her feet tucked up next to her, holding her mug with both hands.

'The tree looks spectacular,' he said, admiring the array of baubles and old-fashioned tinsel which sparkled in the glow of yet more fairy lights, adorning almost every branch with an overall effect which was surprisingly tasteful.

'Thanks, I'm quite pleased to be spending Christmas with it after all.'

The wood in the basket next to the fireplace was nice and dry so it didn't take him long to get the fire roaring. He glanced out of the window and saw that the snow was still falling steadily, reassuring him that he'd made the right decision and that he had no need to feel guilty about not being able to make it to Amy's parents. Amy. He needed to call her to tell her he wasn't coming, and he already knew she would be as mad as hell about it. He had promised Lois not to tell Amy that they were spending Christmas together, so he wouldn't lie but he wouldn't tell her either.

'I'm just going to make a call,' he said, excusing himself and going into the kitchen.

'Hey, Amy…'

'You're not coming, are you?' She sounded angry.

'The snow's really bad. I took the car out in case it was worse in Croftwood, but the roads are awful everywhere, even in Worcester.' She didn't speak so he added, 'I'm so sorry.'

'You should have closed the coffee house a day early as I suggested and then you could have come down with me.'

Or she could have waited for him, and they'd be at home together now.

'I'm so sorry, I don't know what to say. There's nothing I can do, Ames.'

He heard her sigh gently. 'Okay. I'm just disappointed. And you'll be by yourself for Christmas.'

'I got the three-bird roast for when we get back. I'll cook

that, it'll be great.'

'We'll do presents when I get back?'

'Yes, good idea. And say sorry to your mum and dad for me. I was looking forward to seeing them.' He'd been nervous about seeing them again after everything that had happened, so he was grateful to the snow for that.

'I will. Love you, Oliver. Call me tomorrow?'

'Will do. Bye.'

He breathed a sigh of relief. Now he could relax. He went back into the lounge where Lois had put the television on and was flipping through the Radio Times Christmas edition.

'So, we can watch *The Holiday* or *Elf*.'

'That's all that's on? On all those six pages of today's listings?'

'No, it's Christmas Eve which means there are three, maybe four days more to watch Christmas movies before the Christmas spirit disappears and then they'll just make you sad. By a process of elimination, those are the two we have on offer this afternoon. Luckily, we can watch them both on catch-up so either way we're okay.'

This was exactly the kind of Christmas he wanted. He had such a full-on life with the coffee house and the cinema, that Christmas was almost the only real break he had all year. It would have been fine at Amy's parents but he'd have had to make an effort all the time and being with Amy at the moment was enough of an effort all by itself let alone having to make sure they could get through three or four days with no disagreements in front of her parents.

He sat down in the armchair next to the fire and poked it to bring it back to life.

'Okay if I put my stuff upstairs?' he asked.

'Sorry, yes. Let me show you.'

The spare room looked onto the small courtyard garden which was covered in a perfect blanket of snow. It had a double bed, a bedside table with a quirky-looking table lamp on it, and a huge chest of drawers.

'There's no room in the drawers,' called Lois from the landing where she was rummaging in the airing cupboard for some sheets. 'Sorry, they've got all my sewing stuff in there.'

'No problem. I'm happy to live out of my bag.'

In silence, they made the bed together. Oliver tried to catch her eye, but she was steadfastly not looking at him for some reason. Was it too intimate making a bed together? Maybe. He'd never made a bed with anyone but Amy.

'I think we should watch *Elf*,' she said as she left the room.

It seemed so natural to be in Lois's house, as easy as their relationship had become before he'd ruined it by telling her that Amy was cheesed off. Why he'd done that he had no idea now. It wasn't Lois's problem, he'd just panicked. But the fact that he was here, about to watch his favourite Christmas film with Lois in the most Christmassy house he could imagine, meant that at least she wasn't avoiding him anymore. That would do.

He changed into some suitably festive flannel tartan pyjama trousers and a soft black jumper and added some reindeer socks which he'd shoved in his bag as an afterthought.

'Will Ferrell's a genius.' Lois said a couple of hours later as she stood up and stretched. 'Sorry if I talked too much. I don't often watch TV with anyone else at the moment. I was making the most of it.'

'Don't worry about it.' It had been endearing and it didn't matter as he'd seen *Elf* so many times before and agreed with most of Lois's commentary on which bits were her favourites – most of the film qualified on that score. 'Can I make dinner for us?'

'You can... but most of my shopping this week was frozen festive party food so we may have to have some kind of buffet. Come on, let's have a look.

It was going to be a great couple of days. Lois was back to normal and the awkwardness he'd thought they'd take a day or so to get over hadn't materialised at all.

40

Lois crept past Oliver's bedroom door. It was closed so he must still be asleep. She had thrown on a woolly jumper over her pyjamas and she tiptoed down the stairs, trying to avoid the squeaky bits.

Oliver was already in the kitchen, busy peeling carrots.

'Merry Christmas!' she said.

'Merry Christmas.' He paused in his vegetable prep, put down his peeler and came towards her.

As he took the last couple of steps towards her, she knew what was coming. He was going to hug her, and she made a split-second decision to go along with it. It was Christmas after all, and she didn't want to start another drama like the hand-holding episode.

He wrapped his arms around her and nuzzled into the top of her head. She laid her head on his chest and hugged him tightly. It felt so natural, as if they'd done it a hundred times before rather than just once or twice.

'You don't have to do all the cooking,' she said, pulling away. 'Although it smells amazing so I'm not going to object that hard.'

'Cinnamon bun and Christmas coffee?'

'I don't know what Christmas coffee is but yes.'

'I've put some gingerbread syrup in it. I had a tiny bottle of it in the coffee house which I remembered to bring.'

'Do you think Father Christmas has been?' she asked him, semi-seriously as she sipped her coffee.

'Do you want me to check?'

She laughed. 'God, I love Christmas. All the traditions you should have grown out of seem completely acceptable.'

'Do they?' he grinned. 'What's on the agenda for today?'

'Hmm. I'm going to light the fire so I was thinking we would check out the Radio Times and basically that all day. Oh, and Christmas lunch at some point, obviously.'

'But the snow, Lois.' He had a glint in his eye. 'It's fresh, just begging us to have a go in it.'

'Have a go in what sense?' The idea of getting dressed and then going out in the cold wasn't that appealing.

'I don't know, not sledging or anything but we should go for a walk at least. Just think how lovely and cosy it'll be when we get back. And it is Christmas. We could pretend we're in a Christmas film.' He grinned a lop-sided grin at her.

'Okay, but I don't want to get wet.'

'Deal. We'll start by walking into town, we could go through the park, it'll be really pretty.'

'You sound like a girl. No offence.'

'It's Christmas Lois. Don't judge me.'

She went into the lounge, cleared the ash out of the fireplace and laid a fresh bunch of Christmas kindling and logs. She'd made her own kindling with pinecones, dried orange peel and cinnamon sticks. It smelled delicious and was good at starting the fire which was a bonus. While she waited for the flames to take, she opened the curtains and looked out to the street. It had stopped snowing, but the road was covered in a deep blanket which only a couple of intrepid cars had driven through. She hugged herself. This was just what she wanted Christmas to be like. Cosy, snowy and with someone to share it with. It was so odd having him here in her house. The weirdness between them had gone, they weren't quite back to the pre-Amy friendship level but maybe that was never going to happen anyway. This was good, having a friend to share Christmas with when neither of them could go anywhere else. The view from the window confirmed that. She added another log to the fire, put the guard around it and went to get dressed.

The walk into the city centre was magical. Lois loved how everything had changed because of the snow and she and Oliver had plenty of opportunities at being the first to forge a path across the swathes of virgin snow. Lois couldn't remember the last time it had snowed so heavily since she'd lived in Worcester. She also couldn't remember ever going anywhere on Christmas Day except to her nan and grandad's house for lunch when she was little.

Once they'd crossed the bridge, instead of heading into the city centre, they walked along the riverbank and headed through College Green to the Cathedral.

'Do you fancy it?' Oliver asked, tilting his head towards the building.

Lois's family never went to church at Christmas. They'd been to nativity plays and things like that but never gone to actual church on Christmas Day. 'I'd love to.'

He grinned at her and led the way inside where the service had already started, and the congregation were in the middle of singing 'See Amid the Winter's Snow'. They snuck into the back row and Oliver grabbed a hymn sheet from further down the pew.

'I love this one,' said Lois.

'Obviously,' he said, rolling his eyes and smiling. 'It's got everything. Christmas and snow. What more do we need?'

They stayed for the rest of the service which was very traditional with readings of the Christmas story and many more of Lois's favourite carols. Every time she sneaked a look at Oliver, he looked at her as if he could tell somehow that she was looking at him even though she tried hard not to move her head, or she pretended she was looking at something else. Watching him doing something so mundane as just sitting next to her was surprisingly charming and Lois allowed herself to think for a moment that Oliver was hers. This is what it would be like to be his girlfriend. They'd do things like this together, things that seemed unimportant and unimpressive, but which meant more than anyone could fathom.

When the service was over, they hung back, waiting for everyone else to leave before they made a move.

'Wow, it's lovely in here.' They headed towards the altar where a nativity scene was laid out.

Oliver smiled back. 'I haven't been inside before.'

'It's a while since I have and never for a service. I loved singing the carols, it sounded amazing, especially with the choir doing the descants.'

'Are you ready to head back for lunch?'

'I think it might be dinner at this rate. And we need to watch the King.'

'Dinner is fine. We can eat after the King,' he said, easily as they walked slowly down the nave.

It was snowing again when they got outside so they pulled their hoods up and took the walk home at a much quicker pace than they had on the way. Lois enjoyed walking past other people's houses and having a peek into their Christmas Day lives. It was snowing, on Christmas Day and she was with Oliver. No-one's Christmas was better than that.

When they came in from their walk, Oliver took his boots and coat off and then went straight into the lounge to see if the fire was still going. There was just enough of a glow for him to think that he'd be able to liven it up again. He sat cross-legged in front of it while he tempted it back to roaring with some of Lois's unusual kindling.

'So,' she said, sitting down on the sofa and picking up the Radio Times. 'It's Christmas Day so we have to watch *Love Actually*. Unless you've already seen it this year?' Her eyes were wide with alarm which made something surge inside him, it was so endearing.

'No, not seen it yet. What do you think about *White Christmas* for later?'

'Perfect. Any thoughts on *It's a Wonderful Life*?' she asked him with a very serious expression on her face. How he answered that question meant something to her.

'Okay, this might be controversial so I'm going to need assurance that you're not going to throw me out into the snow.'

'You don't like it, do you?'

'Sorry.'

'Neither do I! I've never told anyone that before. I don't know why there are Christmas Eve screenings of it everywhere when people, not all people obviously but me and you at least, would much rather see something more Christmassy. It's just not festive enough.'

Amy loved the film. He'd never understood it. He'd bet good money that she'd watched it last night. It was another sign.

The fire was back to its former glory. 'Right. I'm going to put the dinner on and make some mulled wine to have with the film. Do we need snacks?'

'Shall we have some Twiglets?'

'No. I'll suggest Cheeselets instead and accept that we

don't agree on everything.'

He could still hear Lois laughing when he got to the kitchen and he realised he had a huge grin on his face too. He couldn't remember the last time he'd laughed like that with Amy. This unexpected Christmas was highlighting all the differences between his life and this try-out life he had for a couple of days with Lois. Yes, it was skewed because of the season and because of the snow but it still niggled him. He'd rather be with Lois.

He put the roast into the oven and put the potatoes on to boil. The mulled wine smelled fantastic. He'd added some orange liquor which Lois had found in the cupboard the day before and a sachet of mulled wine spice which he had brought with him. While it was heating gently on the stove, he took out his phone. There was a missed call from Amy. He'd called her first thing that morning, so he was surprised she'd called again.

'Hi, how's it going?'

'Where were you when I called?' There was no let-up at all.

'I went out for a walk and forgot to take my phone. Sorry. Are you having a good time?' He tried to take the weariness out of his voice.

'Yes, it's been lovely. I went sledging with Mum and Lottie,' her niece, 'and we're just settling down to watch a film. I miss you.'

'I know, me too.'

'What are you doing tonight? I bet there's not much going on in Croftwood is there?'

'No, it's going to be a quiet night in. I'm going to watch *Love Actually* and open a bottle of wine.'

'I'm sorry we weren't together today, Oliver. I should have stayed in Croftwood until you were ready to leave and then we'd be together now.'

'Just enjoy being with your parents, Ames. Next year.'

'Yes, next year will be our year. And Oliver, I'm sorry I've been such a bitch about the book club and things. You know I love you, I'm just a bit insecure.'

He assumed the 'things' were Lois. Most of the arguments they'd had recently revolved around the book club and Lois and whatever he thought was going to happen with him and Amy, he was glad that she could see reason.

'It's fine, Ames. I know things have been difficult. Maybe these couple of days apart will help.'

'Maybe.' She sounded uptight again.

Perhaps he shouldn't have said that. 'So, have a great evening and I'll call you tomorrow?'

'Happy Christmas, Oliver. I love you.'

'Happy Christmas, Ames. Talk to you tomorrow.'

He exhaled. He might have been holding his breath for that whole conversation. He felt like he was lying to Amy for the first time since he'd got to Lois's. Before, he'd felt justified in being secretive because he knew, or thought he knew, what Amy's reaction would be if he told her the truth. But now, he wondered if he'd made the right decision because however amazing the past two days had been, it had cast huge doubts for him over his relationship with Amy and that was not going to be easy to navigate.

41

Lois lay in bed wondering whether Oliver was up yet. She had planned to make some eggy bread for breakfast so she needed to get downstairs first. She didn't want him to start breakfast before she had the chance, but she was so cosy, it was hard to drag herself out of bed. Christmas had been brilliant. Going from thinking she'd be alone as she stood on the platform at Foregate Street station only two days ago to having what she truly felt was the best Christmas she'd ever had, it seemed unbelievable.

She had to admit that she'd put Amy out of her mind entirely. She and Oliver had existed for the past two days in a little bubble. It was fleeting, unexpected and Lois knew that she'd feel absolutely gutted when it was over because whatever she'd told herself, she'd allowed herself to get close to Oliver again. To almost imagine that they were together. The only thing missing was the physical side of things. Otherwise, it was exactly as she imagined their relationship would be if they'd been able to find out.

She sighed and threw back the duvet. The jumper which she'd worn the day before was on the chair but even though they'd both been in their pyjamas for most of the past couple of days she needed to give the appearance of having made a slight effort, so she pulled a different one out of the drawer.

Oliver was still asleep, or at least the door was shut. Lois put her ear to the door, just to check and could hear him talking in hushed tones.

'You should have said you were planning to come back today. I would have made sure to be there when you got back... I know, I know... just a mate in Worcester...No, I'll leave now... no, no...Ames...look... okay.'

Lois crept as quickly as she could down the stairs and started making the eggy bread. A few minutes later, Oliver appeared in the kitchen with his coat on and his bag over his shoulder.

'Oh, you're making breakfast.' He looked frazzled and ran his hand through his unbrushed hair.

'It's only eggy bread. Are you leaving?'

'I'm so sorry Lois. Amy's back at the flat. I didn't know she was coming back today but the roads are better now, so she left early this morning. I'm so sorry.'

She couldn't have felt sadder, but she didn't want him to feel bad about having to leave so suddenly. 'Honestly Oliver, I can easily eat your share. Go, it's fine.'

He came over to her. 'Thanks, Lois. It's been the most amazing Christmas.' He leant towards her and kissed her gently on the lips.

It was the only good thing about him leaving. The kiss was perfect. A perfect ending if there had to be one.

'It has, thanks for suggesting it,' she said brightly. If he didn't leave soon, she was going to start crying right in front of him.

'Okay. Well, come into the coffee house when you're back at work.'

'Yep, I will.' She managed to smile.

'Bye.' He backed out of the kitchen, pulling the door to behind him.

Lois managed to finish cooking her eggy bread and get settled on the sofa before the tears started running down her cheeks.

She'd known it would end like this for her, but she didn't care. It hurt but she wouldn't have changed a single thing about any of it. The last two days had been worth what was to come, and the memory of the kiss would stay with her for a long time. Today and maybe the next day, she'd let herself wallow while she could still use the excuse of Christmas to get away with lying on the sofa all day watching television without feeling the need to get dressed. And after that, she'd go back to pretending she wasn't in love with Oliver and hope that eventually, she'd start believing it.

42

Steph was at the Hive loading the library van. It was New Year's Day, and she wasn't feeling a hundred per cent after a heavy night of drinking and endless talking with Tom but the van needed loading ready for the next day. At least she had the place to herself, and she had managed to get the books ready the week before so it wasn't anything she needed to think too hard about. Tom had offered to come and help her, but he was in the middle of lesson planning and they'd seen enough of each other over the past two weeks. She was ready for some time to herself.

'Hey, Steph.'

'Lois! You made me jump. What are you doing lurking around here?'

'I thought I'd come and give you a hand.'

Lois looked pretty miserable. Steph felt a pang of guilt that she'd hardly given her friend a thought since before Christmas.

'Good Christmas?'

'Yes, amazing actually.' Her face lit up for a second but then went straight back to glum.

'So, what's up? You wish you were still at Jim's?' It seemed unlikely.

'The trains were cancelled because of the snow so I had Christmas at home.'

'By yourself? Oh, Lois, I wish you'd rung me, I would have come and hung out with you after Christmas.'

'I wasn't alone.' She looked furtive. 'Oliver came to stay for a couple of days.'

'Oliver? Bloody hell, Lois! He finally got his act together and dumped Amy?'

'No. But Steph, we had the most amazing time. We watched Christmas movies, went to the Cathedral on Christmas morning, he cooked the most amazing Christmas dinner, and it was just the best two days of my life.'

'So, what's with this glumness?' Steph waved her hand in front of Lois's face. Sometimes it was like getting blood out of a stone.

'It was like a stolen Christmas, so unbelievably unlikely and I knew what it was, I know he's with Amy, but I let myself forget about that and now…it's shit. I feel worse than I thought I would about it and I can't seem to pull myself out of this slump. And it's that bloody awards evening in London next week and I'll be with him again and I just don't know if I can do it.'

Steph hadn't seen Lois like this before. She'd breezed through her relationship with Alex taking all the crap he threw at her in her stride, almost not noticing. But this was different. She was in love with Oliver and Steph wasn't sure there was any advice she could give that would help.

'You can do it. You have to approach it like you would when you tackle Rosemary. I've never seen you be so firm and matter-of-fact as you are in those meetings with her. Look how you sorted it out when you first started at Croftwood and she'd turned up for work as if nothing had changed. You need to be like that, Lois. Stand your ground, don't let him know you're feeling like this, put on a persona that shows him you can handle being with him. Be breezy.'

'It's all very well saying that but the only way I almost got over him in the first place was by avoiding him. Just being with him, Steph.' She sighed. 'He smells so good and he's going to be wearing a suit.'

Steph laughed. 'It's so funny that Oliver in a suit does it for you whereas Tom in a suit does the opposite for me.'

Lois looked slightly more cheerful and even managed a chuckle. 'Oh, god Steph. You're right. It's a work thing, I can just be professional.'

'See? Steph knows. Come on, we need to get these shelves filled.'

They'd finally called it a day at four o'clock. All the books were in, there were just a few things to sort out in the morning. Lois seemed a lot better, it had probably taken her mind off things. It also made Steph realise how lucky she was to have found Tom. Being together almost solidly for the past two weeks had been great, if a little smothering compared with what she'd been used to in previous relationships but after spending the day away from him she was looking forward to spending the evening together and was relieved that she wasn't full of angst like Lois.

She rang the bell when she got to his house. They hadn't got quite as far as exchanging keys; it had only been a few weeks after all.

He opened the door and beamed at Steph before taking her into his arms and kissing her as he pulled her inside and kicked the door shut behind her.

'You're pleased to see me,' she said breathlessly.

'Longest day of my life.'

Oh god, she fancied him so much.

43

'What are you going to wear?' Linda was giving Lois the third degree about the plans for the awards ceremony.

'I've got a dress, it's midnight blue, long and has tulle sleeves.'

'And shoes? Not boots, Lois. Even under a long dress.'

Lois grinned. She had thought about it. 'No, I've got some heels. Black patent boots with high heels and pointy toes. Boots are the only kind of heels I can walk in.'

'Do you know, David emailed me asking if he could use the pitch I used for the competition entry for his speech. Isn't that brilliant? He said it 'evoked the spirit of Croftwood'.'

'That's great, Linda. I'm sorry again that we can't all go. We all deserve to go but we'll have a proper celebration of our own soon.'

'I'm glad you and Oliver are going.' Linda looked pointedly at Lois. She had been rooting for them all along however futile that was.

'Right. Well, I'd better check the emails.' She took refuge in the office.

She hadn't seen Oliver since the kiss in her kitchen on

Boxing Day. She'd not been to the coffee house, and he'd not been to the library. Thankfully the next book club wasn't until after the awards ceremony so she wouldn't have to see him at all until they got the train to London together. She'd considered booking seats in separate carriages on the train but that would just postpone the awkwardness until the actual event so maybe it was just as well to get that out of the way on the train journey.

Aside from the anxiety she had about going with Oliver, she had started to get excited about the awards ceremony. It was being held in the London Library, a private library in the West End and somewhere she'd always wanted to go. That in itself was a once-in-a-lifetime opportunity and if they did win, it would be the icing on the cake.

Would she be able to get through the whole night being friendly to Oliver without betraying how she felt? She had played the events of that last morning in her kitchen over and over in her mind. He hadn't been honest with Any when she'd overheard him talking to her. She'd asked him not to tell anyone and he was sticking by that promise, at least then. But she was worried that face to face, he wouldn't be able to avoid telling her the truth about Christmas. Had he told her? Every time Lois left the library, she worried about bumping into them. She had to get a grip. After the trip to London, she would avoid him and then it would only be a couple of months until the library closed and she went back to her job at the Hive and that would solve the problem for good.

There was a knock at the door and Linda popped her head in. 'Rosemary's just arrived. Some sort of problem with the book club.'

'Thanks, Linda, I won't be a sec.'

She took a deep breath. Enough about Oliver. She was going to forge her own way, be by herself and enjoy that freedom for a while and the awards dinner was going to be her starting point.

'Hi, Rosemary, Happy New Year.'

'Hello, Lois. Yes, and to you. There is a problem with the book club. We have had some unwanted social media contact which needs addressing.'

Linda looked like a rabbit in the headlights and disappeared into the children's library. She obviously knew what was coming.

'What's the problem, Rosemary?'

'We have had several tweets from people who are under the assumption that we will arrange dates for them. At the book club.'

'Haven't we been through this before? If people want to use the book club to meet people that's okay.'

'This is a little more salacious, Lois. People are implying that we are a dating club for pensioners. Apparently, the Worcester News ran a story about William Templeton meeting the new love of his life at Oliver's and now we are being inundated with requests from people wanting to join the date night at Oliver's. Not the book club, Lois, date night!'

Rosemary had turned quite red; such was her indignation. Lois had to turn away to allow herself a quick giggle before turning back with a straight face.

'I think we have to go down the 'no publicity is bad publicity' road, Rosemary. It's great for us and Oliver that the paper ran that story. Some people have just got the wrong end of the stick, that's all. No harm done. We'll ask Linda to reply with a friendly reminder that it's a book club.'

'It's the name, Lois. Date-with-a-book. I knew we would run into trouble.' She stood, shaking her head.

'Rosemary. The library will be closed two months from now. There's no point changing the name now.'

Rosemary gave a gentle harrumph and picked up her bag.

'I hope you know what you're doing. It could ruin the reputation of the library. Forever.' Then she turned on her heel and left.

'I'm so sorry,' Linda said, appearing at the desk. 'I had no idea she'd take it like that. I thought the tweets were really funny and the article about Eunice and Bill was wonderful. I should have remembered to tell you about it, so you were ready for Rosemary.'

'Don't worry. No harm done. Rosemary's been desperate to tell me she told me so for ages. It could have been about anything. Is that true about that couple getting together from going to the book club?'

'Well, it's got a bit of spin on it. They were both on Steph's mobile library visit to the book club and Eunice recognised Bill from a film he starred in in the 1960s or something. Very romantic.'

'Wow. Perhaps we should get David to add that into his speech.'

'That would send Rosemary right over the edge!'

'She'll never know.'

'I think she's asked Oliver to film it on his phone for her. Although, if we win, will it not be you and Oliver who go up for the award?'

'I doubt it. At this stage, I think David thinks it's down to him that we got nominated at all.'

'All the people that matter know that's not true, Lois.'

'Exactly. And that's why we'll have our own party afterwards that everyone can come to.'

44

It was already noon and the coffee house had been so busy that Oliver still hadn't made it upstairs to change and he was supposed to meet Lois at the station at one.

'Sorry Pats, I'm going to have to leave you in the lurch. I need to go and get ready.'

'It's fine, go on,' she said, good-naturedly in the face of an ever-extending queue. 'I know how long it takes you to get your hair right.'

He grinned and flicked at her with a tea towel. 'Thanks. Are you still okay to open up in the morning?' They were getting the last train back from London and he knew he'd need a lie-in.

'No problem, boss. Alice is covering tonight at the cinema, so I'll be up bright and early. Have a great time if I don't see you before you go.'

He raced upstairs where Amy was sitting in the corner of the sofa watching the end of This Morning.

'Ames, did you have a chance to iron my shirt?'

'It's hanging on the wardrobe door,' she said without taking her eyes away from the screen.

'Thanks. And do you think the navy tie or the green one?'

'Does it matter?'

He sighed. Things had been even worse between them since Christmas, if that was possible. After the Christmas Day phone call, he'd thought she'd resolved to be more understanding but after she'd come home on Boxing Day to find he wasn't there, well, that seemed to have taken her insecurity to a whole new level.

He whipped off his clothes and jumped under the shower, being as quick as he could. As he was in such a hurry, he blow-dried the worst of the water from his hair before he got dressed and then finished off by sorting out his quiff – it had to look good today – and splashing some aftershave on. He decided on the blue tie. It was a Liberty floral print and he thought Lois would like it.

'That's the aftershave I got you for Christmas,' said Amy, leaning against the door frame.'

'It's nice, isn't it?' he said as he tied his shoes.

'It'd be even nicer if you were wearing it to go out with me.'

He looked up, hoping to see that she was smiling even though there had been no humour in her voice.

'Sorry, Ames. I didn't think.' And he didn't have time for this now.

'I thought you were going to take me out as I'm letting you go to this awards thing.'

Letting him? 'I am going to take you out but let's get it straight, I'm not going because you're letting me, Amy. I'm going because I want to.'

'And you always do what you want.'

'I don't have time for this. I'm going to miss the train. We'll talk about it tomorrow.' If they had to. He shrugged his smart black wool coat on and made sure he had his wallet and phone. 'Right, I'm off.'

'Aren't you going to kiss me goodbye?'

He pecked her cheek and then ran down the stairs.

The taxi he'd booked was waiting outside and he slumped gratefully into the back seat wondering how he had got himself into this mess with Amy. He'd thought they were picking up where they left off, but she wasn't the Amy he'd known before. He'd understood that things would be different, but this? This was unbearable. If she wasn't feeling the same way, he'd be amazed. The antagonism between them was there all the time and yet they still hadn't addressed the issues they had. All the arguments they had were superficial, always about something he had done that she was unhappy about. In the beginning, he'd thought it was natural that getting back together would throw up problems as they tried to fit back into each other's lives but as time went on it had become clear to him that it was more than that.

Over Christmas, he had come to realise something that he had only just begun to admit to himself. He loved Lois. He'd tried to ignore it, tried to get things on track with Amy but it wasn't working and even though he didn't know whether that was because of how he felt about Lois or whether things would have been hard with Amy anyway, what he did know was that this feeling he had wasn't going away. Lois was in his head all of the time. Everything that happened with Amy, he played through his head how Lois would have behaved in the same situation. It wasn't fair on Amy, he knew that, but it was hard to be sympathetic towards her when she gave him nothing but grief. He couldn't deny, his imagination painted a very rosy view of a life with Lois, and he was smart enough to know that real life wouldn't match up to that, and yet it had. The few stolen days at Christmas had been like a dream. A dream that he wanted to live every day.

The train was waiting on the platform when he arrived at

the station. He jumped on and heard the whistle go a few seconds later. It was close. He checked his ticket for his seat number. C28. He exhaled. Tonight was about work. Whatever he felt for Lois, he had to behave just as he had at Christmas because at the moment, they were friends. But he was going to speak to Amy tomorrow and end it, and having decided that, he felt like a weight had lifted off him.

'Oh my god, I thought you'd missed the train!' said Lois as soon as she saw him.

'Sorry, I did cut it a bit fine. We had an early lunch rush.' He took his coat off, folded it and put it on the overhead rack then sat down next to her.

'I'm so excited,' she said, her eyes sparkling. 'Even if we don't win, it's going to be amazing.'

The London Library was everything Lois had hoped when she had looked at the images of it online. Because of the awards ceremony, it had been closed to the public for the afternoon and evening which only added to the anticipation.

The entrance, off St James's Square near Piccadilly, belied the size of the library within.

'There are seventeen miles of shelving,' said Lois, as they walked into the foyer, forgetting that she was going to be business-like with Oliver and letting her excitement get the better of her.

'Wow, it's incredible. I've never seen anything like it.'

Lois looked at him, expecting to see that he was making fun of her, but he looked genuinely amazed.

They picked up their programme for the evening and a glass of something bubbly and were invited to explore the library for the next hour until it was time to take their seats for the ceremony.

The library had been described as labyrinthine and that

was exactly right. Lois had read that it had expanded over the years into many of the adjacent buildings and the narrow iron walkways and stairs which led to little nooks and crannies that were crammed with volumes and volumes of books as far as they could see was a testament to its organic growth.

'I'd move to London if I could work here.' The feeling that she got from this place was incredible. It was like the nostalgia of her childhood library experiences on speed and she wanted to drink it all in knowing that she may not get another chance to visit.

'It's a far cry from the Hive or Croftwood Library, that's for sure,' said Oliver.

They walked through what felt like a tunnel of books, although shelves were stretching above and below them far higher and lower than they could reach until they came upon a gap in the shelves where there were a couple of easy chairs. It was a reading nook.

'Shall we?' asked Oliver.

Lois smiled and sat down, enjoying the feeling of being in a secret corner of the library where maybe no-one else would come across them.

'I was a bit worried about tonight,' she said, realising that the bubbly had loosened her tongue. 'I thought things might be awkward between us.'

'Oh. Why?' He looked bemused.

'Well, Christmas was so great and then we had to go back to normal...' She stopped to gather her thoughts. 'And I thought it might be weird for us to try and be friends again after having Christmas together.'

'You haven't been to the coffee house. Is that what you mean by normal?' He looked sad.

He had noticed. She hadn't thought it would be that obvious.

'I loved Christmas, Oliver.'

'I know, so did I.' He reached out his hand. She took it.

'The hardest thing I've ever had to do was settle for being friends with you,' she said, trying to convey how she felt as she looked into his eyes. 'I told myself I'd be all aloof and cool tonight then I would avoid you until the library closed and I'd never have to see you again.'

'That's not what you want is it?' He was stroking his thumb across the back of her hand.

'No, it's not what I want but it's the only thing I can do. Being here tonight is so magical that I can't pretend to be aloof. I can't pretend there's nothing between us.' She watched his face for a sign, anything that would tell her he felt the same way.

'I'm glad, Lois. I want you to have the night you deserve and make sure we enjoy every minute of this together.'

What he was saying was perfect, but it wasn't going to end up like that.

'Just for tonight.'

'For tonight.' He leaned in and kissed her on the cheek. It was a lingering kiss, not in the same league as the kitchen kiss but more than she could have hoped for. Enough to give her the collywobbles from the smell of him and she suddenly realised she had nothing to lose. Maybe it was the bubbly or maybe she was finally ready to try and get what she wanted for once instead of settling for whatever was on offer to her.

'Actually, tonight isn't enough.' She closed her eyes briefly so she could pretend to herself that she wasn't talking to Oliver. 'Trying to carry on like normal since Christmas has been the hardest thing I've ever done. Being friends when I want it to be more than that is killing me. I'm not doing it anymore, Oliver. I think there's something special between us and if you think the same, then I'm here. If not, I've made the biggest idiot of myself and thank god I'll be moving on from Croftwood soon.' She held her breath, stunned by what she'd blurted out but really proud of herself.

'I do feel the same. I spent Christmas with you, pretending that I didn't have a life with Amy, and I've been miserable since. I'm going to talk to her tomorrow.' He put his finger to her lips as she opened her mouth to protest, 'I'd decided before I got on the train. I'm not doing it because of us, Lois. I'm doing it for me. Amy and I, we're not working. I don't know what I was thinking by letting it go this far. We've both been unhappier than we were when it ended last time.'

Tears sprang to her eyes when she heard him say he felt the same. She'd hoped but it had seemed impossible and admitting her feelings had been the last resort to find some closure for herself. She hadn't dared to hope that he would be ready to change his life for her.

'Okay. But you have to speak to Amy before anything else happens.'

'Deal.' He gave her the briefest of kisses on the cheek and they grinned at each other like fools until an announcement over the tannoy broke the spell.

They managed to find their way back to the reading room where the event was being held. Worcestershire County Libraries had a table to themselves which was near the back of the room. Was that a bad sign? David and his people were mingling around the table.

'Lois! Welcome,' he said, flamboyantly. He was dressed in evening dress as were the rest of his entourage, none of whom Lois had met before.

'Hello, David.' He insisted on doing the double kiss thing. 'This is Oliver.'

'Good to meet you, Oliver. Amazing contribution to the Croftwood book club,' he said, pumping Oliver's hand.

'Thanks. It's all Lois, though.' He beamed at her with a look that summed up everything they'd said to each other. The best thing was, she knew he was proud of her, and she didn't think anyone had thought that way about her before.

45

The libraries that had been shortlisted for the Community Spirit award were displayed on the screen behind the host of the ceremony, Sue Perkins.

'So now we move to my favourite category, the award for Community Spirit. I know you shouldn't have favourites, but this award shows which libraries make the biggest difference to their communities and we have some fabulous contenders tonight.'

She went ahead, listing the other five libraries in the category. Then said, 'And Croftwood Library. I have to say this is my favourite entry, and I can say that because the actual result has already been decided.' She waved the envelope. 'Any library that uses books as a matchmaking tool is a winner in my mind.'

Everyone laughed and clapped. Oliver took Lois's hand under the table and squeezed it, his other hand holding his phone up to record the moment. David crossed his fingers dramatically and grinned at his colleagues around the table.

'And the winner of the Community Spirit award is...' Lois scrunched her eyes shut. She wanted them to win so badly but it seemed so unlikely.

'Croftwood Library in Worcestershire!'

Everyone around the table stood up while the rest of the room erupted with rapturous applause. David made his way to the stage with a huge smile on his face and shook hands with Sue Perkins, reaching into his pocket for his speech as he waited for the applause to die down.

'No offence David,' said Sue, looking his name up on her cue cards, 'but you don't look like the kind of chap who would have been the mastermind of this date-with-a-book club.'

Everyone laughed and David blushed. If he'd been involved in it, he probably could have made a witty comeback but Sue was right and he knew it.

'Come on David, who do we have to thank for this genius idea?'

Oliver stood up and began clapping as he looked down at Lois who stared at him in a state of mortified embarrassment. The rest of the room joined in, and Sue began gesturing for Lois to join her on the stage. Oliver grabbed her hand and led the way between the tables to the front of the room.

'What's your name, my love?' asked Sue, once Lois had climbed the couple of steps onto the stage, thankfully assisted by Oliver because the heels were a hindrance.

'Lois Morgan, I'm the manager of Croftwood Library.'

'And who's your handsome friend? And did you meet at the date-with-a-book club, more to the point.'

Everyone laughed apart from David, who Lois could feel seething next to her having had his moment of glory snatched away.

'This is Oliver Jones. He runs the coffee house in Croftwood where the book club started,' explained Lois.

'Marvellous! And wonderful to meet a success story from your book club.' She made her hands into a heart shape and

Victoria Walker

won another laugh from the audience.

'Thank you to everyone who voted for us,' said Lois into the microphone. 'We love Croftwood Library and all our customers, and we hope that the date-with-a-book club carries on even after it closes.'

Lois was past caring that everyone was misunderstanding the book club and thought it was a dating service and instead was enjoying the fact that Sue had thwarted David's speech-making opportunity. And what did it matter if everyone knew that Croftwood Library was due to close? It was wrong. This award should help to celebrate and save the library. That was what was important, not what the County Libraries PR people said.

'Well done Croftwood Library!' The room erupted again and Lois, Oliver and David returned to their seats.

'God, David looks cheesed off,' Lois said to Oliver while the room was still noisy.

'This is your night, Lois. Serves him right for trying to gate crash our party.'

After another hour or so, the category awards were over, and it was time for the big overall Library of the Year award. David had lost interest now, sure that Croftwood wouldn't have a hope in hell of winning the main award and Lois was inclined to agree with him. The competition was stiff, very stiff, so she was just enjoying the rest of the night with Oliver while it lasted.

All the same, while the contenders were being listed by Sue, Oliver squeezed her hand when Croftwood Library was mentioned again.

'And now I hand over to Sebastian Caulder from the British Library who will present the award.'

Sue melted into the shadows at the side of the stage while Sebastian stood at the podium.

'The British Library was delighted to be represented on the

judging panel for this year's awards. We were incredibly impressed with the standard of entries we received this year which truly represents the valuable work being done in libraries right across the country. This year's winner was chosen because we believe it illustrates the resilience that libraries have had to demonstrate over the past few years. Many libraries have been lost to cost-cutting and the digital revolution but there is a way forward. Our winner for Library of the Year is Croftwood Library in Worcestershire.'

The room erupted with applause and cheers while Lois sat, dazed, not sure whether she had just hoped for him to say Croftwood Library or whether he actually had. Then David appeared at her side and held out his arm for Lois to take. He had clearly got over his annoyance now that he was on the winning table.

She stood up, looked at Oliver who took her face in his hands and gave her a big kiss, with tears in his eyes as he pulled away.

'Go on, Lois. This is your moment,' he said.

Lois took David's arm and they walked to the stage, people congratulating them as they went.

'Congratulations! David, your time has come,' said Sue Perkins gesturing that he should take the stage.

'Thank you,' he said. 'I am beyond thrilled that Croftwood Library has won this award. As you may have heard, this library had been due to close in March. The pressure to save money is immense for any county library service. Worcestershire is no different and sadly, Croftwood was an easy target. This young woman, Lois Morgan has turned its fortunes around in just a few months by making it valuable to its community again. This award is hers. Lois.'

David stood aside to let Lois speak. She had no idea what she was going to say, she hadn't thought there would be the remotest possibility of winning but once she stood there, looking at Oliver who was standing at the back watching her and smiling, it was easy.

'Thank you for this award. I've only worked at Croftwood Library for a few months. When I arrived, I was supposed to look after it until it was closed down for good. But there was something about it that made me want to do my best for it. It's the library of my childhood and I'm sure yours too. I can still remember the moment I realised that I could take these precious books home with me, books which give us all hopes, dreams, ideas, and access to worlds we would never know otherwise. But people started to find their dreams in other places, they found other ways to discover new things, and Croftwood and lots of other libraries lost their place in the world. What we've done over the past few months was to show that even in this age where many libraries have reinvented themselves for the modern world, there is still a place for libraries like ours that could so easily be written off and closed. People will always love books even if they can buy them without leaving the house and if we have found a way to engage people with our library when there is less reason than ever for them to need to, it's because some things can never be replaced and there is a whole new generation of people who are discovering the magic that a library can give them. I'm delighted that the judges have seen Croftwood Library the same way that we do. Thank you.'

Everyone in the room stood up and applauded while Sebastian kissed Lois on the cheek and presented her with the award; a glass book with 'Croftwood Library – Library of the Year 2023' engraved on the front. She walked back to the table in a daze, with David following behind her.

'I underestimated you, Lois,' he said once they had made their way to the back of the room. 'I have to admit I thought we had no chance but Library of the Year, well. I think we'll have to look at our closure decision in light of this.

Congratulations.'

'Thank you, David.' It wasn't a promise to save the library, but it was at least in a less precarious position than when they'd arrived that evening.

Oliver was on cloud nine, so he couldn't imagine how Lois must be feeling having won the Library of the Year award. It was astounding and he was so proud of her.

Knowing that they needed to catch the last train back to Worcester, he was keeping half an eye on the time, but every time Lois came back to the table, someone else came to ask her to meet someone or other and time was ticking on. It got to the point where they had to leave within the next five minutes to have any hope of getting to Paddington in time and Lois was deep in conversation with Sebastian whatshisname from the British Library. She was having the time of her life. He could see from the expression on her face that she was talking passionately – probably about libraries or books. Either way, he was loath to interrupt her because how often did anyone have a night like this? So he made a decision. They would stay in London.

'Oh my god,' she said, sitting down next to him and taking a large sip of wine. 'I can't believe I have been talking to Sebastian about Croftwood. It's insane! He was asking me all about what we'd been doing, even the date-with-a-book club which he absolutely loved. He thinks they might try it at the British Library to encourage younger people in, so I told him about Eunice and Bill and he thought that was wonderful!'

Her face was a picture of happiness. She looked beautiful, sparkling and full of delight. More than anything, he wanted to tell her that he loved her. At this very minute, he loved her. The whole world had melted away and they were here together, and he loved her.

'Lois, I think we should stay in London tonight.' He wanted to break it to her gently that they'd already missed the last train.

'Oh, no. I'm ready to go whenever you are. It's fine.' Whatever she said, he could see that she was sorry the night was about to come to an end.

'Well, the last train left half an hour ago, so I don't think we have any choice.'

Rather than being alarmed as he'd feared, she threw her head back and laughed. 'Oh god, we missed the train? I don't even care. We won!'

She threw her arms around his neck and hugged him. 'This has been the most amazing night,' she said pulling away. 'I'm so glad we came together.'

'Me too.'

The rest of the people at their table left, as did many of the other people, but not before David arranged a meeting with her for the following week. Sue Perkins also came over and congratulated Lois again before she left.

'I suppose we'd better find somewhere to stay?' she asked Oliver.

'I've booked a room at The Cavendish, it's around the corner from here. A twin room, if that's okay,' he added.

'Thanks, that sounds great. I can't believe I didn't notice what time it was.'

Some music began playing and some of the staff began clearing the tables away.

'I think it's our cue to leave,' said Oliver. But then a few people began dancing in the space that was being cleared and no-one seemed to mind. 'Or shall we have a quick dance before we go.'

'Definitely,' said Lois, leaning down to unzip her boots.

'Oh, you're planning on some serious dancing?'

'Is there any other kind?'

He led her over to the small space where the handful of other dancers manoeuvred around to allow them in, then he put his hands on her waist and pulled her towards him.

'You were amazing tonight.'

She buried her head into his chest and when she looked up, she was grinning. 'Thanks. I can't believe tonight. It's been insane. I so wish that Linda and Rosemary had been able to come.'

That would have made it an entirely different night for him, so he didn't wish the same. He had loved every minute of the day since he'd stepped onto the train that afternoon. The decision he'd made to end things with Amy was the right thing to do.

46

Lois felt so embarrassed having to travel home on the train in the outfit she'd worn the day before, with no make-up and her hair a tangled mess on the top of her head. It was a far cry from the glamour of the night before and she also had a terrific headache.

She was at least sat with Oliver who didn't mind that she leaned her head on his shoulder and closed her eyes as soon as they got on the train that morning. She'd texted Linda the night before and asked if she would hold the fort and she knew that Oliver had Patsy opening up for him, so they'd had a lie-in and a lazy breakfast in the room.

The dancing had gone on at the London Library until 2 am by which time Lois and Oliver were the only actual guests left, everyone else was either catering staff or people who worked at the library.

They'd got to the hotel minutes after leaving the library, it was that close, and because Lois was clutching her award, had been upgraded to an amazing room on the 15th floor with a balcony.

They'd raided the minibar for a nightcap and sat on the

balcony talking until neither of them could keep their eyes open any more.

When they'd finally fallen into bed, she and Oliver had lain, watching each other until they'd fallen asleep.

The morning had been fairly awkward. Taking turns to use the bathroom, both avoiding looking at each other until they were both showered and dressed. At least Oliver looked amazing still with his shirt unbuttoned and his hair pushed back, slick from the shower. Lois thought she'd never looked worse. Having nothing with her, she couldn't even put a dash of mascara on or sort her hair out properly.

As she dozed on Oliver's shoulder, she wondered how things would play out once they got back to Worcester. He was going to call it off with Amy, and then what? She supposed they might start dating properly, picking up where they'd started. That's what she hoped.

They hadn't talked about Amy last night. They'd both talked about everything but that and what would be in their future together. It hadn't seemed right to start making plans when Amy still didn't know what Oliver was planning to do and Lois was keen that it didn't look as if he was doing it for her.

But now, as she snuggled into his side, feeling her award in his coat pocket next to her, she couldn't believe how lucky she was that he was going to be hers. Finally.

The taxi dropped Lois at her house in Worcester and then continued to Croftwood. Oliver went into the coffee house through the front door and was greeted by an enthusiastic Patsy.

'So, the library won?'

He nodded. He'd sent her a text letting her know he wouldn't be working that day until later than he'd planned.

'God, that's amazing! No wonder you decided to stay the night, I bet you were celebrating hard.'

'Yes, it was brilliant. They had an impromptu after-party, so we stayed there until late. Mind you, we'd already missed the train by the time we found out about that.'

'The trains don't run very late though, do they? It can ruin the end of a good party.'

'Exactly. Any sign of Amy this morning?'

Patsy shook her head. 'All quiet on the western front,' she said and went back to loading the dishwasher.

Oliver climbed the stairs with a feeling of dread in his stomach. He had decided to talk to Amy straight away. There was no point in dragging it out. He let himself into the flat and found her lying on the sofa watching the end of Homes Under the Hammer.

'Morning,' he said as brightly as he could muster.

She sat up and glared at him. 'I can't believe you didn't come home last night.'

'I'm sorry, I did leave you a message, but it was late when we decided. I didn't plan to.'

'When you and Lois decided? Who else was with you?'

'It was just us.'

'Just you. Exactly. And you think that's okay, Oliver? When I didn't want you to go anyway? You think it's fine to stay out for the whole night with Lois!' She almost spat at him.

'Amy, look. We need to talk.' If ever there was a time to end things, it was now. She was making herself crazy with thoughts of what she imagined was going on. Now that he was closer than ever to that being the truth, it wasn't fair on her to let things carry on. He sat down next to her on the sofa. 'I think we both know this isn't working. It's not working for me, I do know that much and I wanted to try so badly because it was what you wanted but I'm not sure even that's true anymore.'

He could see the fight go out of her. Maybe this was going to be okay. Maybe she could see it too.

'I'm pregnant.'

Lois had another shower when she got in so that she could sort out her hair properly and she changed into her dungarees which were her favourite item of clothing and the complete antithesis of the dress she had been wearing for too long.

The bike ride into Croftwood was lovely. It was a crisp bright January day and any ice that would have been on the road that morning had disappeared by the time she set off which made for a much more relaxing journey than she'd had on most mornings recently.

She had the award in the basket on the front of her bike, wrapped in a jumper, having insisted to Oliver that she needed to have it with her when she got to the library rather than going with his suggestion that he would drop it in later that day.

She locked her bike up outside as there was no chance of rain, took out the award and went inside. Linda was at the desk and gave a huge whoop as she saw Lois holding it aloft.

'Oh my goodness! I watched the whole thing on the Facebook Live feed! It was amazing! Oh, Lois, your speech.' She gave Lois a fierce hug.

'It is amazing, Linda. I can't believe we won! We won the whole thing!'

'What do you think will happen now? They can't close down the Library of the Year, can they?'

'I've got a meeting with David next week, but he seemed to suggest they couldn't. He was very magnanimous. I don't think he realised that what we've done means so much to people.'

'Good! It's about time they all realised. And you had a lovely time? You looked wonderful in that dress, Lois.'

'Thanks. It was brilliant, the whole thing. The London Library is unbelievable, full of nooks and crannies and just crammed with books from floor to ceiling.'

'And Oliver enjoyed it?'

Lois knew that her face was incapable of being cool about it. She nodded. 'He did. We had the most amazing time.'

Linda squeezed her hand. 'Good, and not a moment too soon. Coffee and cake to celebrate?'

'I'd better not…'

'I'll go,' said Linda, matter-of-factly.

'That'd be lovely. Thanks.'

Late that afternoon after Linda had gone and Lois was about to lock up, Oliver came into the library. He didn't look great. Maybe last night was catching up with him.

'Hi,' she smiled and went around the other side of the desk.

He took her in his arms and hugged her, nestling his face into her neck and giving her a tender kiss. But when he pulled away, he had tears in his eyes.

Lois locked the door and led him to the beanbags where he slumped down into one with her next to him.

'What happened?'

'I tried to tell her, Lois.'

'Oh.' He hadn't managed to do it. She'd thought he was going to, that he'd made his mind up even before what had happened last night.

'She's pregnant.'

Lois knew without him saying anything else, what was going to happen. He was going to stay with Amy because he was that kind of person. Loyal.

He wiped his eyes with the back of his hand. 'I can't believe it.'

'Are you happy about the baby?' Because even if he was being forced down a road he didn't choose, that at least was something positive to come out of the whole mess.

He looked at her in despair. 'I don't know. It's such a shock. I thought I'd have kids one day but… not like this.'

Lois was torn between giving Oliver the support he needed and telling him that it would all be okay, and self-preservation. Because her world had seemed perfect for almost a whole day and now it was crumbling.

'Plenty of people have surprise pregnancies when the timing isn't perfect.'

Oliver looked at her as if he couldn't believe what she was saying. She totally understood and she wanted nothing more than to plunge into the depths of his wretchedness with him, but she also understood that he was never going to walk away from his child, or Amy. Her platitudes were an attempt at protecting herself, and him, from thinking about the life they'd thought they were about to begin together.

'But I don't love her, we're not in love. I want to stick by her, for the baby but I can't be with her. It hasn't changed the way I feel about her. It's… terrible timing.'

Even though he wasn't going to be with Amy in a relationship anymore, they would forever be bound together by the baby. Lois already knew what he had come to tell her.

She stroked his cheek, rubbing his tears away with her thumb while her own coursed down her face. 'It's okay. You don't need to say anything.' But all she wanted was for him to tell her that she was everything he needed, that they still had a future together, come what may.

'I'm so sorry, Lois. So sorry.' He pulled her to him, taking her into his arms. Her head was against his chest, and she could hear his heartbeat. But his heart wasn't for her anymore.

'I do understand. I know that we thought our time had

come, but it hasn't. Not yet and it might not.' If ever she felt the odds were stacked against her and what she wanted, it was now. 'Let's accept that fate's not on our side.' She tried to smile through her tears.

'I want to be with you more than anything, Lois. But I don't want to come to you with so much baggage that we don't have room for our own suitcase.'

She managed a small laugh.

'Last night was... perfect. I'll never forget it.'

'Neither will I.'

They stood up, having to acknowledge that it was over. The conversation, the friendship, the future for them.

Oliver took her in his arms. 'I would have loved you, Lois,' he whispered into her hair. Then he left.

Lois managed to bolt the door behind him before she let out a sob and collapsed to the floor.

47

The meeting with David was being held at County Hall, on the outskirts of Worcester, rather than at The Hive. It was a bit more formal than Robert's office although Lois knew Robert would probably be invited too.

She caught the bus to Worcestershire Royal Hospital and then walked through Worcester Woods Park to the County Hall offices. The trees were bare, and it was rather muddy until she came to the tarmac portion of the path but the air was fresh and cold and seemed to match her mood.

As she waited in the reception area, Robert arrived. She stood up and they had a quick hug. It was strange to see him anywhere but The Hive. He looked different here, in unfamiliar surroundings; a little lost.

'Wonderful news of the win, Lois,' he said enthusiastically.

'Thanks, Robert.' She managed a smile although she felt so low that even the thought of the award wasn't enough to cheer her up. And the fact that the memories of that evening were so intertwined with memories of Oliver made it even harder.

'Lois, Robert!' David came striding across the reception to

greet them. They all shook hands and then followed him to a conference room where three other people sat waiting. Lois recognised one of them from the awards ceremony although she couldn't remember his name.

'Here we have Connie Perks from Human Resources, Lee Fielding our Finance Manager whose responsibilities include the library function and Sue Wilkes our administrator. This is Lois Morgan from Croftwood Library, and you all know Robert from the Hive.'

Everyone said hello and settled themselves down around the table.

'So, Lois. On the back of your fabulous win at the Library Awards, we have reconsidered the position regarding Croftwood Library. The fact is, we can't close down the Library of the Year, at least not this year.'

Lee chuckled and David grinned at him.

'Fortunately, the publicity from the win and the growing interest around your book dating club, particularly the press we've seen from that elderly actor, William Templeton, well frankly it's worth its weight in gold.'

'So Croftwood is safe? Is that what you're saying?' She needed to be sure.

'Yes. And there's more. We'd like to make you the full-time manager of Croftwood Library and we'd like you to take on the project of launching your book dating club at libraries across the county.'

Last week, Lois would have bitten his hand off because he was offering her dream job but the reality of having to avoid Oliver and Amy, risk bumping into them every time she left the library, she wasn't strong enough to deal with that. The further she could be from Croftwood the better.

'That's an amazing offer but I can't accept. I'd like my old job back at the Hive, please.'

David's face dropped and Lee and Sue looked very

uncomfortable.

'Are you sure, Lois?' Robert asked gently. 'This is a wonderful opportunity for you.'

'Is my job still open at the Hive?' Suddenly Lois realised they may have assumed she would take this role given that Croftwood won the award. Why would she leave if she didn't have to?

'Of course, of course,' he said, shooting a look at David who started muttering something to Connie the HR woman.

'Thanks. Because that's what I'd like. As soon as possible.'

'And what about Croftwood?' asked David, looking confused.

'Give it to someone else,' said Lois and she ran out of the room, out of the building and across the road back into the woods.

She'd almost had everything she ever could have wished for. How had it come to this? She'd never get a chance like Croftwood again and she'd never find anyone like Oliver. She hurt more now than she had the night in the library with Oliver. She couldn't see how anything would be okay ever again. She was going to have to go back to the Hive, to a job and a life she'd grown out of. There was nothing else she could do.

If only the trip to London hadn't been so magical, she might not be feeling as bad as this. It was so much worse than she'd felt after Christmas. So much worse than she'd ever felt.

It had been a tough day in the coffee house. Oliver had to cope with customers who were unhappy with the coffee blend, someone who had so many food intolerances that he struggled to offer them anything other than a glass of water and his order from the wholesaler had been delivered somewhere else, so he was suddenly short on napkins and dishwasher detergent.

He was glad to see the back of the last customer but when he locked the door a new sense of dread crept over him knowing he was going upstairs to Amy.

Since she'd told him she was pregnant and he'd told Lois, things had been awful. She'd seen the state he'd been in when he got back from the library although he hadn't told her where he'd been. He'd sat down that night and carefully explained to her that although he would do whatever she needed in terms of the baby and that he would be involved in all aspects of the child's life, that he would do anything for their child, he couldn't be in a relationship with her anymore. Since then, she'd refused to talk to him, leaving them both in dreadful limbo.

As he trudged up the stairs to the flat, he was fully expecting her to be in bed, where she'd been for however many days it was since he'd got back from London. He didn't even know how long it had been.

He opened the door to find her sitting on the edge of the sofa, a pile of bags and suitcases by the door. She had her hands clasped on her lap and she was incredibly pale and drawn.

'Oliver,' she stood up quickly as soon as she heard him come in. 'We need to talk.'

'What's going on?' he asked, gesturing to the bags.

'I'm leaving.'

He was torn between his natural reaction of pure relief and the sense of responsibility he felt towards her again now that she was pregnant.

'You don't have to go.' He didn't mean it and she could tell.

'I do. I'm not pregnant.'

'What?' He ran his hand through his hair, looking at her in disbelief.

'I'm sorry, Oliver.'

'You lost the baby?' He sat down on the sofa, feeling guilty at being relieved about something so dreadful. He looked at her, expecting her to confirm what he'd asked but instead found her looking shifty. With sudden clarity, he knew what had happened. 'You lied to me.'

'I'm so sorry.' Tears were running down her face and she was kneading her hands together as she stood in front of him.

'Why? How could you lie to me about something like that?'

'That night, when we met in Bolero, I saw you talking to Lois and her friend. Until you'd seen her you looked like you were having the worst night of your life and then, you came back over to me and smiled, and I knew it was because of her. I see how you look at her Oliver and I couldn't bear to think that you would look at someone else like that when it should have been me. I didn't know how much I wanted you until it was too late.'

'Ames…' He took her in his arms and held her for a moment then led her to the sofa and they sat next to each other.

'I'm so sorry Oliver. I know things have been awful between us. I thought we could go back to how things were in the beginning, but it hasn't worked at all.'

'It hasn't,' he agreed, handing her a tissue from a packet he pulled out of the drawer in the coffee table. 'We had our time, Amy. I knew that but I wanted to give you the chance to see that too and it hasn't worked out like that at all. It wasn't fair of me to let you think there was a chance for us.'

'Because you were already in love with Lois.'

He wasn't going to deny it. 'I am now,' he said. 'But not when you first came back, I'd never have done that to either of you.'

'I know,' she said softly, taking his hand and holding it to her face. 'You're a good man, Oliver.'

'You know what Ames, you'll be okay. Moving on seems like the hardest thing in the world but without me to remind you of the bad times, you'll be great.'

She smiled at him through her tears. 'I will. Seeing how happy you were when I came back, I can see how that could happen to me.'

'It just takes time, and you have to let yourself be happy. None of it was your fault, Ames. You know that.'

She sniffed and nodded.

'So where are you going?'

'Mum and Dad's. My house is rented out for another few months, so I'll go back there and try to get a job.'

'That's a good plan. Come on, I'll give you a hand with your stuff.'

They loaded her car with all her things and had another hug before he waved her off.

He went back up to the flat and poured himself a stiff whisky.

48

Lois caught the bus to Croftwood for her last day although she planned to leave as soon as she could just in case Oliver came into the library looking for her. The last time she'd seen him had felt like a goodbye, but he'd tried to call her a few times over the past couple of days – she'd rejected the calls – and she couldn't risk seeing him. It hurt too much to even think about how wonderful it would be.

Linda was sitting behind the desk when she walked in.

'Lois, how are you?'

'I'm fine, thanks. You? Did you get the email from Connie?'

'Yes.'

'And is that okay?'

Lois had been given the okay to start back at the Hive as soon as Linda agreed to be the interim manager of Croftwood.

'Oh, Lois. Are you sure? The place isn't the same without you. After everything you've done, maybe take some time to decide. There's no rush.'

'Thanks, but I can't. So, you'll let Connie know that's okay?'

'If that's what you want.' Her eyes were full of concern. 'If you're sure.'

'I am. I hope you don't mind but I'd like to go over to the Hive today.'

'No problem. I'm so sorry about how things have worked out. I thought he'd...that things would be different.' She squeezed Lois's hand.

Lois hugged her, put her keys on the counter and left before she started crying all over again.

She sat on the bus back to Worcester, surprised that she was feeling a bit better just by knowing that she didn't have to worry about running into Oliver or Amy on a daily basis. There was always the chance that she'd see them in Worcester, but it was a lot less likely.

It felt very strange being back at the Hive. She wasn't quite sure what to do with herself as Robert had suggested it might not be a good idea for her to be manning the information desk until she was feeling better. Andrew had been keen for her to take on some of his tasks, most of which he hated, so she had been doing quite a bit of re-shelving and organising the short loan items for the University students.

'I hope you're sad for a couple more weeks,' he said to her later that day when they were both sat on the first floor sorting some medical books into piles. 'I feel like I'm on holiday or something being able to get you to do all my jobs.'

'Thanks. I'm glad someone's benefiting from my mess of a life.'

'Oh, Lois. You know I don't mean it. I'm just doing a terrible job of trying to cheer you up. Anyway, you haven't cried yet today. Things are looking up.'

'I've just been over to Croftwood, so I suppose that's the end of the chapter. I do feel a bit better.'

The internal phone rang. 'Lois,' whispered her friend, Sarah, who was manning the information desk. 'A guy has come to the desk asking for you. I said I wasn't sure if you were in.' Everyone knew what had happened in Croftwood, or a version of it at least.

'Hang on a sec.' Lois put the receiver down on the desk and went over to the balustrade where she would be able to look down at the ground floor. The man who was standing at the desk had brown hair and it was very nicely quiffed. It was Oliver.

She ran back to the desk. 'Sorry Sarah, can you tell him I'm not here, please?'

'No problem, leave it to me.'

Lois put the phone down and rushed back over to the balustrade. She could see Sarah talking to Oliver and he was nodding. Then he asked her something else and she shook her head. He tilted his head back as if he was sighing and Lois thought for a moment that he might see her, so she ducked down for a second. Then she saw him say something else to Sarah and walk out. Lois wove her way through the stacks to the windows on the other side of the library where she knew he would be walking. The need she had to see him was overwhelming. What did he want? He probably just wanted to make sure she was okay. He certainly looked like he was doing better than she was. He looked back to his normal self. Things must be better between him and Amy.

She watched him until he was out of sight then went back to the desk and carried on with her sorting.

'He's here looking for you?' asked Andrew.

Lois nodded. She didn't want to talk about it. She had to get used to him not being part of her life and endlessly talking about the whole sad episode was not going to help.

'Gosh, he's persistent. Are you sure it's over?'

'Absolutely certain.'

That evening, Lois pulled out the blouse she had started making before Christmas. Now seemed like as good a time as any to restart her hobby. After all, that's what she'd started it for in the first place; to take her mind off Alex rather than Oliver. It would hopefully work for either.

The sewing machine was whirring away when she stopped, thinking she'd heard something. The doorbell rang. Then someone started knocking.

'Lois, it's Oliver!' She could just about hear him.

She started sewing again, trying to take as long as possible over the seam she was finishing so that he would have given up by the time she got to the end. Also, if he heard the machine, he would know she was sewing and may not have heard the door, which was somehow better than if he thought she was just ignoring him.

Her phone started ringing. God, Andrew was right. He was extremely persistent. She turned it off and carried on with another seam. By the time she'd finished that one, she was fairly sure he'd gone.

She sat in the lounge unpicking the terrible job she'd done of her side seams while her heart had been beating ten to the dozen, when Steph rang.

'Hey, how are you doing?'

Lois was starting to get annoyed at the sympathetic tone everyone was using when they spoke to her.

'Fine thanks. You?'

'Yeah, great. Eunice and Bill were on the van today. Oh my goodness, they are revelling in their newfound love, and I think Eunice is secretly thrilled that she's dating a film star.'

Lois smiled. 'That's lovely, isn't it? Are they going to the next book club?'

'Yes, I think Dottie's driving them. I wouldn't be surprised if they're at all of them from now on. How about you? Will you be braving it?'

The book club was one of the hardest things about the whole situation. 'No, I don't think so. I don't want to see

Oliver or Amy. I think it's better to stay away. You know he came to The Hive looking for me today?'

'I know, Andrew told me.'

That's why she had phoned. The calls between them were much less frequent now that she was with Tom, but it didn't matter to Lois, she understood and she was glad for Steph because Tom was perfect for her.

'And he came round here about half an hour ago. God, I just need to be away from him. I mean, I don't want to be, but I have to for my own sanity. Even seeing him today. It's wonderful but terrible at the same time.'

'Look. Why don't you crash at mine for a few nights? I'm mostly at Tom's anyway. Think of it like a holiday. No-one will know where you are, you'll have complete peace.'

Lois didn't need to think about it. Steph lived in a flat overlooking the river at Diglis. It had a little balcony, and she would be very happy whiling away the hours between her shifts at The Hive watching the boats turning in the basin.

'That'd be brilliant, thanks Steph.'

'No problem. Pack your bags and I'll drop the keys into you at work tomorrow.'

Yes. It was the perfect solution to give her a bit of space until Oliver realised he ought to leave her alone.

Oliver had been into The Hive, yet again, to try and find Lois. She had been down in the archives for the morning and luckily, Andrew was on the desk and told Oliver that she wasn't there. Lois was grateful to him for his quick thinking, especially because he didn't know what Oliver looked like, but it was unusual for anyone to come in asking after her. Andrew also reported that Oliver didn't leave straight away, instead, he headed upstairs and probably had a good look around so maybe he was onto her, and she may not be so lucky next time.

'You didn't tell me he was gorgeous, Lois,' he said over lunch which she insisted on eating in the staff room just in case Oliver did show up again. Maybe it was his day off.

'Hmm,' she said through a mouthful of marmite sandwich, 'I love his hair.'

'Yep, that probably is his best feature. But his eyes, Lois. Beautiful brown pools you could lose yourself in,' he said with a faraway look in his eyes.

Lois was not unaware of all Oliver's lovely features. Trying to put him out of her mind was proving difficult when all she was doing was worrying he was going to spring out on her from behind a stack or follow her back to Steph's.

That evening, she sat on the balcony looking out over the river, huddled in her biggest jumper, with a blanket over her lap. She wrapped her hands around her cup of tea and seriously started to think about what she was going to do next.

Being at Croftwood Library had changed her and she had been missing that freedom and energy since she had left. Maybe there were other libraries out there just like Croftwood that could be saved? Perhaps she could move somewhere else and do the same thing again. But would it work anywhere else unless there was a huge cheerleader in the form of a coffee house owner, a cantankerous but ultimately kind-hearted old librarian and a steadfast, loyal sidekick who was enthusiastic about everything. Lois smiled to herself. That was why it wouldn't work anywhere else.

She picked up her laptop and found the internet browser open on the London Library website. A fresh pang of sadness washed over her as the memories of that most perfect night came flashing back as the smells and atmosphere of the place were momentarily all around her again.

Scrolling down the page to look at all the pictures, with

renewed interest since now she'd seen it in real life, she noticed at the bottom of the page in minuscule type – Work for us.

Suddenly full of curiosity, she clicked on the link and came to the vacancies page. There was just one job being advertised and it was for an assistant librarian. It would be a step down from where she was now, but it was such an amazing place that she couldn't even believe they'd need to advertise for staff. Maybe it was a sign.

She clicked through to the application form and spent the next hour filling it in before she pressed send and sat back with a smile on her face. For the first time since she and Oliver had spoken in the library, she felt like there was a glimmer of light in her life again.

The next morning, Lois managed to engineer a trip out with Steph on the school run. Despite having left Tom that morning, Steph was already excited about seeing him.

'I'll have to call him Mr Reeves, it'll be so funny,' she said, smiling and shaking her head as if she'd never called him Mr Reeves the other hundred times she'd seen him on the mobile library.

'Mmm,' said Lois. 'So funny.'

'Come on Lo, let's have a laugh. Forget you're down in the dumps. It's a girl's day out! God, imagine if we were doing the Old Hollow stop today. This is just the kind of day when you need a pick-me-up session with Zoe.'

Lois's phone pinged.

'Oh, my god! They want to meet me!'

'Who? Why have you gone from sad to excited because of one text?'

'I applied for a job at the London Library last night.' Lois couldn't stop grinning. It was so soon to have heard and now she was going to get to go back to that wonderful library. Her heart sunk a tiny bit – it did hold those lovely memories. It might be hard and the last thing she wanted was to start crying in front of them. But she was getting ahead of herself.

'You what?' Steph put her foot on the brake and Lois was sure that if it wasn't for the fact that you had to plan about a mile ahead of needing to slow down, they would have ground to a halt. As it was, Steph pulled into the side of the road, put the hazard lights on and faced Lois. 'You're joking? You can't let this thing with Oliver drive you away. What about… me?'

Lois laughed. Steph looked so forlorn. 'I only applied, Steph, I'm sure it'll come to nothing. It's everything with Oliver that's brought things to a head but I'm ready for a new start somewhere. Croftwood made me realise what I can achieve, and I didn't know until I worked there how much I love challenging myself.'

'They might snap your hand off now you're an award winner.'

'I'm not going to get the first thing I apply for, am I? It's been ten years since I applied for a new job. All that happened was that I was sat there last night on your balcony wondering what I was going to do next, and I opened my laptop and the page for the London Library was still there from when I'd googled it before, and there was a vacancy.'

'And they've already contacted you? That's a good sign.' Steph was looking more enthusiastic now.

'Hopefully. It doesn't say it's an interview though, just a meeting.'

'I think a meeting means it's in the bag, to be honest.' Steph got ready to pull out again, probably worried now that they'd be late. 'And you're right, Lois. You nailed it at Croftwood, and I've never seen you more ballsy at work. You were brilliant.'

'Thanks, Steph.' It meant a lot that her friend had noticed. 'At the very least it'll be nice to have a day in London and get to visit there again.'

'And don't think I don't get it about Oliver. I know how hard you fell for him, but you'll be okay. And even though I'll miss you like mad, you deserve an amazing opportunity like that, Lo. Go for it.'

'You'll be okay too, Steph. Now that you've got Tom.'

'Mr Reeves.'

'Okay. Mr Reeves.'

49

Oliver had run out of ideas. He had been to Lois's house every evening for the past week and aside from the first time, when he'd been pretty sure that she was there, the lights had been off and there was definitely no-one home.

He'd made a nuisance of himself at the Hive. He was pretty sure all the staff knew who he was and had been primed not to let on where Lois was. She had to be there, Linda had said she'd gone back there but there was no sign of her, even though he'd given up asking for her at the desk and instead wandered around the place every day for half an hour or so just in case he came across her.

'Give her some time, Ollie.' Patsy was trying to be kind but had no idea what Lois would be thinking. She didn't need more time to mull over the fact that she thought he and Amy were having a baby and that he couldn't take the added complication of a relationship with her as well. And now none of that was true.

'I can't, Pats. I need to tell her.'

'Well, I'm not complaining about the extra hours I've had to work while you've been off trying to stalk her but maybe just relax. She'll turn up when you least expect it.'

'I'm sure she's avoiding me, so I doubt it.'

'You don't think she'll come to the book club?'

'Are you joking?'

'Well, she might love it more than she wants to avoid you.'

He shrugged. 'She might.' It was a very remote possibility, but he thought he'd hurt her so badly that she almost certainly wouldn't set foot in Croftwood again let alone in his coffee house.

'You must know her friends. Maybe they can get a message to her or something?'

'That's not a bad idea, actually.' It was a good idea but the only one of Lois's friends he'd met was Steph and that was very briefly. He knew she drove the mobile library. Maybe he could find out where it was going to be and intercept her.

'So, are you back for the day?' Patsy looked expectantly at him, wanting to be able to go but all he could think about was the mobile library.

'Give me ten minutes.'

He ran upstairs, trying not to imagine Patsy rolling her eyes behind him, and trawled through the county library website until he found a mobile library page. Frustratingly, he could only search by an A to Z of stops rather than just see the whole list, but he supposed anyone looking at it for normal reasons would be perfectly happy with that. He picked a random nearby village and checked that. The timetable for the third Thursday of the month popped up. What date was it according to that kind of timetabling? He'd already missed the third Thursday. After picking several other villages at random, he eventually managed to track down the mobile library timetable for the following day. It was visiting Old Hollow, near Malvern. Perfect.

'Hey Pats, you're good to go,' he said, tying his apron as he came to stand behind the counter with her.

'Great, thanks. You look like a man with a plan.'

'Are you okay to work tomorrow?' He asked with a sheepish grin. 'I can open up.'

'Okay. I'll be in at nine, but tomorrow is it, Ollie. At this rate, we'll need to find another manager for the cinema because I'm here more than you are.'

'Thanks, you're a star,' he said, hugging her. 'I massively appreciate it and I'll do some of your shifts at the cinema to make up for it.'

The following morning, he left as soon as Patsy arrived. The mobile library was only at Old Hollow for fifteen minutes from 10 am. He arrived way too early, but that was better than missing it and having to trail around after it to stop after stop.

At five to ten, the mobile library van turned cumbersomely into the car park. Oliver watched Steph open the doors and lower the steps down before he got out of the car and walked over. He was nervous. He stood outside for a minute, thinking how best to phrase things to Steph. Should he ask where Lois was? She probably wouldn't tell him if the response he'd been getting from the Hive was anything to go by. What else could he say? Why had he come? He couldn't even remember now. Patsy had said something about giving a message. Okay, so he'd ask Steph to pass on that... he loved Lois? No, that was too much. He needed to talk to her first.

'Are you going in?' A woman came up behind him, then pushed at him with her elbow. 'Come on, don't be shy.'

He followed her into the van. He'd never been in a mobile library before and hadn't known what to expect.

'Morning Steph, I found this one lurking outside.'

'Morning Zoe, cup of tea?' asked Steph as she walked over to him without having looked to see who it was. 'Oh, Oliver.'

'Hi, I wasn't sure if you'd remember me.' He looked around awkwardly to avoid Steph's gaze.

'Oh, I remember you.' She crossed her arms and stood in front of him.

'Who are you, Oliver? And what have you done to piss Steph off?' Zoe was intrigued even if Steph looked like she was going to forcibly eject him.

'He broke my friend's heart, Zoe. So I don't know what he's doing here.' She said this while giving him the evils, not taking her eyes off him.

'I need to see Lois I need to explain. I know she doesn't want to see me but honestly, I think she'd want to if she knew.'

'Knew what?'

'That it's over with Amy.'

Steph raised an eyebrow. 'Really?'

'Look, I don't know if Lois told you everything—'

'She did.' Steph cut him off.

'Right... well, Amy's not pregnant. It was a mistake.'

'And?'

'And I need to tell Lois.' He could see that Steph was still unconvinced, but he didn't want to explain everything in front of Zoe.

'You've let her down one too many times. Christmas was bad enough—'

'What happened at Christmas?' asked Zoe. Steph raised a finger and carried on.

'But then the night in London when she thought that was it for you two followed by literally the worst time of her life. Now she's lost the job she loved and ...you.'

'You're right and I know it's no excuse, but I thought I had no choice. I think Lois will understand if—'

'That's the problem, Oliver. She probably will understand but that just leaves her wide open to be hurt. Again.'

This wasn't the way to find her. He wasn't going to manage to get Steph on his side.

'Okay, fair enough. You're a good friend to her.'

'Damn right, she is!' piped up Zoe.

'Thanks. Bye.'

He went back to sit in his car not knowing what he was going to do next but knowing he wasn't going to stop trying.

Steph watched Oliver slump over the steering wheel. Seeing him, she could tell how broken he was. It wasn't just Lois who was hurting.

'Hold the fort for a minute, Zoe?'

'Where are you going?'

'To make sure he's okay. Look at him.'

They stood in the doorway watching Oliver. He had at least sat back up but wasn't making any move to leave.

Steph knocked on the passenger side window, making him jump. He opened the door from the inside and she got in.

'I can see that you mean it, okay? But she's my best friend. She's always been treated like shit by men who just take her for granted and she deserves better than that.'

'I know. But believe me, the only reason I let her down was because I was trying to do the right thing by someone who I loved once. I know now that I love Lois more than I ever even imagined I could love anyone but before I knew that, I was trying to give the person I used to love the closure she needed.'

He looked at Steph, his eyes pleading with her to understand, and she did. And for Lois, that undeterred loyalty was a great thing now that he loved her. She could see that he did. He was trying to fight for her, and he'd won Steph over.

'Okay. You need to talk to her properly and you can't blindside her by rocking up when she's at work. She's staying at my place. Come round tonight about eight. I'll have spoken to her by then and I know she'll at least hear you out. Hang on.'

Steph ran back to the van and wrote her address down then ran back to the car and handed it to Oliver. 'Wait downstairs and I'll come down when I've spoken to her. Don't let me down.'

Steph invited herself to her own flat that evening to have dinner with Lois. They ate pizza and drank a couple of bottles of beer each. She wasn't entirely sure how Lois would react to the news she'd invited Oliver round so she waited until just before eight o'clock to tell her.

'I need to get off in a minute, but I need to tell you something first.'

Lois, quite rightly, looked dubious. 'Okay…'

'Oliver's coming round.'

'Round here? Christ Steph, I go to all these lengths to avoid him and then you invite him round?'

'Look. I know. I know how he treated you, but you need to hear what he has to say. Trust me.'

'I can't carry on letting him in when he won't choose me. I need to be the only person he wants. I deserve that.' She carefully wiped a stray tear away.

'You do. And that's why you need to hear him out.' Steph took her hand. 'He came to see me, and I roasted him, believe me, in front of Zoe too. I sent him off and he just went and sat in his car. He didn't leave and we were watching him and then he laid his head down on the steering wheel and I had to go out to see if he was okay. Anyway, let's just say that the man is beyond sorry, Lo. All he wants to do is to talk to you. Please.'

'Okay. So where is he?'

'He'll be waiting downstairs. I'm going round to Tom's so you two can talk. Are you going to be okay?'

'Yes, it'll be fine.'

Steph hugged her. 'It will be. But don't just fall back into his arms. Make sure it's on your terms.'

Oliver was indeed waiting downstairs. He was pacing back and forth in front of the door and looked terrified when he saw Steph come out.

'Go on then.' She held the door open for him.

'Thanks. I appreciate this.'

'Well, like I said, don't let me down.'

50

Lois heard a gentle knock at the door and went to open it. Oliver looked so worried that she couldn't help but feel sorry for him.

'So, you got Steph on side?' she said as she stood aside to let him in.

He looked a bit sheepish. 'I needed to see you. To explain that things have changed.' He unbuttoned his coat but looked unsure as to whether he was actually welcome and didn't go as far as taking it off.

'Things have changed for me too, Oliver. I've got a meeting at the London Library tomorrow about a job.'

'Wow, that's amazing, you said you'd love to work there.'

'I did.' She sat down and he tentatively perched on the edge of the chair opposite her.

'You know, I'm not with Amy anymore. The pregnancy, well, she wasn't. It was a mistake.'

'A mistake?'

'A last-ditch attempt, I think. But it's over. Completely. And I know I've messed you around, Lois. I treated you badly and I hurt you and I have no right to expect you to turn around and forgive me, but I want you to know, there's only you. For me.' His eyes were pleading with her as he spoke, trying to convey to her how sorry he was.

It was everything she'd been wanting to hear but she needed to be sure and to make sure he understood.

'I've hoped you would say that to me since we first met. Dreamed of it. Christmas and then the awards night were the best times of my life but only because I let myself go along with you, even though I knew it was going to come crashing down around me afterwards. I'm not the person I was before, the person who just settled for whatever was on offer and was happy with that. Working at Croftwood Library and winning the award showed me that I can expect better for myself. Christmas with you showed me that that's what I need to hold out for. Those days were amazing, just the two of us and I want that kind of feeling in my life all the time. If it's not with you, then so be it but I know I can be the person who gets exactly what she wants and I'm going to make that happen for myself. I don't need to wait until the time is right for you to be ready. And I wanted to be with you, Oliver, more than anything. But I can't worry that there might be someone more important to you than me.'

'Lois, I can promise you now that there is no-one more important to me than you are. I want to be with you and I'm willing to do whatever that takes. I'll move to London with you, I'll be a barista at Starbucks while you work in your dream job because you'll land that, no question.' He smiled briefly and Lois could see how much he believed in her.

'What about the coffee house?'

'I mean it. I can make it work if that's what it takes.'

She could see that he did mean it and she wanted to believe him. And he was offering to move to London of all things. Leave his business for her, his life in Croftwood.

'Well, let's not get ahead of ourselves,' she said. 'It's just an interview.'

'They'll want you. They'd be mad not to.' He took her hands in his. 'I love you.'

It was what she'd wanted to hear for so long. What she had known was true on the night of the awards ceremony even though neither of them had said it. Now that she finally had it in her grasp, why was she faltering? She could have thrown herself into Oliver's arms as soon as she'd known it was over between him and Amy but she hadn't.

'The thing is, I need to do this by myself, Oliver. I can't keep living my life around what everyone else is doing and fitting in with that.'

'I meant what I said. Whatever it takes, I'll do it.'

'I know you will.' She didn't think she'd ever met anyone as fiercely loyal as Oliver. 'But I need to go to London and see what happens next for me, by myself.'

Oliver's face fell but although Lois felt guilty for turning him away and terrified that now she was the one throwing away the future she had thought she wanted, she wasn't going to change her mind. She needed to know whether she could get the job in London. It was the first time she'd ever reached for something she'd never thought would be within her grasp and now that she knew how fulfilling it was to succeed at work, she wanted the challenge of seeking out something else just as special on her own. So that it would be her win, not something that had happened because she was the only person who couldn't say no to Robert.

'Look, I need some time. I'm not saying that to hurt you,' she said, squeezing his fingers in hers as she saw the despair in his eyes. 'When I saw this job listed a couple of days ago, it felt like fate. Like a light at the end of the tunnel when everything else was going wrong. I have to see it through.'

'I understand, Lois, I do.' He dropped her hands and gave her a fierce hug.

She could feel his breath as he sighed into her neck, and she pulled him closer.

'I'll be back for the next book club,' she said into his chest. 'Let's just see what happens. Is that okay?'

He pulled away, kneaded his brow with his fingers and nodded as Lois prepared herself to watch him leave all over again. It was hard, but this time she knew whatever happened was in her hands and it made the moment bittersweet rather than heart-breaking.

'Bye Oliver.'

'Bye Lois. Good luck tomorrow.' He managed to smile although his eyes were full of tears, and she hoped she wasn't breaking his heart.

Lois stood outside the London Library looking up at the facade which hid the magic it held within. She'd spent the train journey from Worcester trying to decide what she would do if she got the job and then what would happen if she didn't. There was no clear thinking involved at all, it was a huge seesawing of decisions whirring around in her mind and it was all she could think about.

She went inside and headed to the desk, announcing herself to a friendly-looking man who asked her to take a seat.

As she waited, she couldn't help but think back to the night of the awards ceremony. She'd felt the same when she walked in today as she had that night which could only be a good sign and the thought of actually working here sent a thrill right through her.

'Lois? Hi, I'm Georgie, great to meet you.' She held out her hand for Lois to shake. 'Follow me, can I get you a coffee?'

'That would be great, thanks.' Lois followed Georgie through the library to a small room which was lined with bookshelves and had a large, low table surrounded by three well-worn leather armchairs. Georgie had a very sleek, shiny ponytail which swung from side to side as she walked. She didn't look like any librarian Lois had come across before, wearing skinny black jeans with high-heeled knee boots which Lois could only dream about being able to walk in and a long, cream, cowl-necked sweater but she felt at ease despite her underlying nerves at it being an interview.

'Take a seat,' said Georgie, leaving her phone and sheaf of papers on the table. 'I won't be a sec. Milk and sugar in the coffee?'

'Oh, just milk, thanks.' While she waited, she tried to imagine what it would be like to be here every day. Would it still seem as amazing? Did Georgie feel like that about the place?

'Right, here we go.' Georgie set the coffee on the table, picked up her papers and put them on her lap. 'So, Lois. To introduce myself properly, I'm the operations manager of the library. My background is in business, and I'm sure you know that because this is a private library, we have slightly different priorities.' She smiled in a way that Lois found slightly patronising. 'I have to admit I was super-intrigued when I saw your application. You've worked in libraries for your whole career so you know this is an entry-level position but the last part of your CV was the most interesting part, I mean, what you've achieved at Croftwood Library, that was a major turnaround. I guess I was curious, that's really why I asked you to come in.'

Lois's nerves cranked back up to the level they'd been that morning. Did Georgie think that she had some clever agenda?

'Well, I'm at a point where I need a change. What I've done at Croftwood has come to a natural end, so it feels like time to move on. This library is amazing and when I saw the job advert, I had to apply.' Lois smiled. 'There's nothing more to it than that. I came here for the awards ceremony and fell in love with the place.' Might as well be honest.

'Because I have to be honest with you, Lois. I hate to assume anything about your situation, but the salary is less than you're on now so unless you're secretly a woman of means,' she said grinning, 'I think you would struggle to make the move to London. Obviously, that's none of my business but I just want you to be across all the facts.'

Lois had known that would probably be the case but hearing it for certain dashed her hopes somewhat. And Georgie was right; it was none of her business whether Lois could or couldn't afford to live on the salary they were offering.

'But all of that aside, what do you think you can bring to us?'

'The past few months have made me realise how libraries can bring the community together and make a difference. I'd love to be involved in setting up some initiatives to broaden the library's offer beyond day-to-day lending.' If she could do something here along the lines of what she'd done at Croftwood, it might be so perfect that the pay cut and the possibility of having to live somewhere dingy could be worth it.

'Lois, I love the enthusiasm you have for reaching out to the community. I guess it's slightly different here than with municipal libraries.' She gave that sympathetic smile again as if Lois had no idea how anything worked. 'We are a paid membership service and we don't do community outreach in the same way as you've been used to.'

'I think it would be great for your members if they could get some added benefits to their membership in the form of genre-specific book clubs, maybe specialist talks from academics on current interest topics.' Lois was determined to make Georgie see that she would be perfect for the job even though she was starting to think it wasn't the right move for her after all.

'Some of the things you are talking about could be paid-for extras,' said Georgie. Lois could see the pound signs in her eyes. 'Do you have any business experience, Lois?'

'Coming up with any initiative is about business, whether or not someone's paying for it. It's good business for me to get more footfall into Croftwood Library so anything we do that makes that happen is good business sense.' Lois was hitting her stride now. She felt quite strongly that Georgie and the library, beautiful as it was, were not for her and now she knew that, her confidence came streaming back to the surface. 'The date-with-a-book club that we started has made a huge difference to two of the coffee shops in our town and that wasn't even the intention.'

'Hmm,' said Georgie with a dismissive edge to her voice. 'Well, I'm not sure that kind of initiative would be what our members are looking for anyway. They're very discerning.'

Georgie's superior attitude was grating on Lois and was almost certainly what led to Lois saying, 'Thank you for your time, but I'd like to withdraw my application. I've heard about another position which I've decided to accept.' Lois stood up and held out her hand towards a flustered Georgie.

'Oh, right,' she blustered. 'Um, well thank you. And if you change your mind, do get in touch.' Her demeanour changed suddenly. 'The library director was keen to get you on board.'

And now Lois had Georgie on the back foot because she was supposed to have been attracting her to the job that she was over-qualified and over-experienced for and instead had succeeded in alienating her because... Lois didn't have the first idea why.

'Well, I'm sorry that you didn't feel that I would be a good fit. No hard feelings.'

Georgie just stood there with her mouth open, but Lois wasn't in the mood to try and alleviate the awkwardness because, having finally realised what she wanted, she was leaving.

She still loved the thought of working in the London Library, but it wasn't what she wanted because what she wanted was in Croftwood. She wanted Oliver and wherever he was, that was where she wanted to be. She hoped it wasn't too late to beg David for the job at Croftwood Library. She knew that Linda was filling in as a favour to her until they could find someone else, so she hoped they hadn't found anyone yet.

Rather than rushing back to Paddington, she strolled along the streets, enjoying the bright, cold day and the feeling of not having anything pressing to do. Now that she had decided what she wanted, she felt happier than she had since the night of the awards and she knew, she hoped, that there was a lot more of that feeling to come.

51

Lois hadn't seen or spoken to Oliver since before she went to London. Part of her had wanted to throw herself into his arms once she'd made up her mind to stay in Croftwood but another tiny part of her was scared that he had changed his mind again over something else, and he would deem her less important again. She needed to see the whites of his eyes before she declared herself, so she kept to the tentative plan they'd made to see each other at the next date-with-a-book club.

Linda and Rosemary had insisted that this book club was to be a celebration of the reprieve for Croftwood Library as well as the celebration of the award win they'd always planned. Patsy had insisted that they hold the event at Croftwood Cinema since it could easily hold more than Oliver's and the Courtyard Café put together. She had programmed a rare night where they wouldn't be showing a film so that they'd have the run of the place.

When Lois arrived in Croftwood, she locked her bike up outside the church and walked through the park to the cinema. The woman who was manning the door smiled at her and directed her through the auditorium doors towards a door at the side of the screen. The stalls were empty, the lighting soft, and Lois could hear chatter and laughter coming from the backstage area.

'Lois!' Linda exclaimed when she walked in, as if she hadn't been expecting her.

'This is amazing!' There were so many fairy lights strung across the ceiling, that's all that was lighting the space and it was beautiful. The mirrored shelves behind the bar reflected the twinkling lights and made everything look more magical.

Patsy and Oliver were behind the bar serving drinks and Patsy gave her a wave and then nudged Oliver. He looked up and seeing it was Lois, came out from behind the bar.

'You made it,' he said, looking at Lois in a way that made her melt. It was okay, he still felt the same.

'She did, and with good reason,' said Rosemary, appearing next to him. 'You can't miss out on our big celebration of the win, Lois. If it wasn't for you, we wouldn't have a book club and Croftwood Library would be gone in a few weeks.'

'It was all of us,' said Lois. '

'Hey, Lois!' called Steph from a table she was sharing with Tom at the back of the coffee house, 'Get over here!'

Lois headed over to them, accepting congratulations from some of the regulars as she made her way between the tables.

'So, you're really doing it?' asked Steph.

Lois nodded. 'I'm so nervous. Do you think he's going to be okay with it all?'

'I have a feeling he'd be okay with anything you wanted,' said Tom.

Lois was surprised that Tom weighed in but was glad that he and Steph had the kind of relationship where they took an interest in each other's lives and friends. None of her other boyfriends would have been like that.

'Let's hope so. Here goes.'

Lois headed over to the bar and took a glass of wine. Oliver was facing away from her, busy opening more wine. It was best to say it before they had any more chances to talk to each other. Otherwise, there was a risk she would blow the surprise.

'Ladies and gentlemen!' she shouted. There was an immediate hush. 'Welcome to this special date-with-a-book club night. Tonight, we're celebrating our win at the Library of the Year awards and the fact that we've saved Croftwood Library!'

There was a cacophony of cheers and claps. Lois glanced over at Oliver who was looking at her in much the same way he had when she made her speech at the awards evening, and it gave her shivers that made her want to scrunch her eyes up and squeal.

'We couldn't have done it without all of you supporting us so loyally and spreading the word to all those people from the Courtyard Café who are here tonight.' Everyone laughed. 'We also couldn't have done it without some other amazing people, Linda and Rosemary.' Everyone cheered and Lois produced two bouquets which she'd asked Patsy to sort out for her.

Linda and Rosemary were thrilled with their flowers and accepted them with blushes and tearful eyes.

'And I also need to thank someone else. He was behind me from the minute I set foot in Croftwood. He championed every idea I had, telepathically knew when I needed coffee and muffins and was by my side on one of the best evenings of my career, and one of the best of my life.' She looked over at him, seeing in his eyes how much he loved her and knowing he could see the same as he looked at her. 'Oliver.' The room erupted and Lois widened her eyes and tipped her head to the side to tell him to come over to her.

He came and stood by her side, taking her hand and

squeezing it.

'Oliver. I have a surprise for you which I hope you're going to like. I've got a new job as the manager of Croftwood Library.'

While the room erupted again, Rosemary ushered them both over to a table for two. In contrast to all of the other tables, it was laid with two champagne glasses and a mass of flickering tea lights.

'Where did this come from?' Oliver said in surprise.

'I'll fetch the bubbles,' Rosemary said as she left them.

A smile spread slowly over Oliver's face as he sat down. 'So, we're not moving to London?'

'No. We're staying. If you want to?'

'Of course I want to!' He reached for her hands across the table. 'What made you change your mind?' he asked, his eyes sparkling.

'You. Everything good in my life happened here. I want to see what happens next.'

'What happens next is that I can't believe it's possible to love you any more than I do right now.' Carefully avoiding the candles, he leant over and kissed her tenderly on the lips.

'What happens next is that we finally get to have our date-with-a-book.'

'I don't want to burst your bubble but I never read the last book we picked.'

Lois gasped in mock horror. 'Oliver Jones, you're going to have to rethink your priorities now you're going out with the manager of the library.'

'Is it too soon to admit that I only chose the romance book to try and win you over?'

'It's definitely too soon,' Lois laughed. 'But it worked.'

The End

Author's Note

When I was little, my dad used to take me to Malvern Library on a Saturday morning. I was allowed to choose three books, which were never enough to last a whole week, and I remember loving the chairs which were formed orange plastic and just the right size for a six or seven-year-old. Now, knowing how little my dad reads, I appreciate even more that he took the time to introduce me to reading and the library as it's something that has stayed with me. The library in Croftwood is heavily based on the Malvern Library of my childhood, before it was refurbished.

Thank you to fellow writer and member of the Romantic Novelists' Association Emma Bennet who was my anonymous reader when this book went through the New Writers' Scheme a few years ago. When Summer at Croftwood Cinema was published, she messaged me to ask what had happened to the library book since this was originally planned to be the first in the series. The belief she had in the book was invaluable to me in deciding to turn it into a series.

Thank you to my fab friend Catrin for editing and proofreading again and to Berni Stevens for another beautiful cover design. Thank you to Pam for being my biggest cheerleader! Thanks James for reading it, freaking me out with a small suggestion for a plot change which would have unravelled everything, and to Claudia who reassured me he didn't know what he was talking about.

And last but not least, thank you so much, from the bottom of my heart, to everyone who has read and reviewed my books. It means the world.

* * *

If you enjoyed this story, I'd be so grateful if you had a couple of minutes to leave a review. It helps other readers find books they might enjoy and makes all the difference to authors too.

The best way to keep in touch is to sign up to my exclusive mailing list at victoriaauthor.co.uk. I'll send a newsletter every month or so to keep you up to date with what I'm up to, as well as any special offers, new releases and exclusive content. You can also find me in all of these places:

Instagram @victoriawalker_author
    Facebook Victoria Walker - Author
    Twitter @4victoriawalker

Printed in Great Britain
by Amazon

27442220R00182